PLAIN JANE AND THE HITMAN

TMONIQUE STEPHENS

Copyright © 2019 Tracy Stephens

All rights reserved under International and Pan-American Copyright Conventions

By payment of required fees, you have been granted the *non*-exclusive, *non*-transferable right to access and read the text of this book. No part of this text may be reproduced, transmitted, downloaded, decompiled, reverse engineered, or stored in or introduced into any information storage and retrieval system, in any form or by any means, whether electronic or mechanical, now known or hereinafter invented without the express written permission of copyright owner.

Please Note

The reverse engineering, uploading, and/or distributing of this book via the internet or via any other means without the permission of the copyright owner is illegal and punishable by law. Please purchase only authorized electronic editions, and do not participate in or encourage electronic piracy of copyrighted materials. Your support of the author's rights is appreciated

No part of this book may be reproduced or transmitted in any form or by any electronic or mechanical means, including photocopying, recording or by any information storage and retrieval system, without the written permission of the publisher, except where permitted by law.

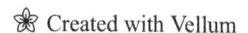

❦ Created with Vellum

ACKNOWLEDGMENTS

Thank you to my critique partner, Cynthia. Your sharp eye for plotting and attention to detail has saved my ass many times.

Also, thanks to Belinda, Karen, and Kathy.

To my drinking buddy, beta reader, and bestie, Charitee, what would I do without you? Don't answer that question! Your friendship has kept me sane.

Thank you to my editor, Nadine Winningham, and my cover artist, Cover by Combs.

I couldn't do what I do without all of you! Writing is a solitary endeavor, but it's not a journey any author takes alone.

For my daughter, Cyré.
Some of the best moments of my life, I've spent with you.
You continue to be my inspiration and my reason for striving forward.
For my Mother.
Decades later and I still miss you.

UNTITLED

Books

Plain Jane Series
  Plain Jane and the Hitman
  Plain Jane and the Marine (Spring 2019)
  Plain Jane and the Hitman's Wedding (Summer 2019)
  Plain Jane and the Billionaire (Fall 2019)

Descendants of Ra series
  Entrapped Prequel (coming soon)
  Eternity Book 1
  Everlasting Book 2
  Evermore Book 3
  Encore Book 4
  Forever Novella Book 4.5
  Entwined (Book 5 coming soon)

The UnHallowed Series.
  Only The Fallen (Book 1)

Only One I Want (Book 2)
Only You (Book 3)
Only One I'll Have (Book 4)
Only One I Need (Book 4 coming soon)

CHAPTER 1

*I*n the shadows of a rusted I-beam, in the corner pocket of an abandoned furniture warehouse three miles outside of Atlanta's city limits, Emmet Streeter blended into the fabric of the night.

Something he did exceptionally well.

Positioned at the far end of the building, he had an adequate view of the expanse. Not much to see except a rotted sofa, moldy mattresses, destroyed dressers, and other household goods from past decades littering the place.

Head on a swivel, gun in his hand, Emmet studied the dark corners and blind spots, even the birds nesting in the rafters. A lot of birds by the number of droppings. They came and went via a busted sunroof on the northern side of the building. Permanent ventilation, it had rusted open. Off to his right water dripped on something metallic, the soft pling a metronome he could set his watch by.

Slow and quiet, Emmet stayed in the shadows and took a circular route around the periphery. His tread silent. He peered out of a cracked, dirty window, careful to keep his body hidden.

Nothing moved in the parking lot overgrown with enough vegetation to hide a bus or an army.

His attention shifted to the rafters as a bird cooed overhead, combined with wings fluttering. Pigeon? A flash of white in his peripheral caught his eye. Hank and that damned cashmere coat. Wouldn't be an issue if they weren't tracking one of their own. One who would see that white coat as a target and not the white flag of surrender.

Splitting up was stupid, but Hank ordered, and Emmet obeyed. Some things changed, and some things remained the same. Hopefully, none of those things would get Hank killed.

Sometimes, Emmet believed that's exactly what Hank wanted, a quick, brutal end to a long, brutal life. Not while Emmet still breathed.

Quietly, he backtracked using a line of credenzas as cover. Precise placement prevented glass from crunching under his feet. He made it to the end of the line and faced a glass field taking notice of the abnormal quiet. Everything had stilled. His heartbeat drumming in his ear was the only thing he could hear until he refocused on the outside instead of the inside.

Not a single sound in the entire building. Even the pigeons had ceased to move as if they knew death was near.

He had to go back, find Hank and approach another way—wait... What happened to the dripping water? He dropped low and swung thirty degrees to his left, his gun leading the way and squeezed the trigger twice.

The sound of a body hitting the wall, fabric ripping, and feet doing an awkward shuffle in a vain attempt to escape made him smile. A flash of white came up on his right, Hank rushing in. Not this time.

Emmet darted in front of his mentor, prepared to take a bullet, and if it came to it, die for the man who'd save his life.

"Move, Emmet." Hank elbowed him in the gut.

At fifty-eight, Hank was no out of shape lightweight, but

neither was Emmet. He used his two-inches and thirty pounds of muscle advantage to shove Hank out of the way and kept plowing forward. If the target was down, he needed to stay down.

Emmet leapt over a stack of pallets and landed on Bryan Hardwick's—AKA Hardware—chest. Member of an agency that had no name. Correction: former member. Bryan twisted, throwing Emmet off and into a stack of barstools. Bryan was halfway to his feet, hand pressed to his side when Hank shot him in the knee. Screaming, Bryan toppled onto his one good knee and his free hand. In his other, he brought his gun up with a clear shot of Hank.

A barstool to the back of his head took care of the threat. Hank landed on Bryan like vengeance incarnate. Emmet let Hank have his way for another couple of seconds, then cleared his throat. A little reminder that they needed Bryan alive…for a bit longer.

The interruption worked. Hank eased up on the beating and grabbed two fistfuls of Bryan's coat and tossed him into a rotted wingback. With a roll of duct tape he happened to have in an inside pocket of his white cashmere coat, Hank bound the unconscious man to the chair.

Emmet snatched up a rusted umbrella stand full of filthy water and emptied it over Bryan's head. The man came to cursing and fighting against his restraints, which held fast. He wasn't going anywhere.

"Motherfucker, you are mine," Hank yelled in Bryan's ear. From another inner pocket, Hank retrieved a switchblade and flicked it open with grand flare as Bryan panted.

Not that Emmet was concerned. Bryan's time on earth was down to a collection of seconds, and that's only if Emmet could leach Hank long enough to get the information they need.

Hank dropped to his haunches and freed a tactical knife from another hidden pocket in his coat and got down to business. He sliced through coat and shirt to expose Bryan's chest and started with shallow cuts across the pecs and abs to get the party started on the right foot. Not shallow enough by the cast-off splatter on Hank's white cashmere coat.

White. May as well be wearing a bullseye with a coat that color in the dead of night. Couldn't tell Hank that. Original member of their little group, he spewed orders with no reciprocation.

"We need him alive," Emmet decided to remind Hank over the screams.

"A piece here and there won't kill him." He sliced into the man like a side of beef.

Grim work. Emmet stayed focused. Unlike their usual signature tap to the forehead routine, this kill was a personal statement to those who had betrayed them. A statement to Rogers, the bastard.

A bit of wet work was needed to get the point across. He fucked with the wrong men. Emmet had to admit, this exercise was probably cathartic for Hank. Emmet wanted to get to the killing. All those traitorous bastards bit the hand that fed them. They would all die. Painfully.

Hardware was just the latest.

The screams escalated after Bryan's right hand landed with a solid thump to the filthy floor. Took a while for them to die down.

The ring of blood circling Bryan's chair expanded. "You haven't asked him anything yet." All the cutting was a preamble, but at Hank's cutting rate, he'd soon be dead.

"I'm working on it."

Bryan coughed and sprayed a good amount of blood all over Hank and his pretty white coat.

Hank cocked his head at Emmet. Jesus, his face would've made for a great Halloween mask with the blood clinging to his crow's feet and frowns line, speckled in salt and pepper hair, running down his clean-shaven cheeks to drip off his chin. "I think he did that shit on purpose," Hank muttered.

He snatched up a heavy-duty pipe wrench off the floor and hefted the rusted tool onto his shoulder. Bryan whimpered. Emmet wasn't sure how Bryan could see out of two swollen eyes. Yet, was impressed with the feat.

The pipe wrench connected with Bryan's ribs. The satisfying crunch echoed in the abandoned warehouse. Hank stood and leaned on the wrench, his breath hard gasps of frosted air. Hunched over like that, he seemed older than his fifty-eight years, seemed ancient. Fifty-eight multiplied by ten. A façade. There was nothing old about Hank.

"Now that I've softened you up… Tell me where Rogers is hiding."

Emmet arched an eyebrow. Hank had done more than softened him up. Granted he wouldn't have survived this garden party anyway. Emmet didn't like wasted energy, and he preferred tidy over messy. A kill was supposed to be clean, untraceable, professional. After six months of hunting the traitors, a bit of a mess was the least of their problems. Besides, a nice gasoline fire would clean up the evidence.

"Tell me where he is, and I'll make it quick." Hank bargained.

That was a lie even a novice could see through. Bryan was a pro. This was gonna take a while.

Bryan coughed up another wet glob of blood. "He's close."

That got both of their attention. Hank chuckled. "Close, huh? Is that chill I feel on the back of my neck the wind or his breath?"

A red spot appeared on Bryan's forehead. Emmet dove for the ground while Hank, the fucking idiot, stayed put even as Bryan's gray matter tasted air.

"He's in the rafters." Hank emptied his nine-millimeters into the rafters, but a second red dot appeared on his left shoulder.

From the angle it originated, the shooter wasn't in the building but perched somewhere outside. Probably in the overgrown parking lot.

Emmet launched himself at his mentor/father and took the shorter, slightly smaller man to the ground with his body shielding him. He wasn't fast enough. Blood bloomed above Hank's left collarbone.

"You're hit."

"I'll live." Hank snapped and shoved Emmet off.

"Surprising for how big of a target you provided. You see a red laser sight, you don't stand there and gape at it." Emmet dragged him behind an overturned credenza that barely shielded one person, never mind two.

"Don't you think I know that?"

"No. I don't." Not since the internal war began. Friend against friend. Partner against partner. Men he'd known for a decade, some more than that, were now in his crosshairs. No one was neutral. Everyone had taken sides.

Two weeks, four men dead, and Emmet still didn't understand why. What caused the unexpected rift? Why did steadfast partners in an exclusive membership suddenly turn on each other? Friends to enemies. Regardless, his loyalty belonged to Hank, the man who saved and raised him. Whatever caused the rift, only Hank knew for sure, and he would share when he was good and ready.

"Instead of ducking, you stood there. Whoever's out there could've blown your brains out." Emmet yanked off his scarf, balled it up and pressed it to his wound. Hank grunted but didn't stop Emmet as he felt around for an exit wound on his back. The sound of a motorcycle revving and speeding away gave him a second of relief.

Emmet's hand came away bloody. "Clean, through and through. We have to get you to a doctor." He wrapped the scarf around Hank's shoulder and knotted it as tight as he could.

"Get off." Hank pushed Emmet again. "I'm not going to any doctor." On his feet again, he marched over to Hardware and glared down at the dead man.

"Want to check for a pulse?"

Hank turned his hard glare on Emmet, who ceased being intimidated by the age of fourteen. "I've been robbed."

"Get over it."

Hank stepped over Bryan's body. "I'm disappointed."

"I'm sure Rogers feels horrible about your disappointment."

Hank's snort was his reply. "You think he was a decoy?"

"That would be a yes. What a shitty way to use a friend."

Hank shook his head. "They weren't friends. None of us are friends."

A sentiment he'd drilled into Emmet's head time and again. No, none of them were friends. But two of them were closer than any friends could be.

A low hum alerted Emmet to Hank's phone ringing. Hank fished it out of his pocket. A few swipes and a video began to play. Emmet angled his head for a better view. It didn't take long for him to realize it was a video of the house he grew up in. A home thirty miles away.

"Someone's in the house?" The video continued up the central staircase and veered toward the master suite, Hank's bedroom.

"I'm going to kill Rogers, have a doctor save him, and kill him again," Hank growled.

Emmet studied the video while Hank railed. The videographer was in the bedroom now and at Hank's Matisse, which hid his personal safe. The image shook, and it took a second for Emmet to realize why. Hank's hand trembled, something Emmet would've sworn he'd never seen or would ever see. He clutched his gun tighter.

"What's in the safe?" What's has Hank so rattled?

The safe swung open soundlessly. The video pulled back to

show a gloved hand reaching inside for a manila folder, then the video ended.

Hank gripped the phone in his hand tight enough to crack the screen. Emmet waited. Hank would share when he was ready. It didn't take long. "I need a favor."

Emmet had an idea where this was headed. "Not if it takes me away from guarding your back."

"I need you to head to Jamaica."

This wasn't the first time Hank had tried to brush him off and take on Rogers by himself. It wasn't the second time either. The argument was past old, and Emmet was tired of it. "Not happening, old man."

Hank went into his email account. Emmet bent down to rifle through Bryan's pockets for any clues. His phone vibrated, and he looked up at Hank. "Did you just send me an email?"

"Yes." He spun, bloody coat flapping from the breeze he created. He headed for the rear of the abandoned building and the cars they'd parked in the bush.

Emmet caught up to him at the Range Rover. "What's in the email?"

"Everything you need to know about my daughter."

What?

Hank turned slowly as if to give Emmet time to absorb his last word.

And Emmet needed a few seconds to absorb that word. *Daughter.*

Hank retrieved two gas cans from the trunk of the car and handed one to Emmet.

"Since when do you have a daughter?" And how old was the kid? Had to be recent. *God, he wants me to babysit an infant, or worse, a toddler.*

Hank pulled out his wallet and retrieved a picture from inside. He held it up for Emmet to see.

Holy. Fuck. "You have a grown daughter that I know nothing about? A grown daughter." With black hair and blue eyes. She was in a park on a skateboard, wearing board shorts and a wife beater with a ballcap on backward. The picture was taken with a telephoto lens unbeknownst to the girl—woman. "Why the secret?"

Hank pressed into the center of Emmet's chest. "Everything you need to know about her is in the email I sent you, including how to find her. Go to our storage unit on Lexington. There you'll find everything you need in the black duffle bag on the back shelf." He turned away, but Emmet grabbed his arm, hard.

Angrier than he'd ever been with his mentor, he got in Hank's face. "I need more than a fucking email." *You owe me more than a fucking email.*

Hank pried Emmet's hand from his arm and growled, "Rogers has all of the hard copies on her. Everything I've compiled. She's out there, exposed. I can't protect her and round up my allies. That's why I'm sending you." He headed back into the warehouse.

But—but. Emmet heard everything Hank said, yet his brain struggled to wrap around this twenty plus-year-old secret. He followed Hank into the warehouse. Together, they doused the interior with gasoline and lit a match when they exited the building.

Hank climbed into the Range Rover and started the engine. Emmet knocked on the window. It whirled down, and he stared at his mentor/father/friend. "Don't get yourself killed."

A fraction of a grin lifted one corner of Hank's mouth. "Same goes for you."

Emmet had a list of questions that wouldn't be answered today. But soon. If he couldn't get it from the father, he'd get it from the daughter.

Hank has a daughter. What the fuck?!

Emmet threw himself into the Lexus GX that had been parked next to the Range Rover. He started the car and followed Hank out of the overgrown parking lot. Hank went right. Emmet went left. He drove the speed limit, his gaze darting to the rearview mirror for any tails, and carefully merged onto the highway.

And that's when it hit him. He didn't even know her name.

CHAPTER 2

Two Days Later

"What about that one?" Daisy tipped her head at the group of men gathered by the bar. Not as nonchalant as she'd like since they'd seen her. Actually, the men hadn't taken their eyes off her since she and Bailey had arrived at the pool. "I want the blond one." She grinned at the man.

"Of course you do," Bailey said without removing her attention from the book in her lap. "Like you said, you want blond, blue-eyed babies. Just like you."

Daisy glared at her over the rim of her glass. "Do I hear censure in your voice?"

"No." People in glass houses etc., etc. She wasn't one to judge, especially not her best friend.

Bailey spared Daisy a glance and took in the perfection of her heart-shaped face, pouty, bee-stung lips, her long, blond hair pinned to the top of her head with curls cascading around the face. "You have a type and never deviate. Golden-haired Adonises. Others need not apply."

Daisy giggled. "You have a point. But you never know." She gave a forlorn glance at all the barely clothed bodies frolicking in the Olympic-sized pool and sighed wistfully, "Out there, somewhere, is some dark-haired, suave, hunk of a man who will entice me away from my blond obsession. Until the time, he comes along to sweep me off my feet, I'm gonna have fun, and you should too."

Here we go. Bailey gave a nonchalant shrug and focused on her book.

Daisy snatched the book out of Bailey's hands and tossed it to the foot of the lounger. "We are not here to read. We are here to have fun with men our own age." She stressed the last word.

Bailey knew where this was going and had no way to stop the Daisy train. "I know that, but I'm just not interested."

Daisy rotated her body and faced Bailey. She crossed her legs, folded her arms under her ample breasts, and twirled her finger around a strand of hair. Diamond hoops twinkled in her ears. She shouldn't be wearing them, but when money was no object because Daddy footed the bill... "Why? Because there are no geriatric men in sight?"

Low blow. Bailey rolled her eyes.

"Don't try it, girlfriend." Daisy continued. "Ninety-three is the combined age of your last two boyfriends."

Damn it, why did she have to bring that up, *again*.

"You have a daddy complex, and I bet some fresh, young dick will cure you of it." Daisy waggled her sculpted eyebrows. "That is why we're here, right?"

That was the initial plan, Bailey admitted to herself.

Daisy harrumphed as if she'd read Bailey's mind. "We've been here three days, and you haven't even said hello to anyone with a penis and a set of balls."

"And they haven't said hello to me either." Thank God. She liked her men with more substance than worrying about their next blowjob and a more than general idea of what to do with a clit.

"Could be your resting bitch face. You're scaring the men away." Daisy side-eyed Bailey.

Please. "If a man is that easily intimidated by a look, he's not worth the effort."

"I want a man I can intimidate into buying me anything I want," Daisy said with supreme confidence. Why Daisy would need anyone to buy her anything when her father was on the *Forbes* list of wealthiest men in the world was beyond Bailey.

"Good grief, Bailey." Daisy made a circle around Bailey's entire head. "I actually think it hurts you to smile."

Bailey wasn't surprised Daisy ignored her. It was her usual M.O. when Bailey said something logical. "I smile when I have a reason to. Only idiots prance around with a permanent smile attached to their face. No one is happy all the time." *And I'm not one to fake it.*

Daisy tossed back her drink and stood. "Fine. Don't smile and don't be happy. I did not come to a tropical paradise full of gorgeous men to be miserable and mopey. Enjoy the book. I'll see you later." She stretched her curvy body clad in a barely-there white bikini and headed for the bar. The hottest guy met her with a Corona. All Bailey could do was shake her head. Daisy hadn't bought her own drink since she turned sixteen.

Bailey studied the group of men. All handsome. All muscular and tanned. Sexy as hell. And she wasn't interested. They came to the exclusive resort in Jamaica for uncomplicated fun and sun. Translation: sex and a tan. It's what the resort specialized in, "A private getaway for a private affair."

Daisy sold Bailey on this trip after they were both dumped within weeks of each other. In truth, Daisy dumped her boyfriend because she was bored. Bailey didn't dump Richard. She just stopped trying. Trying to see him, talk to him, reach him on a level deeper than skin.

Yeah, they were great in bed, but after the exchange of bodily fluids, they had nothing else to say except everything they'd already said. Six months of the same repetition. Richard was cute enough, worked middle management at a marketing firm, and liked kids and small pets. He was older, settled, safe. A future with him promised a four-bedroom home in the suburbs, two kids, one purebred dog, and cat. Sex once a week, pot roast every Sunday, membership at the local country club which they probably couldn't afford, and a minivan.

She thought it was enough. It wasn't. Not for her.

On the one hand, it was good to know what she didn't want. On the other hand, what did she want? She couldn't keep a nine to five. No patience, short-tempered and with a bank account in the love seven figures thanks to a biological mother she never knew, not joining the workforce hadn't left her on the street.

She had a Bachelor of Liberal Arts she never used. Started and stopped her master's degree three times. Bought a massage and yoga franchise and sold it after eighteen months because she was bored. Nothing interested her. Rather, nothing fit her. She was a square peg in a round world. She had yet to find her niche and had no idea what that niche could be.

A floundering boat was how she silently described herself, and she had no idea how to right whatever was wrong.

Studying the group of men fawning over her best friend, Bailey knew *that* wasn't what she wanted either. She gathered her book, floppy hat, and returned to her bungalow. Knowing Daisy wouldn't miss her for hours, Bailey showered and dressed in a pair of long shorts, a loose shirt, and her comfortable Teva sandals.

She took in her appearance and mumbled, "You are so sexy." A laugh bubbled up as she slapped a baseball cap on her head. Her jet-black pixie hair curled at the edges of the cap. Dressed like this she was a ringer for a teenage boy, which was easy with her thin frame and minuscule boobs. Losing thirty pounds over a man was stupid. Though, it wasn't so much Richard that sent her into the breakup spiral. It was the lack of anything tangible in her life.

At twenty-five, she'd expected to have a career and a husband who adored her as much as she adored him, the possibility of a child, maybe even the four-bedroom house in the suburbs. With Richard, the thought of all that domesticity made her nauseous. But with the right man...

He'd have to be adventurous. She wasn't talking about skydiving, but there were a few places in the world she hadn't visited, and she wanted to do so with a partner. He had to be funny. A sense of humor was paramount. He had to be able to laugh at himself. Not take life so seriously. Sex wasn't that important, as long as he was adequate in bed, he'd do.

With her camera hanging around her neck and her fanny pack on her hips, Bailey exited her bungalow. She skirted the pool area, bar, and spa. A quick hike to the front of the resort, she got a ride on the hospitality shuttle to the open market in the middle of the town the resort bordered on.

Her phone rang as they bounced along the roads. It was Theresa. She turned the phone off and zipped it inside her fanny pack.

"The resort recommends all guests do not stray from the market," the driver said in a thick accent. "Watch your belongings carefully and do not give to beggars. It only encourages them."

"Thanks for the pep talk." This wasn't her first foray off the beaten path. She stepped from the shuttle and uncapped the lens of her camera and started clicking.

The market was more like a bazaar filled with every colorful item imaginable and every exotic scent she'd ever inhaled. But it was the people that fascinated her. The pleasure on their faces when she asked for permission to take their photos. The joy at viewing the result. She loved taking pictures of the children.

Something about capturing their youth, a moment when happiness is all they felt, inspired her.

She bought a beef patty with coco bread from a vendor along with a ginger beer to quench her thirst as she wandered the stalls purchasing decorative earrings, a seashell necklace, and bracelet. A dance troupe sashayed by in their colorful, yet scanty outfits. She captured the fluidity of their bodies, their gaiety and the ecstasy in their movements. They danced around her, made her join in, though she couldn't keep up and made a complete fool of herself.

And she loved it, this small piece of faux freedom where nothing mattered except the sun on her skin, the wind in her hair, and the good food in her tummy.

Something tugged on her waist, and her fanny pack slid free. She spun, expecting it to be near her feet. Instead, it was running away, carried by a kid as fast as a cheetah. She took off after him, darting around people, pushing some out of her way and screaming an apology as she struggled to keep the kid in sight. A woman blocked her, and the kid vanished down an alley off the main square.

This was a bad idea, but she followed. Her passport and wallet were in her fanny pack. She had to get it back. The alley was filled with a network of shanties made of leftover aluminum and wood and anything else the occupants got a hold of. That's how it was on most of the island. Luxury and poverty residing feet apart. Present, yet tucked out of sight away from the tourists. The boy ran into one of those shanties. Ordinarily, she wasn't one to barge into someone's house unannounced, but the kid had her shit.

At full speed, she barreled toward the open doorway, and nearly bounced off the chest of a man. She backed up and noticed the man wasn't alone. Others came out of the shanties to watch.

She raised her hands in mock surrender. "I don't want any trouble. I only want what belongs to me."

"This what you want?" he said in a thick accent as he signaled to someone inside the shanty. The boy came out carrying her fanny pack in one hand and a smug grin on his face.

"It's mine." She held out her hand.

The man unzipped the pouch and peered inside. "Valuable stuff inside. I see a passport. No cash, though. You want it back?"

Nah, you can keep my passport and credit cards. I don't need them. "Yes. I want them back," she said calmly as more spectators gathered to watch. Or to join? She wasn't sure.

"What you give me for it?" He haggled like a professional thief.

"How can I give you something when you have everything?" She gritted out the words through her teeth.

His grin was a black hole of missing teeth. He gave her that "I'm hungry and you're a piece of meat" look that made her want a bath. "I know what you can give me."

Not happening. Bailey stepped back. The man stepped forward, reaching for her. It would be the last thing he ever reached for.

"Step away from the woman." A voice cracked like a whip and echoed in the alley.

She didn't move. She kept her focus trained on the asshole holding her fanny pack. Whoever the voice belonged to, she'd thank him for the distraction later.

Footsteps sounded behind her. Steady, the precise pace brought another man to her right. He swept in front of her without pause. Crisp white short-sleeved shirt stretched over a well-defined broad back. White male, black crew cut fade. Tall, the way she liked them.

She reared back, flustered at his proximity and nerve. One doesn't step into an altercation that's none of one's business.

"Who are you?" her would-be thief asked.

And she concurred. Who was he? She moved to the left for a better view and wasn't disappointed. His profile was as fine as the man. For a fraction of a second, his gaze cut to her—blue, ice blue. A chill ran down her spine, not just from his artic gaze. Everything about the man was hard, cold, and hostile, deadly to anything with a pulse. Yet, contained on a low simmer, under a thin veneer of slightly tanned skin. *I think I've found Daisy's, perfect non-blond man.*

His gaze returned to the would-be thief. And just like that, the Caribbean sun heated her blood. "The pack, it's not worth losing an arm," her newfound protector said. She liked his voice, the sexy, low timbre hummed along her skin.

"I ain't afraid of you."

Liar. She could hear the fear in his voice, even with more people filling the alley. Whoa! Her protector had moved so fast, she'd missed the fight but not the result. The thief was sprawled on the ground. Un-fucking-conscious. Talk about a glass jaw. Her *hero* bent down and plucked her fanny pack free. He still didn't turn to face her. Instead, he stepped in front of her again and pulled a gun from beneath his shirt.

"We got a problem here?" he faced the crowd, meeting their hostile eyes. One by one, they turned away and cleared a path out of the alley.

He took her arm, his fingers rough and warm, and strong on her skin. He didn't give her a choice, not that she would've chosen differently, as he guided her out of the alley. Back on the main thoroughfare, she pulled free and spun.

She'd seen him before. Last night, at the pool party. He sat at a table tucked into a corner in the back, observing everyone while he sipped on a clear drink. Could've been vodka but she suspected club soda. She didn't know why the thought occurred when it and he were none of her business. He'd seemed out of place with his brooding dark looks, intense stare, and general don't fuck with me vibe. He carried himself like he knew how to deliver pain, or pleasure, depending on the circumstances.

No one fucked with him. Including most of the women. Oh, some brave souls sauntered up to him in their bikinis and clear heels. Their breasts high, their pelvises forward, strutting like they were on a runway. With a flick of his fingers, he sent them on their way.

Now, he stared at her with the icy blue eyes. Did that color have a name? "I didn't need your help."

He cocked his head to the side, and she noticed he had a touch of salt mixed in with his coal black hair at his temple. His brow lowered to two angry slashes over those eyes, he stated matter-of-factly, "You did. Accept it and move on." His lips formed a grim slash that she suspected were full if he ever smiled. She couldn't tell if his jaw was squared or sharp due to a full beard and mustache, but she wanted to know.

Hand to the small of her back, he guided her through the throng. She had no idea where he led her and didn't fight it. Out of the crowd was good enough for now. People cleared out of their way when they saw him coming. She didn't like his familiarity, his hand on her body, heating her skin through the thin barrier of her shirt, or her body's reaction to that heat. She certainly didn't approve of the way he took over. For the moment, she kept that opinion to herself.

He guided her out of the bazaar to a small compact car parked on a side road and opened the passenger door. "Get in," he ordered, assuming she'd obey as he rounded the front of the car. Such a gentleman. Not that she cared.

"I was taught to never take a ride from a stranger."

He leaned on the hood, arms splayed, knuckles pressed onto the metal, those cold eyes of his latched onto her. "Good lesson. Doesn't apply today. Get in the car."

"Why?"

An eyebrow shot up, and his head cocked to the side.

She got the sense no one questioned him. That this was a first for him. "You want to stay and deal with that guy when he wakes up since you didn't need my help?"

"Don't threaten me."

His brow arched with disdain. "You consider that a threat? Babe, when I threaten you, you'll know it."

Babe? Hackles rose on the back of her neck. The last thing she needed was to be alone in a car with this man. The hotel shuttle coasted by them and stopped at the end of the street, a block away.

"Thanks for the offer of the ride and getting my stuff back." She slammed his car door closed and headed for the shuttle. Don't know why, but she expected footsteps coming up behind her. There weren't any. She made it to the open-air shuttle and parked her ass on the bench, along with the other hotel guests who visited the bazaar.

Five minutes later, the shuttle pulled away, and she bounced along with the rest of the people, aware of the car trailing them.

Don't turn around. Don't turn around.

She locked her muscles down and refused to give in. Something was wrong. This guy wasn't a Good Samaritan. He didn't *rescue* her out of the kindness of his heart. He had an agenda. What she didn't know, but whatever it was, he would be disappointed.

His name! She hadn't gotten his name. Also, he hadn't asked for hers, yet he ordered her around as if he had the right to do so.

She hopped out of the shuttle as it coasted to a stop in the circular drive of the hotel and noted the compact continuing down the road to the rear of the hotel.

Her gut churned. He may not know her name, but how difficult would it be to find out when they were staying at the same hotel? Especially for him, a handsome asshole used to getting his way.

CHAPTER 3

*D*inner was a fantastic affair Bailey shared with Daisy, her new fuckbuddy, and fuckbuddy's bestie who stared expectantly at Bailey. Did he think she would strip down and spread her legs for him in the restaurant? Apparently so. Other than her name, he hadn't asked her a single question. Instead, he talked to the guy at the next table about the beach volleyball game they'd played earlier, then his workout routine. He was very proud of his over-stacked, greased muscles and his musky body spray.

Big mistake letting Daisy rope her into this. At least the grilled sea bass and vegetables were delicious, though her appetite had fled soon after the men had joined them.

Daisy laughed at something her fuckbuddy whispered in her ear. He was cute with his lean body and sun-bleached long hair. He draped his arm around her chair and angled his body toward her, the epitome of attentiveness to his companion. As opposed to Bailey's date.

Do you really want his attention? A quick no followed.

She also didn't want to be alone. After the bazaar, she returned to her room for a shower and a nap and ended up staring at the palm ceiling fan spinning over her bed. Anxious and on edge, she considered packing and leaving two days earlier than her planned return to Atlanta.

But why, why the urge to run when none of the hardships she'd suffered in her twenty-five years had ever caused her to cut bait and swim? Something about that guy unnerved her, and she didn't like it.

She wasn't a runner. Had never been and wouldn't start now. Besides, she'd left her room hours ago and hadn't seen him.

A beefy hand landed on her knee and squeezed. She grabbed his middle finger and bent it backward in response.

"Hey!" Her date snatched his hand away. His startled glare was all about "What. The. Fuck."

She crooked her finger and waited for him to lean in so she could whisper in his ear. "I'll tell you when you can touch me." She tossed her napkin onto her unfinished seabass, downed her third drink, and shoved her chair back. She snatched up her purse, gave Daisy the silent code for "I'm outta here," and headed for the exit. By the time she hit the atrium, Daisy was next to her.

"Chicks before dicks," she singsonged.

And that's why they were best friends because, at the end of the day, they always had each other's backs.

They shared a high five and a laugh as they followed the reggae music to the bonfire on the beach. Bailey kicked off her sandals and let her toes sink into the warm sand as she hiked over the dunes with Daisy. She had the right idea wearing a short flowy skirt that allowed her to enjoy the cool breeze on her toned legs. Bailey wished she could roll up her palazzo pants, but that wouldn't keep them from rolling back into place. At least the warm air caressed her back and shoulders in the lacy halter top she matched with the pants.

Daisy's fuckbuddy showed up and snatched her away before they got to the bonfire circle. Not so much a bonfire, but more like a large firepit. Still, with the music, and the cold drinks, and the dancing bodies, it was nice.

A guy separated from the circle and came to her. He was young and cute, with cut abs she couldn't help appreciating.

"Dance?" Not waiting for her reply, he hooked her waist and grooved to the music.

She kept it PG-13, though didn't mind when he pulled her close and pressed his body into hers. Daisy, on the other hand, went full rated R, bordering on XXX, as were most of the couples grinding on each other. Bailey slipped her phone out of her purse and snapped a pic. Daisy saw the flash and posed for another one.

"Crazy!" Bailey screamed at her bestie and slipped her phone into her pants pocket for easy access.

Her dance partner's hand moved from her waist and cupped her ass. He was really slick about it, easing her into him to cop a feel. You know, any other day, he would've gotten a fist down his throat. Maybe it was the liquor humming in her blood, blunting the remaining edginess over her strange day. Whatever the reason, she went with it when he brought their pelvises together.

His erection poked her. And instead of being turned on, she giggled. Not at his erection. The absurdity of the situation struck her. She'd come to Jamaica with a box of condoms for a week of uncomplicated sex, the same box she'd opened and used once with Richard six months ago.

She extricated herself from her would be lover's arms. He was a gentleman and let her go. "Thanks for the dance. I'm gonna go home, alone."

He pressed his hand to his heart and gave her a sad puppy dog look she almost fell for. "Aww. You sure? We could dance some more. No strings."

Maybe she should… "I'm sorry. I'm exhausted. You won't

be alone for long. Those ladies over there have been eying you." She patted him on the shoulder and strolled away.

She found Daisy still shaking her ass and signaled that she was turning in, then made her way around the fire pit to return to her bungalow.

Sandals dangled in one hand, palazzo pants fisted to keep from tripping, clutch braced under her arm, Bailey paused. Between the dancing flames of the fire pit, the guy from the bazaar appeared.

Not the thief, but her rescuer. He stood there watching her while people danced around him.

Buddy. You are fucking with the wrong girl.

Bailey continued her way, her pace deliberate. She had options and utilized her first one. "Excuse me," she called to a security guard standing near the entrance to the hotel, her pace unchanged as she approached. "There's a man following me." Wasn't quite true, but the guard didn't need to know that. "I believe he's a guest, but I'm feeling very uncomfortable."

The guard looked over her shoulder, peering into the night. "I will speak to him right away. Can you point him out to me, please?"

She didn't expect him to be standing under a streetlamp, fully illuminated, waiting for her to point a finger labeling him a stalker. Though, it would've made things easier. "He's six-three, dressed in a white shirt with dark jeans. Dark hair with a beard and mustache, silver watch on his left wrist, no jewelry. Don't go alone. I saw a gun in his waistband."

The guard unclipped his walkie-talkie. "Need back up. Man with a gun on the property." He gave the description Bailey provided as he jogged into the crowd.

Three more security guards dashed out of the building. That gave her some breathing room, but she wasn't stupid enough to believe she was out of the woods.

She waited for the guard to return but spotted another guard moving through the crowd coming at her. "Ma'am, I will escort you to your room."

"Did you find him?"

"Not yet ma'am, but I'm certain we will. For your safety, I will see you to your quarters."

That was a good idea. She nodded and cut through the hotel, taking the long way through the full lobby, the restaurant, and the conference center. Her guard's phone rang. He turned the volume down and gave her an apologetic smile.

They exited out of a side door on a path leading to the private bungalows lining the beach. Hers was next to Daisy's, the last two bungalows out of ten.

She loved the privacy when she arrived three days ago. Now, all she saw was the danger. Isolated, with dim lighting, the music from the firepit and the outdoor club on the second-floor terrace would drown out any scream.

"Have they found him?" she asked the guard.

"Not yet," he said quickly with another smile.

How would he know that when he hadn't checked in. Clipped to his shoulder, the walkie-talkie was silent. He just kept grinning.

Bailey let her sandals slip from her fingers into a potted plant lining the walkway. The flat thongs wouldn't help, and the guard didn't notice as he rechecked his phone. She opened her clutch and rifled around the inside.

"Trying to get this keycard," she mumbled to herself while pushing the keycard out of the way. "Small purse, but I've got everything in it." Lipstick, comb, gum, credit card, and a pen.

Her bungalow was up ahead. She didn't have much time. Palming the Bic with her last three fingers, she pulled out her keycard, tucked her purse under her arm, and switched the keycard to her other hand.

Slow breath in. Slow breath out. The door to her bungalow was up ahead. The guard cut in front of her. "Allow me, ma'am."

He pulled a keycard with a black strip down the middle and swiped it through the lock. A low snick, a turn of the knob, and the door swung open to the softly lit interior.

He stepped back, giving her plenty of room to sweep past him and enter. Then, he would follow her inside. She wondered how much he was paid to what? Keep her here and tenderized her for the main event? Rape her? Kill her? Both? Was the man who'd rescued her at the bazaar behind this? She didn't buy that last train of thought. He wasn't the type to need help to take what he wanted whether it be a woman or a life.

Bailey stepped into her bungalow. The maid had tidied up. Fresh sheets, fresh mints on her pillow, a towel twisted into the shape of a palm tree. Lamp, towel, chair, coffee pot, and mugs, all the things she could use to defend herself, combined with all her years of training, crystallized in her head.

Adrenalin pouring into her bloodstream, Bailey tossed her clutch onto the chaise, gripped the pen tight in her hand and spun. Sure enough, the guard was inside her room, with his phone pressed to his ear. "Bring da money. I got her."

He nudged the door closed behind him, but it banged open and a big body barreled into him. Stunned by the fast assault, the guard was knocked to the ground. A rubber-soled boot to the throat kept him there, along with a silencer to the temple. Held by the man from the bazaar.

"Who sent you? Answer fast. I don't have time to waste."

The guard managed a garbled sound until the boot eased off his throat. "Didn't get a name. Promised me money to keep her here for him."

Bailey backed up. She could do a lot of things. Dodging a bullet wasn't one of them. If she could make it to the screen door and onto the beach, she may have a chance to make it back to the hotel.

"Don't. Move." His gaze landed on her and leeched all the heat from her body.

A sharp rap sounded at the bungalow door.

He kicked the guard in the jaw, knocking him out cold, and crossed the short distance separating him from her. His gun still in his hand.

"What do you want?" she croaked, afraid for the first time today.

The knock sounded again at the door, harder, angrier.

He stepped right up to her, towered over her, crowded her, tried to intimidate. "Bailey Michela Monroe."

Body blow to the gut. *How the fuck does he know my name?*

"Your father sent me to save your life, and that's exactly what I'm going to do." He pointed the gun at the door and fired.

CHAPTER 4

"Bullshit. My father doesn't know I exist." She wanted the words to come out hard as an indisputable fact; instead, they were a raspy whisper.

That got his head cranked to the side and his brows furrowed with a silent question. "Henry Murray. Also known as Hank, is your father, is he not?"

He had the right name, but that didn't mean anything.

Shots pierced the cheap wood of the door. Bailey ducked and dove onto the chaise. She had nothing for cover, except her purse which wouldn't offer much. Mr. No Name snatched her hand and pulled her to the screen door. He unlocked it, slid it open a crack, and slipped onto the deck. He held a hand up for her to wait.

A gunman in front of her. A gunman behind her. No other options available, she waited and counted off the seconds. She made it to thirty, then he threw the screen wide and hauled her ass out of the room.

"Run. I'm right behind you."

No shoes on her feet, Bailey ran. The man claiming her father sent him to save her, close behind.

Yeah, claiming.

He shoved her left, she stumbled as a bullet clipped a nearby palm tree. He spun and returned fire while she huddled in the bushes. "Why does someone want me dead?" she hissed.

"They want me dead."

That was a relief.

"So they can kidnap and torture you to get to Hank."

That was bad.

He hauled her up by her arm and pushed her in front of him. They took the long way around the party, through overgrown bushes hiding what the hotel didn't want the guests to see and exited through a broken gate into an alley filled with dumpsters. She ran through filthy, stagnant water, praying she didn't slice her feet open and end up having to amputate a limb.

"Right."

That single word had her veering right into a parking lot.

"The Celica."

She raced up to a battered Celica and hopped into the passenger seat. Her savior dropped into the driver's seat. Gun pointed out the side window, with his free hand he started the car and shifted the gears. The engine roared much louder than any Celica she'd ever heard. A man raced out of the alley and had to dive behind a dumpster or eat bullets. Her savior didn't stop until his gun ran dry and the hotel was in the rearview mirror.

Her heart had relocated to her throat, and sweat coated every inch of her, while the man next to her was as cool as his icy eyes. He sat in his bucket seat as if he owned the world even though his knees hit the underside of the dashboard.

"What is your name?"

Focused on the road, he took his time answering. "Emmet."

Not good enough. "Last or first?"

"First."

She folded her arms and waited for the rest. And continued to wait. Fine. "Prove you know Hank."

"When we get to the airport."

Airport? She was not getting on a plane with him. However, he didn't need to know this yet. "Prove it now."

That got her his attention, well, a quick glance, and then he refocused on the road. "When we get to the airport."

Bailey settled back in the seat and studied the few road signs. Not easy in the dark, on a road cutting through the jungle.

She didn't know this man, and jumping out in the middle of nowhere with another man willing to kill and kidnap her, wasn't smart. But she would be ready. With the airport an hour away, she would have her chance.

Thirty minutes later, they drove through a bustling town she didn't remember driving through when she first arrived. People milled about. There had to be someone willing to help her, get her to the consulate. When the car rolled to a stop at a red light, she took a chance and yanked on the handle.

And nothing happened.

"Lock is disabled."

Bailey cranked her head around at him while he slammed a new clip into his gun. On their left, a police car rolled up next to them.

"I know you're thinking about screaming, slugging me, drawing attention to the car." He placed the gun on his lap and returned his hands to the wheel. He tipped his head in greeting at the lone officer. Focused back on the road, he whispered, "Do so, and that man will die. His blood will be on your hands. Can you live with that, Bailey?"

She swallowed the sudden lump blocking her throat, keeping her from breathing.

Now, he fully met her gaze. "Your father gave me one job, and I will not fail. I will kill without a moment of hesitation and sleep the sleep of an innocent babe afterward. Understand me?"

Yes. She understood perfectly.

Hank had sent a man with no heart, no moral compass, no

conscience. A man who did as he pleased. A man just like him. Hank had sent her a killer.

CHAPTER 5

The car slowed. "Wake up."

Bailey wasn't asleep. She'd rested her eyes and centered herself for whatever came next because she wasn't getting on that plane.

Sitting up, she studied the small airport with a spat of two propeller airplanes parked well back from the runway. The hell she was getting on one of those. Gated, they needed entry, which was provided by a man armed with an AK-47 slung over his shoulder.

"One of your men?" she asked when he waved them through.

"No," he growled, clearly not happy about it. A large hangar came into view. "Listen well. When I get out of the car, you will stay in the car until I come for you. Understand me."

Statement, not a question needing an answer. Why formed on her tongue and stayed there as three men blocked the hangar entrance, two of them armed. Behind them, a G6 waited.

Emmet parked, but he didn't cut the engine. He reached into the back seat and retrieved a duffel bag. As he climbed out of the car, she caught, "Streets, how are you," from the guy in the center before Emmet slammed the car door closed.

Bailey hustled her butt over the gears and eased into the driver's seat. No one noticed, and if they did, no one cared.

She could shift into reverse, spin the car around, crash through the gate to freedom, and no one could stop her. Instead, she hit the window button.

Did Emmet hear the glass lowering? If he had, his attention didn't deviate from the men in front of him. Her foot hovered over the gas, her hand rested on the gear shift. She could be out of there in seconds, simply shift into drive and hit the gas. Except, *what if this Emmet asshole hadn't lied and this wasn't some elaborate kidnapping? What if Hank had sent him to protect me?*

Options. Options.

Emmet moved in front of the car and rested the bag on the hood. He unzipped it and pulled out two bricks of cash. Separated by a windshield, their gazes met. He stared as if he knew her indecision. Should she trust him? Could she? Even if Hank had sent him, which was reason enough to head for the hills. *Fuck.* How could she when she didn't trust Hank, never had.

A fraction of a smile tweaked his lips at the same time he gave a subtle shake of his head.

"What going on?" one of the men shouted, his accent thick.

"Getting your cash." Emmet angled sideways, presenting a smaller target, and allowing her to see the trio. "Send one of your men over to collect."

Middleman motioned for his associate to get moving. He came forward, snatched the cash off the hood and returned to his boss. Money in hand, middleman weighed the brick as if he could tell the amount by touch alone.

Would he question the amount, demand Emmet give him more? Or was there truly honor among thieves?

"What else in dey bag?"

"Dirty underwear."

Middleman chuckled. "Is dat all?"

Emmet's hand slipped beneath his shirt and out came his gun at his side. "Come see." Clearly a threat though spoken softly.

The men carrying the AK's stepped up to the challenge and got a gun pointed at them from Emmet, and the G6 parked behind them. Someone was on the stairs, with a big ass gun. Friend? Foe? Shit could get messy.

Bailey revved the engine of the Celica. "Get out of the way," she mumbled. Running him over would defeat the point. Emmet didn't move.

Run him over.

She hit the gas. The back tires smoked and the souped-up engine, that baby roared. The body may be old, but the heart of the beast was young and ready for roadkill.

Emmet didn't move. Instead, he faced the trio, providing a big ass target. Bailey eased off the gas and switched her foot to the brake. Her hand landed on the gear shift, prepared to slam it into drive.

"You have friends in low places. Wanna keep them? Step the fuck off. Me and who I work for as enemies, ask yourself, is it worth it?"

The trio took Emmet's advice and stepped off. Exit stage right, they got in a black Escalade and gunned it.

Emmet didn't move. He kept them in his sights until their tail lights were in the distance. He gave a thumbs up to the man with the gun on the G6 stairs, then pivoted.

Bailey turned off the car and climbed out. Emmet waited, a silent statue with those artic eyes, for her to close the door. Now she waited for him to say something. They had a moment when their eyes locked with a ton of steel and a windshield separating them. He'd read her mind, and that had never happened before, with anyone.

Without a word or further acknowledgment, he snatched up the duffel full of something worth killing for and led the way to the plane. He played the gentleman he definitely wasn't and halted at the stairs. Bag slung over his shoulder, gun still in the other hand, eyes hooded. She crossed the hangar, her bare feet slapping on the concrete. Staring straight ahead, she ignored his presence and carefully placed her foot on the first stair. She gripped the rail and cranked her head around.

"Where are we going?"

"Miami."

"To Hank?"

His scowled, and a question formed in his eyes. "No."

"Why not? Where is he?"

"Get on the plane, Bailey."

She glanced at the entryway.

"You could've run me over." He tipped his chin to the car. "Roadkill and you would've been on your way back to your umbrella drinks and gropy dance partner." He leaned in and dropped his voice low. "But you didn't."

True enough. "I don't kill children and dumb animals."

A dry bark escaped him. "I don't need to guess which one I am." The low hum of the plane's engine kicked up a notch.

The same guy appeared at the top of the stairs. "What's the holdup? Bad weather is coming. We gotta leave now." He vanished into the interior.

One step at a time, she climbed, fully realizing the precarious position she'd placed herself in. She didn't stop until carpet tickled the soles of her feet.

Wow. So, this is how the rich lived. The interior was done in gray and silver with white leather seats trimmed with gray, Bailey took in the opulence along with her dirty feet and her less than haute couture attire that screamed she didn't belong.

With a solid thunk, the door closed and locked behind her.

Emmet moved past her, deeper into the plane, to take a seat at the conference table. For the first time all day, she was kind of at a loss.

The plane lurched and started taxiing. She sunk into the first leather seat and buckled up. There was nothing to see outside the window at one a.m. with night claiming the landscape.

A bell chimed, and a voice came from overhead. "Butts in seats. We've been cleared for takeoff. We'll be in the air in ten."

She'd only seen one guy, but surely another guy was flying the plane, a co-pilot. Too bad she had no one to ask.

Not going to ask him. Nope.

She loved flying. Especially the lift off to new destinations. Growing up as the child of a diplomat, flying all over the world had become routine. Funny how she always thought of Theresa every time she stepped onto a plane.

Her heart twisted at the thought of her mother's name, and she quickly locked down the memories. Some things were too painful to dig up. Theresa was at the top of that list.

Shit, Daisy! Bailey peeked over her shoulder at Emmet. He had his back to her, ignoring her. He got her on the plane, mission accomplished. She fished out her phone from her pocket and sent a quick text.

Met someone interesting. Left island for more intimate encounter. Don't freak out & yes, it's me. You've finally rubbed off on me.

Bailey chewed on her thumbnail, wondering how much more she should tell her. Not much more, she decided.

See u in ATL in

What was a reasonable time? How long would this misadventure take?

2 days. Love you.

That's how long she'd give Hank. Two days was all she owed him.

The whine of the engines went from idling to full throttle. The G6 rocketed down the runway. She gripped the armrest as her body pressed into the leather and didn't let go until the plane leveled off.

An overhead monitor showed the flight time to Miami. One

hour and forty minutes. Shorter than the flight time from her home in Atlanta. How would he get her into the states without her passport? That would be her chance to get him arrested and get help.

Damn it. She needed information and wouldn't get it sulking near the cockpit. She unbuckled and made the trek back to the man who *saved* her twice.

Bailey found him eating sushi with chopsticks when he hadn't even offered her a drink of water, but there was a beer opposite him, waiting for her she supposed. She sat and hated to admit she felt safer with the solid table separating them.

"There's a stocked kitchen behind you if you're hungry." He hadn't paused his food to mouth exchange, had barely spared her a glance.

"You said when we got to the airport you'd prove you know Hank. We are well past the airport."

Emmet placed his chopsticks on the side of his plate and wiped his mouth on a linen napkin. He took a deep swig of beer, then he leaned back in his seat, king of his domain. All those muscles flexing in his hands and arms, she watched with a dispassionate eye. This wasn't a date, and she wasn't interested.

He pulled his phone out of his pocket, swiped his thumb to unlock it, and pulled up a video. The one person she never thought to see again was on the screen. He'd aged. Gray peppered his hair, along with a wealth of crow's feet and frown lines.

"Bailey. Circumstances have changed. My associate, Emmet Streeter will protect you until the situation is resolved." The video ended.

Emmet picked up his phone, closed the screen and returned it to his back pocket.

Streeter, AKA Streets. "That's it. That's all I get. Three sentences." Which was more than she'd gotten in the last seven years.

"Your father has enemies. They want him dead. *Us* dead. To get to him, they will get to you. I'm here to prevent that."

Her lips curled back from her teeth, and she spat, "I'm a means to an end."

He gave a slight inclination of his head. "Good, you understand your situation."

Yeah, she understood. She was caught in the middle of a war she had no part of and no way out. A long swallow of her beer cooled her temper and allowed her to think instead of reacting. "Who's this enemy?" Maybe she could make him an ally.

"No one you need to worry about." He picked up his chopsticks.

"A mystery man is trying to kill me. I don't know his name. Don't know what he looks like, and I shouldn't worry about it?"

His chopsticks returned to the side of his plate, and he planted his elbows on the table. "His name is Rogers. He's a killer. As am I. As is your father who trained us."

Wow, she'd learned something new. Not that Hank was a killer, that she'd already known and accepted. The latest information, her father trained killers. All these years she thought he followed orders, didn't realize he *gave* orders. Men followed him, not the other way around.

And one of those men wanted him dead. Maybe there was a way she could help him.

She picked up the beer in front of her and took a long swallow, before demanding, "Tell me about Rogers."

CHAPTER 6

God, she was a piece of work. Stubborn, self-possessed, and unflappable. Emmet expected hysterics, anticipated a spoiled, pampered, privileged bitch he'd have to hogtie and carry. He expected to find someone he'd hate.

Instead, he was intrigued. She knew Hank was her father, and by her lack of surprise at his announcement, knew what he was, what he did for a living. However, she didn't *know* Hank, not how a daughter knows a father. Not how Emmet knew him, as the man he admired, respected, loved like the only father he'd ever had.

And Rogers...

"Rogers and Hank worked for the *Company*. Co-workers, you could say." He couldn't call it the agency. It would give too much away.

"The name of the company, what is it?"

He snorted. "You think we have a name? Like Apple or Nike? With a cute logo?" Aww, he'd hurt her feelings. She glowered at him, and he found he liked her glare. There was depth to her blue eyes and not just the navy color. Though she failed to hide it, every hope, dream, and lie resided in her eyes. One merely had to peer deep enough to find it.

"Are you black ops? Part of the government?"

Yes, and no. The government paid them a hefty salary, but no part of the government claimed governance, that's how deeply buried their existence was. However, that was privileged information. He waited for her next question.

Bailey snorted and rolled her eyes. His evasion hadn't escaped her notice. He added observant to her plus column. "Why is Rogers trying to kill Hank?"

"They're having a…procedural disagreement." Easiest way to describe it without the intimate details dragging the story out.

"They disagree on how to file the paperwork? Android vs iOS? PC vs Mac? That can't be why they're killing each other."

Snarky just got added to the plus column. "Rogers wants the company to go a different direction than Hank prefers." He tossed out.

Her gaze narrowed. "Does he want him to go legit?"

Legit had nothing to do with what happened between Hank and Rogers. One woman and a couple of Russians had turned their battleship into the Titanic. Only, instead of an iceberg, a slow leak had their ship dragging them below the surface. The leak being Rogers.

"Not going to answer? That's fine. I don't need one." She stretched and cracked several vertebrae in her neck. It had been a long day for her, and longer for him. He glanced at his watch. Thirty-two hours ago was the last time he'd slept. Wasn't his max. Once, he'd gone seventy-two hours waiting out an asshole who'd locked himself in a fucking safe room.

He needed to rest before they landed because she wasn't gonna be happy. And she needed to stay happy and healthy. Happy for his sanity and healthy for her father.

"We're landing in ninety minutes. There's a bedroom and shower for you to get cleaned up and get some rest."

"What's the point of getting cleaned up when I have no clean clothes. I don't even have shoes." She propped her dirty feet on the table, next to his half-eaten dragon roll. His chopsticks rolled from next to his plate and continued their journey off the edge of the table. Her right eyebrow rose in a graceful arch full of challenge.

Emmet picked up a piece of sushi with his fingers, smeared wasabi all over it, popped it in his mouth, and licked his fingers clean. A little bit of dirt? Fuck, he'd eaten out of wet dumpsters before he met Hank.

She removed her feet and sat up. Next thing he knew, she snagged his last piece of sushi, rolled it through the wasabi, slapped some pickled ginger on top and down the hatch it went. She even licked her fingers, slowly.

How do you taste? The sudden thought struck him straight in the cock and shocked the shit out of him. Tasting her wasn't gonna happen. Hell, she was practically his sister. Practically, except for the lack of any DNA in common. He had to say, the resemblance to Hank was there. They shared the same blue eyes, though Hank's had lost most of his humanity. The same bold square jaw, though hers had an appealing softness. The same straight black hair, except she rocked a messy asymmetric pixie cut, shaved on the left, layered to her shoulder on the right, and had no gray. She was a regular girl. Nothing really stood out about her. In truth, she'd blend easily into a crowd. A ghost.

Yet, everything about her grabbed his attention and kept it locked on target.

She snatched up her beer and took another long draw, her gaze locked on his. Not the first time a woman had tested him over drinks. It was, however, the first time his balls tightened.

"There's more beer in the kitchen." Say yes. He wanted her to accept his offer because of the challenge in her eyes, and the snarky twist of her lush pink mouth, but knew she wouldn't.

Soon she'd be too tired to do anything except sleep thanks to the crushed sleeping pill mixed into her beer.

She slumped in the chair as if the fight had gone out of her. "No. I've had enough liquor for one night."

By the sudden exhaustion etching her face, he agreed. Pointing to the back of the plane, he said, "Shower, bed, and I packed most of the stuff in your bungalow."

"Really? I should be angry, but, thanks." She yawned, rubbed her eyes, and rose to her feet. "What about you?"

He shrugged. "What about me?"

"Where are you going to sleep?"

Aww, she cared. He had a sarcastic reply ready to go and stopped at the concern on her face. She really did care.

Emmet tipped his head to the built-in leather sofa along the left side of the plane. "I've slept on worse."

"Oh, okay." She looked around a bit sheepishly. "Well, I wasn't gonna give up the bed. A quick catnap and I'll be fine."

He watched her shuffle off, stumbling a little when turbulence rocked the plane. She paused in the galley for a bottle of water and continued to the suite in the rear.

Emmet waited for the bedroom door to close to head to the cockpit. "You're clear to alter our course," he said to Blake and Paul, pilot and co-pilot.

"Paris still the destination?" Blake asked.

"No. Switzerland."

"Why Switzerland?" Paul peered over his shoulder at Emmet.

"Just get there." Emmet trusted Paul, just not with this information. That was the reason for the mid-flight destination change. He returned to the cabin. Now that his babysitting duties were done for the night, it was time to check in.

He retrieved his satellite phone from the duffel bag and sent a message. Package secured and waiting.

Bailey wasn't the only one who needed a shower. He could

wait until later. The sounds of movement came from the bedroom. He glanced at the door, imagined her inside, fresh from her shower. Skin wet.

"Don't go down this road," he mumbled. The Sat phone rang.

"Report," Hank ordered.

"As planned, we are on our way to Switzerland. I'll let you know when we arrive."

"Don't. It's too risky. I'll call you when I can."

Risky? "What's the latest on Rogers?"

"The search continues for the hole he's buried himself in. And not just him. Jerrod and Ivan have joined the fruitless effort."

If it were so fruitless, why did those he counted in the friend column continue to join the other side? What were they missing? "What swayed them to join Rogers?"

"I'm working on that."

"You alone?"

"No. Whiskey is here."

"Whiskey?" AKA Dylan McCallan. Once a part of their organization, he'd left on friendly terms. Yet, in these murky days where friends were now foes, could he be trusted?

"I brought him in, not the other way around."

Because I'm on babysitting duty and you have no one else. "I'm coming in."

"No, you're not," Hank hissed. "I need the freedom to move without worrying about—"

"I get it. You can't do what you need to do if you're worried about your kid. I'll take care of things on this end, and you take care of shit on yours." Emmet ended the call and flung the phone across the plane. It was either that or crushing it in his fist.

He lunged to his feet and paced. It was the only thing he could do trapped in a flying tube. Being inside a plane was too much like being inside a cage.

The memory of his father locking him in a dog crate for an

entire night clogged his brain. He didn't need that nightmare cluttering his mental landscape. And he didn't need more liquor either.

Emmet glanced at the closed door to the bedroom suite. He had to check on her, make sure the drug hadn't had an adverse effect. She locked the door. "Good girl." She hadn't forgotten the basics.

He retrieved the key hidden in one of the kitchen cabinets. The lock made a soft snick and opened quietly. Bailey had managed to strip off her clothes and cover her body with a robe provided for her by the agency they used to maintain the plane. Curled into the fetal position on the bottom half of the bed, she looked younger than her twenty-five years. And innocent, even with the smudged mascara from her rubbing her eyes. What happened between her and Hank for them to be estranged.

Emmet hadn't missed the fact Hank hadn't asked a single question about his daughter. Not a fucking one. If he had a daughter, regardless of her age, not a day would go by without him hearing her voice and knowing she was safe. Not a single damn day.

Fuck. "Glass houses, Dude." Who was he to judge. Hank had to have a good reason.

Emmet scooped Bailey up to lay her in the center of the bed and was surprised when a phone tumbled out of her palm. "Sneaky. Sneaky." He was impressed, not mad. That's what assuming her phone got lost in the pursuit got him.

He stretched her out on the bed and covered her with a comforter. Taking the phone from her would be too easy, and after they landed in Switzerland, not Miami, she'd need a security blanket—her phone. Which would last until she tried to make a call. Good thing she wasn't on any social media platforms. Odd for a woman today, but she wasn't, he'd checked. He had his IT person double-check.

He opened the back and removed the chip, and placed the phone right next to her.

Wonder how long it will take for her to find out? Wonder how big the explosion will be? Or will she be the female version of her father and not buckle under pressure...until this unexpected betrayal by the men he'd broken bread with and trained.

Man, he hated being sidelined in the first quarter of the game. It fucking sucked. A soft snore came from the object of his ire. A dry chuckle escaped him. No use being mad at her. Wasn't her fault.

He went into the bathroom for a long hot shower and an overdue shave. She hadn't moved an inch when he exited the bathroom with a towel wrapped low on his hips. He grabbed his to-go bag and dressed quickly in fresh clothing. He cleaned up after himself because why poke a sleeping bear. Enough things were coming down the pike that would piss her off. Knowing he was here, in the shower, naked for a few minutes while she lay unconscious, and her virtue remained intact, call the authorities.

Women got upset over the strangest things.

CHAPTER 7

What time is it? How long was I asleep? Have we landed?

All three questions tripped over themselves inside Bailey's brain as she pushed the blanket off her legs and struggled into a seated position. She scooted to the edge of the bed and flipped up the shade over the window. Sunlight flooded the suite which didn't make sense with a fight time of ninety minutes. They'd left Jamaica around one thirty in the morning and should be landing around three a.m. give or take when headwinds and other atmospheric disturbances were factored in.

"Where the hell are we?"

She climbed out of bed and stretched all the kinks out. However long she'd slept, it had been restful. Her mouth was desert dry, and her bladder was about to climb out of her body and take itself to the bathroom. She went to the bathroom and took care of business at both ends. Water out of the body and water in the body.

She stripped off the robe for a hot shower, picked the cucumber melon body wash over the pine scented one, and damn the water felt wonderful. She didn't even complain about the little bottles of shampoo and conditioner perched on a ledge. She washed her hair and blew it out with the dryer attached to the wall next to the mirror wondering about the sunlight and where Emmet was.

Obviously, he was still on the plane. That didn't stop her from wondering about him. How long had he known Hank? What was their relationship? Had Hank had endeared himself to another human being. She didn't know how to feel about that.

Too tired when she entered the suite to go through her suitcase for something to sleep in, she had enough energy to strip and throw on a robe. Now she emptied the bag onto the bed to see what her savior had decided to pack.

Hmm. She had a lot of underwear. Not sure how she felt about his hands all over them. Three pairs of jeans, two pairs of yoga pants, one sweater, socks, sneakers, and boots she'd worn to Jamaica—also her box of condoms and her vibrator. How considerate of him. Lastly, her winter coat lay on the corner chair. Was it there earlier?

Bailey had slept the sleep of the dead, and if Emmet or anyone else had entered the room, she'd had no idea. The lock on the door was still engaged, yet…

The trip down the rabbit hole had to wait. She brushed away her unease, dragged on her functional, plain white underwear, her skinny jeans, tank top, and sweater. He was kind enough to pack her toiletries so her pits, breath, and body didn't stink. She styled her hair and finished her routine with her usual eyeliner, mascara, and lip gloss.

So why was she checking herself out in the mirror?

Because I'm human, that's why. And to take a note out of Daisy's playbook, "When going into war, pack your armor."

Bailey flung her hands up. Who was she kidding? Her armor wasn't her sex appeal, it was her wits, and those didn't need a makeup tutorial.

She repacked her suitcase for a quick getaway and pulled her phone out from beneath the pillow. Had she put it there before she fell asleep?

Wait a sec. She'd fallen asleep at the foot of the bed...*hadn't I?*

Bailey moved to the door, it was still locked. She didn't buy it. Emmet had been in here, with her. She clutched her phone, now uncertain about it, uncertain about everything.

Opening the back cured her uncertainty. The chip was gone.

Motherfucker!

Stay calm. Stay calm.

Fuck calm. Nobody made a fool out of her.

One deep breath and she opened the bedroom door. The scent of coffee, eggs, and bacon smacked her. Her stomach let out a howl which she ignored because Emmet stood in the middle of the cabin with a mug in his hand. He'd changed into new clothes, replacing the dirty linen shirt and slacks with a black tee and black jeans. Not only was he clean shaven, displaying his cleft chin and arrogant jaw, his hair had a shine to it that it didn't have before she fell asleep at the *bottom* of the bed.

Circumstantial evidence, all of it. That didn't stop her from marching up to him, fisting his shirt, going up to her tiptoes, and taking a long, deep smell at the crux of his neck. Sure enough, a hint of pine clung to his warm skin.

"What are you doing?" His breath washed over her cheek sending goose bumps down her spine.

Unnerved by him being in her room while she was unconscious, angered by her phone being reverted to no better than a video game, and confused because she shouldn't imagine him naked anywhere within her proximity, she slammed her phone into the center of his chest and stepped back. He caught it before it fell to the floor.

"Am I your prisoner?"

His brow dropped low as he placed his mug carefully on the table and faced her. "No."

"Then first, why did you drug me? I know this because, second, that's the only way you could have taken a shower with me lying in the bedroom. I'm a light sleeper, and I would've heard."

"I drugged you because I didn't want the blowout over our destination until we landed."

What? "Destination? You said we were going to Miami." She shoved past him and ran to the monitor at the front of the plane. And there it was, the graphic of the plane winging its way over the Atlantic Ocean and Europe, on its way to Switzerland.

Switzerland. A lovely country. One she'd visited once during her travels. She spun and marched back to Emmet who hadn't moved from where she'd left him. "Why Switzerland?"

"Breathing room." He settled in front of a plate full of scrambled eggs, bacon, hash browns, and toast.

That wasn't an answer, but she doubted she'd get more. A second plate waited opposite him. And what about the chip. If he'd drugged her to get her on the other side of the world for her protection, he wasn't giving her that chip back. There were other ways to get a message out. She'd be patient.

She sat in front of the plate and reached for the cup of coffee waiting for her. And froze.

"Go ahead. You have my word, nothing is drugged."

"Your word means nothing to me."

"Well, it means everything to me."

They eyed each other, neither giving in until he reached across for her mug and drank a mouthful. Next, he took a forkful of her eggs, a bite of her bacon—

"All right. Enough slobbering over my food."

"Don't worry. I'm disease free."

"I'm relieved." Cream and three sugars made her coffee palatable, but she'd give her right arm for a Caramel Macchiato. A snap of her wrist opened the linen napkin for her to lay it across her lap. The eggs were fluffy and creamy with a bit of chive. Not her usual, but tasty. The bacon was crispy even though it was microwaved. She never liked hash browns. The bread, she buttered and slathered with jam. He watched her while she did it, probably amazed at her limited outburst.

Trapped on a plane, a meltdown would only get her so far. She took a sip of her coffee.

"There's only one bathroom—"

She slammed the mug down, sloshing the brew over the rim. "So, the pilots got a gander of me sprawled across the bed with nothing but a thin robe on?" The thought incensed her.

"—with a shower on the plane and I needed a shower, so I took one." He continued as if she hadn't said a word. "The pilots have their own toilet near the cockpit. The only person who saw you sprawled out was me."

Bailey stared into his cold blue eyes which weren't as cold anymore. Banked heat stoked the depths. Her nipples tightened making her aware of the sudden tension filling the space between them. Flustered, she broke contact first, her gaze dipping to the cooling food in front of her.

Emmet moved his food around the plate. "No need to be embarrassed. I didn't see much."

"Much?" she choked. "What's much?"

With a cool detachment, he said, "Nothing above the knee or below the neck. You were decent."

But he wasn't. At some point he was naked, and she missed it. Her gaze traveled from his face, down his neck to his broad shoulders. His Henley stretched over his deltoids and biceps, defining the muscles instead of hiding them.

"I take it you have my passport." He didn't seem the type to forget that critical document.

He nodded.

Asking for its return was a no go. On a good day, she was just stubborn. Today wasn't a good day.

He leaned back in his seat and with hooded eyes, watched

her eat, assessing her. Something stuck in his craw. She could tell by the slow narrowing of his eyes, and she wouldn't rise to the bait.

"I've known you approximately thirty-four hours and not once have you asked about your father's welfare."

And she wouldn't. "If you have a question ask it."

"Why haven't you asked?"

She leaned back, posing as he did with her arms out and relaxed, breathing steady as if his presence and questions hadn't affected her. "A better question is, has Hank asked about my welfare?"

He blinked, and surprise replaced the speculation in his eyes. She had her answer without him saying a single word. "Yeah, that road travels both ways." They finished breakfast in silence.

Only after she'd swallowed her last mouthful of coffee did he ask, "What happened between you and Hank?"

There was a lot she could say starting with how she felt abandoned, unloved, unwanted, forgotten, a mistake. How she never felt smart enough, pretty enough, good enough at anything and for anyone. How her first lover was old enough to be her grandfather. "Nothing happened between Hank and me. Absolutely nothing."

"Why do you do that?" Emmet asked.

"Do what?"

"You call your father by his first name instead of Dad, Daddy, etc. Why is that?"

"You don't know?" Intrigue replaced her anger.

"Know what?"

"I don't call him dad or any other endearments because he hasn't earned it."

He opened his mouth, probably to ask another question, but she'd had enough. "How much longer 'til we land?"

"Thirty minutes." He gritted the words out between clenched teeth.

She took her plate and mug to the kitchen, washed, dried and stacked everything away. She turned to find him standing silently behind her, always watching. "I'll be in the bedroom until then."

Forty-five minutes later, after they'd landed and taxied to a private hangar. Bailey followed behind Emmet, bundled against the cold with her suitcase in tow. And it was cold. Her lightweight winter coat wasn't cutting it, not at all.

An official from customs met them when they stepped off the plane, stamped their passports without even opening their bags. Good thing she didn't blink because she would've missed the payoff. An envelope exchanged hands.

She parked her ass inside of a lovely BMW SUV and waited for him to finish loading up the car with their luggage and more than a few unmarked boxes. "How much did you give him?" she asked when he settled into the driver's seat.

"Enough to get my money and weapons into the country."

"At least you're honest." She buckled her seatbelt.

"Always. It's my best trait." He started the engine and drove at a sedate pace out of the airport and merged onto the highway. There wasn't much to see with snow covering everything, yet it was serene.

"Where are you taking me?"

He didn't answer, and she wondered why the cold shoulder and if it was gonna be this way, them together, ignoring each other.

"To the mountains where I'll have a three-sixty view."

Seemed reasonable. "Will, um, Hank be there?"

He glanced at her, but she kept her attention on the road. He didn't need to see the hope on her face when even she heard it in her voice.

"No. My job is to take care of you while he takes care of our enemies."

"That's nice. I feel so safe." She drew out the last word and layered that bastard with a healthy dollop of sarcasm even though it was the truth. She did feel safe. Safe and pissed. Hank cared enough to send Emmet, but not enough to talk to her. What the hell had she ever done to the man for him to hate her so much?

Tears misted her eyes, and she focused on the view outside the passenger window. She couldn't remember the last time she'd cried because she made it a point to never think about her father, because she didn't have one.

"Hey? Are you…crying?"

She sniffed and blinked hard, took a moment to clear her throat and gave a mental, *fuck it* and refused to look at or answer him. She owed him nothing which included an answer.

He sighed. "I told you I won't let anything happen to you, so I don't know why you're crying," he grumbled as if her tears were an affront to his male sensibilities.

"Shut up, drive, and leave me alone, okay."

"Fine."

"Fine!"

"Fine!"

They glared holy hell at each other until he was forced to switch back to the road. Blessed silence ruled for the next thirty miles which wasn't long in the BMW.

"Why were you crying?" he demanded. "You've been robbed, almost kidnapped, shot at, had to run barefoot through the street, been drugged and you haven't shed a single tear through any of it. Now, when you're finally safe, you're bawling your eyes out. Why?"

Dumbfounded, she cranked her head around. "Bawling my eyes out? Really? I sniff twice, and you consider that bawling my eyes out?"

He nodded. "For you, yes."

She snorted and shook her head because he wasn't entirely wrong.

"Tell me. Why the waterworks?"

She shifted around in her seat, the words on her lips, but she held back. "How long have you known Hank?"

A muscle flexed in his jaw, and his hands tightened on the steering wheel. "Twenty years."

"Two decades. Wow. How old were you when you met him 'cause I'd guess you're about thirty?"

"I was twelve."

"That's young." She nodded, doing the math. "So, you were twelve when you met him, and you've known him twenty years... When did he tell you he had a daughter?"

His hesitation gave his answer, but she patiently waited for him to say, "Five days ago."

Bailey faced the windshield and studied the landscape whizzing by, the urge to cry completely gone. After all, she'd just proven what she already knew. She didn't exist to her father, never had, and never would. He had cared about Emmet, a twelve-year-old boy, more than he cared about his five-year-old daughter, who—at the time—didn't understand why all her friends had a daddy and she didn't.

CHAPTER 8

"Did you rent this, or do you own it?" Bailey asked leaning against the car.

"Rented," Emmet answered relieved to hear a note of awe in her voice and not tears. The last ninety minutes of the drive had been spent in strained silence. He didn't do well with crying women, especially when interrogation wasn't involved.

He parked the car in front of the house but would move it into the detached garage after unloading it.

"It's gorgeous. I have a thing for old houses. They have character, a soul."

He studied her profile as she studied the house. The joy on her face transformed her usually reserved features into childlike delight. Eyes twinkling, cheeks ruddy from the cold, she rubbed her ungloved hands together And bound up the short steps to the house. By the time he joined her, the excitement had faded, replaced with her usual stone-faced resolve. So fast the transition, it had to be her default setting.

Not that he faulted her for her quiet reserve when he was the same way. It was better than a grinning, giggly idiot who had to share every inane thought darting through their head. He blamed his lack of humor on his chosen profession. Couldn't say the same for her. Or could he? Not that she killed for a living as he did. However, one could argue her father's profession had a direct effect on her.

Yah, think? Why have a child only to ignore her which was the equivalent to abandonment? *At least she didn't end up on the street, eating garbage until his father gave him to the mob to use as a runner. Payment for a debt he wasn't man enough to bleed for.* The job wasn't too bad. He was liked, might've had a career if his father hadn't stopped gambling and hadn't snatched him and made a run for it.

A white postcard was taped to the door stamped on one side with the realtor's logo. She got to it first, pulling it from the door, and flipping it over. "'Welcome Mr. and Mrs. Jeffrey. Happy honeymoon! Please help yourself to the complimentary champagne.'" She looked up from the card. "I take it you're the Mr., and I'm the Mrs.?"

"That's usually how it works." He punched a code into the cipher lock and pushed the door open. He entered first with his gun drawn. It took him seventeen minutes to clear the house and she was with him every step of the way, mirroring him 'oohing and ahhhing' at the circular fireplace and panoramic view of the distant snow covered mountains from the living room, the state-of-the-art kitchen, and the luxurious bedrooms, as they searched each room, each closet, kitchen, pantry, mudroom, and great room. Couldn't say he didn't like it, 'cause he did, more than he should. She even followed him to the detached garage, that used to be a barn.

"I'll get the luggage." She volunteered and trudged over the snow to the BMW.

"I can handle everything. You should go in and get some rest."

"I'd rather stay busy." She opened the rear door and grabbed her luggage and the weapons bag. She slung one crossbody over one shoulder and hefted two other bags up the stairs and into the house.

Bailey may be slim, but the woman had strength, and not just in her body he'd come to realize.

Two more trips and they'd completed the task. They worked well together.

"Do you have a preference over the bedrooms?" she asked, pulling him out of his thoughts.

She'd taken off her coat and his gaze skimmed over the formfitting sweater and the jeans hugging her long legs and tight ass. Yeah, he had a preference on bedrooms, but that wasn't gonna happen. "The one closest to yours, for your protection."

"Makes sense," she murmured, fingering the handle of her luggage. "I like the one with the brass bed. I think it's the master bedroom."

She's rambling, he noticed. Nerves would do that to a person. What she had to be nervous about, he had no idea. He hadn't kept much from her, told her what he could. What she didn't know, she just had to trust him.

"What's in the boxes?"

That, he could tell her about. "I wondered when you'd ask." He flicked open his switchblade, sliced open the first cardboard box and pulled out a handful of the tiny cameras. "Surveillance equipment. I'll place these all over the grounds and house, sync them to my phone, and voila, I'll know who's coming before they get here."

"Nice." She took one of the gadgets and rolled it around in her palm.

"I need to place one or more in your bedroom."

Her head jerked up. "Excuse me?"

"To watch the door and the window. Not to watch you."

"Oh. Of course."

"Come on. You can watch me place them." He placed one opposite her bedroom door and chose a sensor on her window that would alert him if it were opened. "You'll have your privacy."

"What about the rest?"

Together, they placed cameras at all the entries and blind spots in the house. By the time they'd completed the job, night had fallen. There was still so much to do to secure the house.

"I'm starving. I wonder if they have takeout here?" She headed to the kitchen.

He stopped her with a touch to her arm. "No one comes to the house."

A rebellious streak crossed her face, and he prepared himself to be the bad guy, again. A role he'd always relished, until now.

"Well then, I'd better get to the kitchen and start cooking," she snapped. "Just so you know, you are damn lucky I know how." Back rigid, she marched away, and he did enjoy the view.

∾

"Report," Hank ordered.

"We're in. Mr. and Mrs. Jeffrey are on their honeymoon in Switzerland." Fifty yards from the house, peering at the structure through a copse of evergreens, Emmet gave Hank his GPS coordinates.

"Any difficulty getting there?"

Had to drug your daughter, but other than that, "None."

"Good."

In the background, Whiskey's muffled voice came through. Emmet gritted his teeth. He hated that arrogant asshole but couldn't deny he knew how to handle himself. If he couldn't be there protecting Hank's back, Whiskey was the next best choice.

"What's the latest on Rogers?"

"He's on the run. We tracked him to Seattle, think he's headed to the Philippines."

"Why the Philippines?"

"There are seven thousand islands to get lost on."

"Shit." They may never find him.

"That's not the worst of it. If we don't find him soon, Lebold will pull our contract. You understand what that means?"

Yeah. Their shadow connection to the Pentagon would be done, and their necks would be on the chopping block.

"Loose thread must be snipped. It's him or us."

"No. It's just him. Do what you got to do. I'm good here."

"I'll call you in forty-eight." Hank ended the call. And once again, he hadn't asked about his daughter.

Emmet entered the house through the mudroom and paused to take in the scent of rosemary chicken. His stomach rumbled, and he kicked off his wet boots and padded into the living room in his socks.

In the hour since he left to check the perimeter, place a few cameras, and call Hank, Bailey had started a fire in the fireplace, set the dining table for two and by the red light on the oven, dinner was mission accomplished.

She emerged from deep inside the pantry carrying a bottle of white wine which she waved at him like it was a trophy. "We have a wine refrigerator, fully stocked."

"Sweet."

"I picked a chardonnay to go with the chicken."

"Sounds good." He headed for the stove for a peek in the pots.

"Oh no. You made me cook. Don't think you're gonna help me now and get out of doing the dishes."

"There's no dishwasher?"

"Nope. We're roughing it." She handed over the wine for him to open and pour while she served two plates of rosemary chicken paired with grilled purple potatoes and asparagus.

He held out her chair for her to sit, then took his own across from her. "This looks...exquisite." Was that a blush on her cheeks? Her head dipped so he couldn't be sure about the blush or the slight curve to her lips yet was sure he'd seen both.

"Save your praise for after you taste it." She speared a potato and popped it in her mouth.

He cut into the moist chicken and moaned, loudly, when the piece hit his taste buds. "It's as good as it looks. Thanks for taking care of dinner."

Now, she didn't hide her smile and damn if she wasn't sexy with her pixie haircut, magnetic blue eyes, and tempting pink lips. *Drink your wine before you make a fool of yourself. She's like a sister to you. Like a sister.*

"Don't think I'm cooking three squares a day, every day. My skills only stretch so far."

"I can cover breakfast and burgers. We won't starve."

"How long are we staying here?"

He shook his head. "Too many variables to predict how long, but we have the house for a week."

"And after that?" She met his gaze over the rim of her glass.

He had plans in place but wasn't ready to share them. "Things are fluid."

She snorted and sipped her wine. "Not ready to tell me, huh? It's fine. I'm used to being left out of the loop."

"There is no loop, Bailey. I keep things close to the vest. It's my way."

Lips thinned into a mulish line, eyes flashing with anger, she snapped, "Did Hank order you to keep me in the dark?"

Emmet exploded. "What the fuck is it between you and Hank?"

CHAPTER 9

*B*ailey dropped her fork onto her plate. The clank as loud as church bells. Her hands curled slowly into tight fists. This wasn't a memory she enjoyed visiting or topic she liked discussing. Tempted to yell it was none of his business, she paused. It was about time she popped Emmet's Father of the Year impression he had about Hank.

"I've met my father five times in my entire life," Bailey whispered, the emotions clogging her throat too much to process. Each of those five moments, snippets of time, were ingrained in her head.

"The first time, I was on the playground at my school in London. I was about seven and the new kid with an American accent, so a target. They lured me behind the playhouse, and one kid punched me while another pushed me down and kicked me. I don't know where the teacher was when it happened." The pain was still fresh.

"I'm lying there, bleeding, crying, and suddenly I wasn't alone. A man appeared. Don't know how he was there because it was a school for the children of diplomats. We had security, but he was there, leaning over me, watching me cry, not helping me." *And I wasn't afraid, not that time.*

"We'd been trained about terrorists, stranger danger. Before fear could take root... Once I saw his eyes, saw they were the same color as mine... I knew he was my father."

"What did he say to you," Emmet asked.

Bailey sighed. "Nothing. He looked me over, I guess to see how injured I was. He waited for me to get up, didn't help. I ran back inside the school and didn't say anything to anyone. The next day my teacher was replaced, and the kids were gone. That weekend I started learning Taekwondo."

He frowned, and she waited for him to ask about her training and skill level. He didn't. "And the next time you saw him?"

The memory rushed to the surface. "I was twelve and had moved to incorporate karate into my training. It was my first match, and I spotted him in the stands. I got nervous and lost. When I got up from the mat, he was gone. I was so angry with myself, but he was there when I exited the locker room."

"Nerves had me trembling when I walked up to him. He looked down at me. No warmth on his face. No greeting for his daughter. You know what he said?" She didn't pause for Emmet's reply. "'No distraction is worth the loss. I expect better from you.' Then he was gone. I lost other matches, but it wasn't because I was distracted."

Emmet sipped his coffee. "When was the next time?"

"I was fifteen and feeling rebellious. I'd stopped training, started drinking, smoking, arguing with Mom. I met a guy." Her voice dropped to a scandalous whisper. "He was nineteen and had a Mustang."

Emmet's brow dropped low, and his voice roughened. "Oh really."

She smirked as memories teased her mind. "I'd cut school to be with him. Then I started sneaking out at night. Staying out all night." Emmet's face turned dark, but she continued. "Mom was furious. I actually told her to go fuck herself." She closed her eyes and shook her head at her stupidity. "I was a badass...until I crawled back through my window. I'd eased it closed when my lamp flicked on, and my father was sitting at my little computer desk, dressed completely in black. I almost shit myself."

Emmet snorted.

"'I'm disappointed,' he said. Two words. That's it, and he got up and left. Didn't make a single sound. The next day my boyfriend's legs were broken, both, in some freak *accident*. As were his father's legs and his uncle's. Both legs. Each man." She'd never forget how little he looked in that hospital bed, legs in casts, an IV in his arm and tubes everywhere. He said he never wanted to see her again, and she couldn't blame him. She wouldn't want to see her either.

"The next night, I knew he would come. I was wide awake when my bedroom door opened and he strolled inside. He stopped at the foot of my bed, and we stared at each other, sizing each other up. He was not impressed." Her mouth twisted in a sardonic grin. "Then he said, 'Cutting school ends. Disrespecting your mom ends. Martial arts training resumes.' He tossed a business card down on the bed between us. Dicks Weapons and Range. 'Be there on Saturday. Ask for Roy.'"

"'I don't go in and ask for Dick?' I asked. I couldn't help it." Emmet choked on the last of his drink. She'd finally got him to crack. "The look my father gave me peeled an inch off my ass, but I was still feeling like a badass. I asked him why? Why should I go back to school, go back to training, go to Dicks and find Roy?"

Emmet leaned forward and waited for her answer.

"'Because I'm the only thing keeping you alive and I won't be here forever.'" She mimicked his deep voice. "Then he left. I saw him one more time at my high school graduation seven years ago. I thought he was dead, and then you show up with the news. Not that he died years ago, as I had hoped, but that he was alive and well, and now someone is after me. Can't say my father hadn't warned me."

"By my count, that's four times. What was the fifth time?" His words clipped.

Bailey drained and refilled her wine glass to the brim. Eyes downcast, she cleared her throat. In nothing more than a broken whisper, she said, "I turned eighteen three weeks after graduation. He showed up the next day. I'd partied all night with a few friends. We were stationed in Singapore. I had a blast, drinking, eating, smoking weed, fucking." Down another rabbit hole, her memory went until she reeled them back in. "Anyway, I woke up and there he was, at the foot of my bed in broad daylight. Suit, tie, he was dressed as a businessman. I never realized how handsome he is. Kinda startling for a daughter to realize her father has sex appeal. Maybe because I'd never seen him as my father." Down another rabbit hole. Avoidance only worked for so long.

"Anyway. He tossed a folder onto my dresser," and destroyed the little bit of security she'd ever had. "He said, 'Your mother died when you were sixteen months old. Everything you need to know about her is in this file, including all of her assets, which now belong to you.' I jumped out of bed, almost threw up my head hurt so bad. 'Mom's in her bedroom,' I yelled. I knew she was in the bedroom because I checked on her when I sneaked in at six a.m."

Bailey paused to breathe. Seven long years had passed since she allowed herself to wallow in this memory.

"Theresa Clark was hired to be your mother. She portrayed a role I paid her to play. And did a better than average job. But now you're eighteen, and the contract she signed is complete.'" She mimicked his voice again.

"I was a contract. A name on a piece of paper. A paycheck. I didn't cry. I think that surprised Hank. I think he expected me to be hysterical. I wasn't. I picked up the file and skimmed the paperwork. Turns out I had enough money to be very comfortable, if spent wisely, for the rest of my life. No picture of my mother, not even her name. I didn't want to know, to see. Didn't have the courage to face what I'd lost." She sighed, the pain fresh. "When I closed the folder, Hank was still there, analyzing me with those flat eyes of his."

"'How did she die?' I asked. That's all I wanted to know. Not her name, not her picture. 'Car bomb set for me.'" She mimicked Hank again and had to pause at the fresh onslaught of pain. "I asked him if he'd loved her. The question slipped out, but I had to know, was critical that I know."

"'Once, she was all that I loved.'" Even after all this time, the pain in his voice lingered in her mind. "I understood, then. I understood him, why he couldn't love me. And I hated him more for it."

"Thank you, Henry. Please make it a point to never see me again."

"That will not be a problem."

"So, you see, I never had a father or a mother. I was someone's responsibility. Not someone's child." Another long gulp of wine soothed some of the pain.

"And Theresa?" Emmet demanded. "What did she have to say for herself?"

"She cried. Told me she loved me. Begged me to understand. Her life hadn't been easy. Hank finagled the job for her in the state department. It got her out of the country, away from some dangerous men. I forgave her, but it's not the same. I see her differently now. I can't call her Mom anymore. She wants me to, but…I can't." She rose and took her plate to the kitchen. For her, the day was finally, blessedly over. Her evening plans included soaking in the tub and crawling into bed alone.

Emmet blocked her path. Oh, she could walk around him, but she sensed it would be a wasted effort.

"I'm sorry, Bailey. I didn't know."

She snorted and shrugged. "How could you? You weren't there."

"Except I was. Well, kinda, sorta." He sighed and dragged both hands through his hair.

Puzzled, she shook her head. "I don't understand. What do you mean kinda, sorta? What are you going on about?"

His ice-cold blue eyes met hers and seemed warmer as if reaching out to offer her comfort she didn't want or need. "Bailey, I was there. Hank…I've known him over twenty years. He raised me since the age of twelve. He's been a mentor and a father to me. The father I never had. He's saved my life in countless ways I could never repay."

Her insides congealed. "What do you mean he was a father to you? Explain that shit."

His hand landed on her shoulder and squeezed ever so gently. "He took me in, and I lived with him until I turned twenty. He trained me, taught me everything I needed to know. How to fight. How to kill. How to survive. Without him, I'd be dead or wishing I was dead. I owe him everything."

Every word out of his mouth chipped away at the wall she'd built around her heart. "I always suspected he had another family. Thought it was a wife and kids he was protecting from his mistress and bastard child. Now I know it was just me he didn't want."

She had to make it to the bedroom. Make it there where she could break down in privacy.

Bailey knocked his hand off her shoulder and broke to the left. She had to get around him and make a dash for her bedroom before the dam burst, but his arms circled her waist and pulled her into his hard body. The wall she built around all the hurt and loneliness, against the abandonment and disappointment, crumbled.

She clung to him, crying out her pain all over his shirt. Stopping was impossible. Every time she tried to rein in the hysterics, it got worse. Her nose clogged, then ran, mixing with her tears. She tried to suck in a deep breath to steady her nerves and ended up stuck in a series of hiccups. This was why she didn't cry. It wasn't pretty. It wasn't dainty. There was no dabbing at the eyes with a tiny tissue. She produced enough snot to float a boat and blotches sprang up all over her face.

Emmet cupped her cheek and brought her head up. She tucked her head tighter into his chest. He couldn't see her like this when she was an unmitigated mess. He wouldn't let go and kept at her until he had both her cheeks cupped in his rough hands.

"Don't," she cried. "Just don't."

"Don't what?"

She couldn't breathe. He needed to fuck off for a minute so she could breathe. Instead, he did a great impression of a helicopter mom and hovered, and she was too upset to enjoy the moment.

He took a napkin off the counter and mopped up her cheeks and nose. "Tears and snot don't bother me."

"It bothers me." She sniffled and grabbed her own tissue to scrub her face. "I don't do this. I don't cry."

"That I believe."

She blew her nose and glared at him through swollen eyes. Then lowered her gaze because, God, she could guess how badly she looked. "What does that mean?"

He stroked a knuckle down the side of her cheek. "It means you're strong. You know it, and I know it." He hooked her chin and lifted it. "I didn't tell you that to hurt you, Bailey. That's not why I'm here."

He was too close. Way too close. He filled her vision, and

suddenly she couldn't breathe again. The pain in her heart ebbed, replaced with the first threads of desire. "Why are you here?"

His face shifted from concern to a grimace, as if he'd fought something and lost. "Hank sent me to protect you because he knows I won't fail him. Understand me, I won't. But I'm not here for him alone, Bailey. I'm here for you."

CHAPTER 10

*E*mmet's words, the conviction in his voice, the sincerity in his eyes, Bailey desperately wanted to believe him. Needed to believe everything he said. He was the only thing she had, but she didn't really have him. She didn't have anyone.

"I don't know if... How do I know you're telling me the truth? You work for him, the man who abandoned me."

"Yeah. I do." Voice granite, yet his fingers were ever so gentle on her skin. "But I won't abandon you. Ever."

His gaze dipped to her lips. Bailey leaned in. It was an automatic response. She couldn't have stopped herself if she'd tried. His lips traced hers in a barely there caress that sent a tremor racing down her spine and wetness pooling between her legs. Wasn't enough. She tilted her head for more.

He caged her with his body pressing into her, with one hand cupping her cheek, and the other threading through her short hair, all before lowering his head and claiming her mouth. She parted her lips on a groan and didn't stop groaning as he licked into her mouth. He tasted of Chardonnay—hints of vanilla, a touch of caramel—and all man. Lips smashed together, teeth banging, tongues dueling, never stopping. *Don't stop!* He fisted her hair, angled her head and took it deeper.

Emmet kissed her until she no longer needed air because he breathed for her.

Bailey tugged at his shirt, grabbed it, and slid her hand beneath the soft flannel. He moaned into her mouth, and he'd picked her up to plop her ass on the counter.

Did she take his shirt off or did he? Either way, it ended up on the kitchen floor, leaving him in an undershirt that also ended up on the kitchen floor.

Oh, God. She'd seen plenty of muscle-bound men who'd spent a lifetime in the gym, honing their bodies, none were as defined as Emmet. Hand on the back of her head, he brought her in for another kiss and another. He sucked her tongue, licked into her mouth, retreated to nip her bottom lip and soothe it with another long, lick.

Lost, she ran her hands over his shoulders, down the taut muscles lining his back, around his waist to his ripped abs, to dip into his pants, through crisp hairs. His fingers sunk to her scalp and gripped her head. A hard tug pried them apart, left both gasping.

"Are we doing this?" he demanded, followed by another bruising kiss as she shoved her hand deeper into his pants. He was granite, a solid mass in her palm.

She squeezed and earned a strangled hiss. He angled her head to the side to trail his tongue up her throat, to sink his teeth into her earlobe. It was her turn to hiss as the sharp sting transformed into pleasure when he licked the outer shell of her ear. "Answer the question, Bailey." His free hand traveled under her sweater to trace lazy circles on her lower back.

Wherever he touched, licked, bit left a trail of heat demanding she give only one reply. "Yes."

He snatched her to him and lifted her off the counter. Startled, she wrapped her arms and legs around him, holding on as he dumped them onto the sofa. Her sweater went up and over her head. She helped by unsnapping her bra and letting it fall away, while he opened her jeans and pulled them and everything else shielding her from his view off. Naked, she lay in the soft light cast from the table lamp with Emmet looking over her.

She wasn't shy, knew her assets—small boobs, athletic build, no real curves for a man to get hung up on. But the way his gaze devoured her…her shortcomings didn't matter. He wanted her, as much as she wanted him with a desperate edge that cut sharper than a knife. God, he was beautiful from his full sensual mouth, slightly crooked nose, and icy blue eyes.

One of his hands covered an entire breast, his palm warm and rough against her stiff nipple. He teased her, rubbing and squeezing the sensitive peak. Shuddering from the sensation, she pushed his hand lower, down the center of her body.

He slowed, drawing out the torture until she writhed on the sofa, legs splayed, begging him to touch her.

Emmet leaned over Bailey, his weight on his other arm, his kisses as unhurried as his fingers parting her slick flesh and diving into her body. Their groans mingled, echoed, Emmet's harsh, yet triumphant. Bailey's breathy, as if she'd run a race, but the finish line was miles away.

She yanked at his buckle, gripped the bulge inside his jeans. The emptiness inside her demanded fulfillment.

He knocked her hands away and completed the job, yanking the rest of his clothes off. Naked, Emmet was a revelation. He was lean with sculpted muscles under tanned skin. Scarred tanned skin. Most were faded. The one under the ribs on his right side was newest. About an inch long and raised, she wondered what happened, who did it and was that person still alive.

None of that cooled her blood or stopped her gaze from roaming over his broad shoulders, corded arms, ripped abs, and…

His cock was a thick spear of hard flesh that made her core clench. "Condom," she croaked, her throat suddenly dry.

"Not yet."

He dropped down over her and licked into her mouth as he settled between her thighs. Fingers slid between her folds and circled her clitoris. The first tendrils of a blinding orgasm curled through her. She arched into the pleasure, reached for it.

Emmet slid down her body. He traced his lips over her chin, down her throat, and settled on the pulse flickering beneath her skin. She wanted him to mark in some primal ritual she couldn't name.

He continued to the valley between her breasts, nipping, licking. She tugged on his hair in an attempt to guide him to a nipple. It worked, and his mouth settled over the peak. Pulled into his hot mouth, and sucked. She arched into each pull, losing herself to the feel of his tongue, teeth, and lips on her flesh. He switched to the other nipple to deliver the same attention. Only after she was a panting, writhing mess, did he sink lower, his tongue wreaking havoc as he dragged it down her body.

Emmet didn't stop until his tongue spilt her nether lips and his mouth closed around her core in the most intimate of kisses. Back bowed off the sofa, a keening moan spilling out of her mouth, Bailey came apart.

He sat back, a satisfied smirk on his face. "That was fast. When was the last time?"

Panting, she gasped, "Two days ago." Which meant the day they'd met. The heat in his eyes died. "Me and my vibrator had an intimate evening."

Heat flared in his eyes again. "When was the last time with a flesh and blood man, or woman?"

Men and their need to know. "Nine months ago. Do you approve? Or should I have been a virgin waiting for my knight in rusty armor?"

He pushed two fingers into her and brought his thumb up to

tease her clit. "I can't see you waiting for anything." He pulled out of her and licked his fingers clean. She loved the way his tongue worked.

"Do I need to get my vibrator?"

He chuckled and reached for his pants. From his wallet, he pulled out a familiar black and gold square packet.

She barked out a laugh. "Good thing you packed my condoms."

"Good thing." He ripped it open with his teeth and rolled it over his length.

Spreading her wide, Emmet lowered himself to Bailey. The blunt head of his sex parted her slick folds. He drove into her with a series of sharp thrusts, then seated himself balls deep. Together, they trembled. She whimpered at the wounding fullness, but God forbid he stop. She wrapped her limbs around him and swallowed his harsh groan.

A roll of her hips had him fisting her hair and grabbing her ass. She couldn't move and didn't need to because he pumped into her, his strokes unhurried and long, torturous. She clawed at him, rocked her pelvis, and met each thrust. "Harder, harder, Emmet."

He growled, released her hair and buried his head in the crux of her neck. His hands on her ass, his body pressing her into the sofa, while he drilled into her body. Pleasure gripped her and tightened with each thrust. Writhing, gasping, clawing at his back, Bailey splintered, her orgasm so intense she broke apart, crying his name, pleading for him not to stop.

Emmet shuddered, faltered for a split second as if to gather his strength, and slammed into her again, and again until she was a quivering mess. He reared back. Buried within her core, Bailey watched his entire body tense, a taut bowstring ready for release. Then she felt him, throbbing inside of her, pouring his release into the latex barrier.

Looming over her, the epitome of male prowess at its peak,

he was beautiful. His head tipped forward, banked pleasure swimming in his eyes.

So that's how he looks spent. Bailey took a mental picture.

Emmet smiled, a lazy, easy stretch of his lips that had her insides purring.

"Where'd you pack the rest of those condoms?"

CHAPTER 11

"There's no one here."

"Tell me something I don't know," Hank growled at Whiskey and moved around the oak-paneled banquet room decorated for a western style wedding. Not unusual for a modern couple in the Philippines.

"Bad intel." Whiskey circled the room flipping chairs, peering under the table for anything hidden.

"Apparently." Hank paused at the bank of windows and peered out onto downtown Manila. Bad intel, his ass. He trusted his source. The info came from the highest level. If that source was compromised, Rogers's betrayal had leapfrogged him and landed with the ones who gave the orders. "We are in the right place. At the right time. Yet we are alone."

Agitated, Whiskey shook his nearly bald head. "Fubar. This is a fucking set up. We gotta go, Hank." He headed for the door.

"We're staying." Hank pressed a button, closing the blinds. Glass broke, close to his left ear, followed by the air whistling through a tiny opening and the feel of it on his skin. Hank hit the deck with Whiskey right next to him. "He always was a lousy shot."

"Thank whatever god you pray to for that 'cause the inside of your head would've decorated my shirt." Whiskey's laugh held no humor.

"Thank you for the graphics." Hank shot out the overhead light, dropping the room into darkness.

"Can we leave now?" Whiskey crawled away from the window and climbed to his feet.

"No. That's exactly what he wants us to do, run. Which means he has something else set up for us. I'm not running. Secure the door."

"With what?" Whiskey held up his MP5 slung over his shoulder.

Out of the pocket of his leather duster, Hank pulled a small brick of Semtex and tossed it and the detonator to Whiskey. "Small explosion, please. I want to get out of this alive."

Whiskey grinned and got to work, while Hank shoved the chairs out of the way and flipped the table on the side. He used the butt of his gun to bust the camera in the corners of the room. He set up his weapons—an AK-47 with suppressor muzzle to keep their little discord as private as possible, two nine-millimeter handguns, also with muzzles, and four smoke grenades.

"You know there are cameras all over this place, not only in this room." Whiskey shaped the plastic to the seam of the double doors.

"Not worried about them. Whoever set this trap isn't worried about the cameras, so neither am I."

"You that certain, huh. Well, *you're* betting our lives on this, so I guess that's something. Just so you know, I'm not surviving this to end up in a Philippine jail."

Hank snorted as if any jail could hold Whiskey or any of his men. He mounted his semi-automatic on the edge of the table. He lined up the sites using Whiskey's back as a target.

"Tired of me already?" Whiskey griped when he turned and found a target on the center of his chest.

"Been tired."

Deeper into the room, Whiskey righted a chair and used it as a stool to plant a micro-camera on a light fixture well out of the blast radius. After the dust settled and they'd evacuated, it would be interesting to see who showed up. That task complete, Whiskey killed the lights and joined Hank on the other side of the table. "You know. If you're wrong—"

"I'm not wrong." Hank cut him off.

"Of course not, but if you are, try not to break anything when you jump out the window. Five stories. That's a long way down for a man your age." Whiskey snickered.

"I'll make sure to land on you."

"You know, I believe you will." Whiskey shouldered his weapon, the same weapon as Hank's, and settled in.

They didn't have long to wait. A kick to the door and the Semtex did its job. It exploded, taking whoever was the unfortunate fool with it. And hopefully a few others. Smoke filled the room, followed by the blare of an alarm and strobe lights over the exit. Someone coughed.

"Didn't kill them all," Whiskey murmured and adjusted the butt of his weapon against his shoulder.

"Good." Bombs were so impersonal. Hank liked the personal touch. And everything about this was personal.

Fucking Rogers. He just couldn't let it go. Couldn't accept it. Veronica had to die. The kill was clean. She never felt a thing. One bullet to the back of the head. It was a mercy she didn't deserve—that lying, deceitful bitch. She got in Rogers' head and twisted everything to her liking.

She said she'd do it and Hank hadn't believed her. He didn't think any man would be stupid enough to fall for her bullshit, but the power of the pussy.

Shots whizzed through the smoldering opening. Hank

waited, and Whiskey followed his lead. He wanted to see who the lucky bastard was, yet wouldn't get lucky enough to have Rogers waltz into his crosshairs.

A red laser sight appeared through the smoke. Then two. Then two more. Hank tracked them back to the gunmen. He tapped the lead gunman, one bullet to the forehead. Whiskey took care of the other three and had the gall to chuckle.

"Keep up, old man," Whiskey murmured.

A flash grenade rolled into the room. Both ducked behind the overturned table and closed their eyes and covered their ears. It helped. Instead of stunned and writhing in pain, they still functioned enough to pick up their weapons and return fire. Five minutes and all was silent, except for the warble of sirens.

They rose slowly and advanced on the bodies, eight altogether. All male. All head shots, destroying their faces, except for one tall fellow who caught one in the chest and lay doing the fish out of water routine.

"I know him." Whiskey bent over Aquaman.

Hank moved closer and halted on the other side of the body. "So do I." He crouched. "Triad. He works with Gwan Zhang."

"Are you fucking kidding me?" The disbelief in Whiskey's voice mimicked Hank's.

"We have to get out of here."

"No shit!" Whiskey leaped to his feet.

"But not yet." Hank grabbed the chin of the dying man and angled his face toward him. "Who told you to come here?" he asked him in Chinese.

"Gwan Zhang."

"And who told him?"

The crackle of a comm snapped Hank's attention to the man's earpiece. He plucked it free and listened to the voice of the man he had to kill.

"Is he dead? Report back."

Seething, Hank crushed the earpiece beneath his heel. Let the fucker wonder.

Whiskey dragged a hand down his face. "Zhang and Rogers are working together."

"No. My guess is Rogers promised Zhang an inside track to the agency once I'm out of the way."

"Once Rogers takes over."

Hank nodded, aware of the sirens drawing ever closer. "We have to leave."

They ditched the guns, not worrying about fingerprints because of their gloves, turned their outer clothing inside out for a bit of subterfuge, and went for the chopper on the roof. Wasn't difficult to steal after knocking out the security guard and the pilot. Hank took the pilot seat while Whiskey took the co-pilot. They cleared the airspace without any further incident, almost as if he was let go.

"That wasn't as hard as it should be."

Whiskey's voice came over the headphones and Hank agreed. "It wasn't. Zhang wouldn't have sent a skeleton crew, not for something as promising as an inside track to the agency. This was Rogers fucking with our heads again."

Whiskey cursed long and loud, which was completely unnecessary. "He keeps getting ahead of us, every single time. We're always on the back foot. It's gonna get us killed."

"Not yet."

Whiskey's head jerked around. "What the fuck does 'Not yet' mean?"

"He doesn't want me dead yet. He wants me to suffer."

Whiskey snorted. "Like you made Veronica suffer?"

Hank had a second of guilt, then he shoved it away. "It was necessary. She would've sold us out to the Russians if I hadn't stopped her. She had the information I needed and wouldn't give it up. Even after I asked nicely."

"Pistol whipping is nicely?" Whiskey quipped, not hiding his amusement.

"A variation of what she liked in the bedroom." Hank input in a set of coordinates and put the chopper on autopilot.

"Man, you could've kept that detail to yourself... Did Rogers know about you two?"

"Ancient history. We had our fun. It ended three years before the agency reassigned me Rogers." The first of many mistakes. He never should've agreed to a partnership, even though he'd trained the man, and the agency footed the bills, paid for the overhead and his toys. Used to saying yes to the powers that be, he didn't think to say no. Mistake number one lasted a year. A year of two-stepping around each other, which worked.

Until their last mission put Veronica in their crosshairs. They met in Paris after he killed Gregorsky, the rusky who'd hacked into the NSA database. Peering into her gray eyes, he felt something other than lust for the first time in decades. Giving that feeling free rein, instead of yanking it out at the root, mistake number two.

She was the most beautiful thing he'd ever seen, a blond goddess he spent a year pursuing. But when he finally tasted her, had her beneath him, it was only then he realized Constance would always have his heart. No one would ever replace the love he had for her. No one would even come close.

He wished Veronica well and broke it off. "I never saw or thought of her again. Until her name came across in an encrypted email. Our meeting hadn't been an accident. It was planned. I was supposed to be her way in, but I didn't fall for her femme fatale role. Rogers did."

"And now we're on clean up." Whiskey grunted. "That's why he won't give up."

Hank couldn't blame Rogers. If he had killed Constance, there wasn't a rock small enough on the planet for him to hide under.

"Rogers is highly motivated. He's not gonna stop until he gets you. So...I say we give him what he wants."

Interested, Hank spared Whiskey a glance. "Explain."

Whiskey scratched at the stubble on his chin. "The man wants his cock stroked. I say we lube up our palms and help him out."

Hank sighed. "Explain without the sexual metaphors."

"He wants to hurt you. Give him what he needs to hurt you."

It took a moment for Hank to understand. Then another moment for the rage to build as what Whiskey said sunk in. "You want me to hand over my daughter to Rogers? To put the only thing I have left in his crosshairs!" Whiskey was lucky they weren't on the ground because Hank would've wrapped his hands around his throat and ripped his fucking head off.

"Can you think of a better way to draw him out? I can't."

Six months. That's how long they'd been at their little war. Six months heading fast toward seven, and how many dead. Too many dead, friends and enemies. He was a killer out of necessity, not because he particularly enjoyed it, even though he was exceptionally skilled. As their war spiraled—not out of control—but contained to their world, his greatest vulnerability remained hidden. Decades of protecting her, guarding her from himself and the dangers he'd brought by simply being her father, remained in place. No one knew of Bailey's existence. She was safe in her world and her hate for him. Both would've persisted if Rogers hadn't broken into the safe and stolen her dossier.

Hank was a fool. He gave up his daughter, but he didn't let her go. So many things he could've done differently. If he really loved her, he would've put her up for adoption and never looked back. He couldn't. Constance wouldn't let him. Which was little consolation since Bailey despised him, and rightly so. After all, that's what he'd wanted. Her hate kept her safely out of his world.

Until fucking Rogers.

"Hank? Can you think of a better way?" Whiskey wouldn't relent. Not when he was right. Just as Rogers wouldn't relent. He had to die. To make that happen, he had to put his daughter in harm's way.

"No. I can't."

Whiskey's sigh came through the helmet headphones. "How do you want to do this?"

"We leak where she is." *Forgive me, Constance.* "Then move her when we know he's in play."

For the first time since Constance's death, he felt helpless. "Once we've landed and are safe, I'll call Streets and let him know the change in plans." And move heaven and earth to make sure the plot next to his love wouldn't be filled with their daughter's body.

CHAPTER 12

*C*ocooned, Bailey snuggled closer to the furnace warming her front. Something wet and equally as warm circled her nipple. She arched into the sensation, moaning as the teasing was replaced with something abrasive. Whiskers, she realized as the gentle abrasion skimmed her nipple. She arched deeper, offering herself for more of the exquisite torture. A hand traced up the inside of her leg at the same time as the whiskers moved over her collarbone.

"Emmet," she whispered and parted her thighs. His weight settled on top of her, pressed her into the pillow top mattress. Through slitted eyes, she absorbed his sharp features bathed in the cold morning sunlight. His face taut from lust. His eyes half icy blue, half molten from the sun glinting off his irises.

He seemed unaware as the blunt head of his cock parted her slick folds and slid home beautifully. How many times? The question flitted through her brain, only to be lost as pleasure took precedence.

He pulled out and slammed back in, bottoming out, balls grinding into her. "Mornin'." He grunted and slanted his mouth over hers.

Wrapped in his embrace, she couldn't move, couldn't participate. All she could do was receive the thrusts of his body and the lick of his tongue as he kissed her.

This was how sex was supposed to be, raw, slate-clearing, bliss, exactly what she'd been missing.

Bailey came apart in a rush, exploding into fragments she somehow must piece back together. She'd let him in, not just into her body, but into her head. He wasn't some stranger she could leave on an island and think of fondly in her golden years. This was Emmet.

Buried deep within her, all that coiled muscle around her tightened. His back arched, a harsh groan escaped, and he pulsed inside her. Damn, she'd never seen anything sexier than Emmet panting, head thrown back, coming apart as she had.

Shit! This couldn't happen again because… Well, because!

With a kiss to her temple and a soft nuzzle, he released her and pulled out of her body. Bailey rolled away, all the way to the other side of the bed, dragging the comforter with her, her head a mess while her body hummed from her release.

He flopped back onto the bed, splendidly naked. Tanned skin stretched over corded muscles, flaccid cock. *Lawd.* He was a shower and a grower.

"Here we go with the post-coital regrets."

"Excuse me?" She sat up careful to protect her modesty. Why when Emmet had seen everything? That question she'd answer at another time. Right now, she grasped onto the only straw she had and tightened the sheet around her.

He sighed, climbed out of bed and headed for the bathroom. She stared—because he didn't close the damn door—as he disposed of the condom, and turned her head away as he relieved himself. She listened as he washed his hands and did whatever men did after sex and was rattled when he flopped back into bed, still naked.

His hooded gaze skimmed over her as if she lay as he,

displayed for his pleasure. "Are we going to be adults and admit what happened between us or are we going to pretend we didn't spend the night fucking each other's brains out? I vote for the latter." As he lay there looking equal parts dangerous and erotic, he hardened.

Bailey swallowed down the lump blocking her throat and ignored the need to rub her legs together. What the hell. They'd made lo—*screwed* three times last night, including what he did to her in the shower in the middle of the night, and what they just did now. She was not *still* horny!

Focused on his arrogant face, she said, "We've known each other a bit over three days. Don't you think this is a little much?"

He frowned. "You were at an exclusive resort known for its hedonistic tendencies. People go for hookups. Not bible study."

Her brain stalled because technically, he wasn't wrong. That was the reason she and Daisy had journeyed to the island, for casual, uncomplicated sex. Emmet was neither. "But I didn't sleep with anyone."

His gaze heavy, sweeping over her as a tangible caress. "Why? That was your purpose for going."

Well, yeah, but she wasn't going to tell him that.

Emmet scooted closer. Sheets pressed tightly to her front, she didn't protest when he curled around her, molded his chest to her back. It felt so good leaning into all that heat and muscle. "Confess, why didn't you indulge, Bailey?" he whispered in her ear.

She shivered, though cold was the exact opposite of what she felt which happened to be more than anything she felt for any potential island hookups.

'*Your body is your temple and yours to do with as you please,*' was a motto she lived by. Not religious, her moral compass had no sexual hang-ups, so she couldn't blame her noninterest on a pious spirit. She also had no reason to lie, not to him and not to herself. "No one had any depth to them. It was all too superficial which is exactly what a hookup is, but I needed more. Plus..." Bailey cranked her head around and met his steady gaze. "No one made me feel anything."

Like you hung unspoken between them.

Bailey didn't fight him when he pulled the comforter away and flipped her on top of him. She landed with an "Oomph." Boobs smashed against his chest, his stiff cock sandwiched between their bodies.

His hands roamed down her back to the curve of her ass. He palmed the cheeks, shifted so that her legs fell to either side of his hips, then gripped her flesh with both hands. "I refuse to let you go puritan on me and say how wrong this is." His tone dry, condescending.

No chance of that. Bailey raised her hips and rubbed her clit along his length. *How can I still be horny?*

His lips parted on a ragged sigh as his hands glided from her ass to tighten on her thighs. He arched beneath her, aiding in the slip, and slide, and grind.

"Isn't it wrong?" she murmured not believing what she'd said. And putting a nail in that coffin as she sucked his nipple into her mouth. Still, she prodded him with, "You are Hank's prodigal son. Doesn't that make us—"

"It doesn't," he clipped. "I was Hank's protégé, not son. We are *not* siblings. Understand me." To prove his point, he picked her up as if she weighed nothing and dropped her on his face.

Shocked, her gasped turned into a choked moan as his tongue split her. "Oh, *oh!*"

Bailey planted her hands on the wall behind the brass headboard and rocked her pelvis. Yes, she understood him and wholeheartedly agreed.

∽

It wasn't right what Emmet did to her. He fucked her into a coma and then left. She woke starving, not sure of the day or time, though the sun was still up, and she was sore. The last wasn't a complaint, just a commentary on her current state. She'd never had a sexual marathon. None of her partners had been up to the physical demands. Now, she knew what she'd missed, how lacking her life had been in that department.

"Damn you, Emmet," she murmured without an ounce of heat. Her next lover would suffer in comparison.

Bailey grimaced and shied away from thinking about any future lovers. Better to not think about the future at all when someone wanted you dead. *This*, where her life currently resided, was a temporary situation with an ending clearly in sight. Eventually, they would part ways. Eventually, the memory of him would fade. Not today, though. Not with her body still basking in the aftermath of his lovemaking.

"Sex. It was sex, Bailey. You've never confused the two before. Don't do so now." She scolded herself and counted his disappearance as a blessing. She fished her phone out of the lining of her suitcase and took it into the bathroom to plug it in. While it charged, she locked the door and soaked in the clawfoot tub.

By the time she'd dried herself off, her phone had enough of a charge to turn on. Bailey didn't regret much. Right now, she regretted not being on social media. Good thing she didn't need Facebook, Twitter, or Instagram to contact Daisy. An email would do, or Google Hangouts.

But she did need Wi-Fi. Damn it.

She dressed, took some care with her hair and makeup, made herself a chicken sandwich from the leftovers of the dinner she'd made and wolfed it down, along with a glass of milk. Still no Emmet.

She studied the room, angel on one shoulder, the devil on the other. Fuck being a good girl. It had never gotten her anywhere. This was the perfect time for a bit of snooping.

She started with his bedroom and noted the unslept in the king-sized bed. Something that would be rectified tonight. Their trip into crazy land wouldn't happen again. Two nondescript black leather duffle bags, similar to the bag that carried the money lay side by side on the luggage.

One held clothing and several grenades and flash bombs. The other, stacks of cash, two loaded nine-millimeter H&K's, and passports—a number of them. Quite a few with Emmet's picture and different names: Michael Strickland, Donald Bracker, John King. Not surprising in his line of work. She flipped another to find her face staring at her with a different name: Rosemary Brooks. She opened the rest: Laurel Sonders, Paige Rowe, Olivia Vale. The last passport was the original. Next to the passports were credit cards. Half-matched Emmet's fake names, the rest, hers.

Was Emmet even his real name? She filed that question away for later and focused on the stash. A lot of planning went into this that wasn't what got her riled. The when of it did. When were all her different identities acquired? And by who? All the passport pictures were the same as the original which she'd taken last year for her renewal. She flipped open the passports again and checked the processing dates which meant nothing, she realized. Why would the forger put the date he created the forgery? He wouldn't.

Frustrated, she returned the passports to the exact place she found them and in the precise order. He didn't need to know she'd been through his things.

A noise filtered in from outside. Bailey left his bedroom and peered out of the living room window at the back of the house. There was nothing to see except the barn off to the right and the trees leading to the forest and the mountains. The noise came again, this time from the barn. Definitely the barn.

A bit nervous, she pulled a butcher knife from the block in the kitchen, grabbed her coat, stuffed her feet into her boots, and walked out onto the back deck. The noise came again.

Quietly, she stepped down the few stairs, her gaze scanning the white landscape and trees. Could have been an animal, except, there it went again and no animal she'd ever heard of made that soft pop, pop, noise coming from the back of the barn.

Over the packed snow, she crossed to the wooden structure. The front door was closed, barred from the outside. She tiptoed down the side of the building and peered around the back.

"I heard you coming a mile away."

Emmet had set up a wooden plank on top of two barrels he must've found in the barn. An arrangement of weapons lay on top of the table. "I should hope so since you're protecting me. Can't have a deaf bodyguard, can I." She strolled closer.

So many weapons, the one in his hands in pieces as he cleaned it. She didn't like guns, didn't hate them either. They were so…final. You could pull a punch to soften the blow. Not possible with a gun.

"Do you know how to shoot?"

Her head jerked up, and she wasn't surprised his cool gaze was on her. The passionate man who'd spent the night pleasuring her was gone, replaced with the hitman she'd met days ago. She answered by reaching for the Smith and Wesson nine millimeter with the attached silencer. Making sure the safety was on, she checked the clip, slammed it back home, chambered a round, released the safety, and line up a target, which Emmet had provided on a tree fifty yards away. Two-handed grip, a steady breath, and she squeezed the trigger.

Bailey emptied the clip and picked up a pair of binoculars. Three went wide, hitting the fourth ring. The rest were centered in a beautiful cluster.

"Damn, I just sprang wood," said rather matter-of-factly.

"Again?" Came her dry response.

"It's turning out to be a constant state around you." He took the gun from her. "You learn all that at Dick's?"

She shrugged. "Most. I had a boyfriend who was into weapons. Made him feel manly."

"One of the old guys you humped?"

Her head snapped around. "How do you know anything about who I slept with?" She planted her hands on her hips.

His eyes bore into her as he wiped down the weapon. "Do you really think I don't have a background check on you?"

That was a cold dose of water in her veins. It made sense, otherwise, how would he have known how to find her. Call her stupid, she just hadn't thought of it. They'd been on the run almost since the moment she'd laid eyes on him. She folded her arms and hiked her chin in the air. "Anything interesting in there? Anything I should be ashamed of?"

He tossed the gun on the table and gave her his full attention. "It was quite a boring read."

God! That was worse than having something to be ashamed of.

"You traveled a lot because of Theresa's job. Straight A student in your middle school. Scored high on aptitude tests in high school but didn't distinguish yourself in class. You were quite average. The same in college, though you did graduate with a bullshit degree in liberal arts. You volunteer at a homeless shelter twice a month and a woman's shelter. No pets. One best friend whom you met when Theresa was stationed in Germany and you were sent to a London boarding school for a year. You have no job to speak of because you've invested your mother's assets wisely and you're not extravagant. No boyfriend since Richard, the fifty-one-year-old physician you stopped seeing six months ago. Did I get anything wrong?"

"No," she choked out. "You summed me up perfectly. I'm quite boring." She spun, and Emmet hauled her back to him by the arm.

Twisting, she broke his hold. He grabbed her again and dodged the fist she threw at his throat, but not the elbow followup. He flinched, and his smirk was all sorts of "Let's see what you've got."

On the balls of her feet, she danced away, but Emmet followed, he gave her no quarter to gather a plan of attack. He struck with a wide punch she saw coming a mile away. She blocked it and ducked under his arm and clipped the back of his head. Not hard, but not a love tap either.

Emmet whipped around a strange twinkle in his eye. A slow, eager grin spread across his face, and he sank to his haunches in a motion that said, "Bring it."

It had been a while since she sparred, five years at least. But some things you didn't forget. She started with a kick, which he blocked, and followed with two punches, both slower than she would've liked.

He was taking it easy.

She threw a punch, telegraphed it, so he knew it was coming. He moved out of the way, easily. She caught him with her elbow and jabbed it into his chest hard enough to make a point. *Don't fuck with me.*

She followed up the jab with a strike under his chin that snapped his head back. He grabbed her wrist before she could pull back for another strike and yanked her off balance. She went with the flow and barreled into him. Wrong move. Emmet was solid, all muscle. He didn't budge and grinned at her as if he'd won the match and a point.

I'm not done asshole. She brought her knee up and earned a satisfying grunt through gritted teeth when she connected with his ribs. Next, she angled her hip, stepped between his legs and hip checked him, but he grabbed her thigh and flipped her.

Bailey went flying into a snowbank seven feet deep. The snow broke her fall, still rattled all her bones.

Breath sawing in and out, chest heaving, she climbed free.

He was there with a helping hand the last few inches and helped dust the snow out of hair and off her clothes. Damn, snow had slipped beneath her collar and melted down her back.

Emmet eyed her and drew her into him, a strange light in the depths of his black pupils danced. It had been years since she'd had a match, used her training and, damn, it felt good. She'd actually had him the bastard, for a second. Now, they stood locked in an embrace until his hands eased from her body.

"I just proved my point. There is nothing boring about you, Bailey. Nothing." He kissed her slowly, and she lost herself in the feel of his mouth, the taste of his tongue, the graze of his teeth.

"No more humping old men," he whispered into her mouth.

"Excuse me? Richard was a nice man. We had a relationship. Not a hump." She licked her lips for another taste of him.

His eyes narrowed a fraction as he tracked her tongue. "Sounds like you miss him?" Emmet growled.

She didn't but also didn't have any animosity for the man. "Like I said, he was a nice guy."

Emmet released her and kept any further opinions to himself. Whatever they'd shared a moment ago was gone, replaced by awkward silence again. She joined him at the table.

"Are you almost finished here?"

He picked up an empty clip and started loading it. "Why?"

"I'm bored."

He frowned at her.

"Yes. Even after whipping your ass, I'm bored."

He slammed the clip home into the gun. "I'm not here for your entertainment, Bailey." Back to Mr. Grim.

Fine. "I'll go into town by myself then." She headed for the car inside the barn.

He stepped in front of her, faster than he had before. Faster than he had when they sparred. "You're not going anywhere. We are not on vacation." His voice, sharp and low.

"And I'm not a prisoner." By his scowl, he did not like what she said. "I would like the company. You can protect me while I eat dinner. It's easier to agree with me than have me annoyed all night."

His nostrils flared, and his eyes turned flinty. "Don't try to blackmail me."

"Who said anything about blackmail?" He released her and continued cleaning the weapon. She lined up next to him. "How much more do you have left?"

He tipped his head at the pieces displayed. "Three more to go."

Bailey picked up the soft cleaning brush and got to work. "I'll help, and we go to dinner afterward." He didn't agree, but he didn't disagree either. She called that progress.

Two hours later they strolled into a pub off the main thoroughfare. Leather booths, soft lighting, the place smelled of roasted meats and cigars.

They drew some curious stares as Emmet led her to a table in the back, by a large picture window showing the parking lot with a view of their car. She pulled off her coat, hung it on a peg and slid into the booth. Two rings came sliding across the polished tabletop, a round cut diamond engagement ring large enough to make her eyes pop out their sockets paired with a plain gold band. She caught both before they dropped into her lap.

"W-what are these?" She held the radioactive jewelry in her palm.

His mouth twisted into an arrogant grin. "They're what you think. Put them on."

Pissed, Bailey shoved the rings onto her finger. "This is not the way I thought my first proposal would go."

"This isn't your first proposal. This is pretend."

His snarky reply was a dose of reality she didn't need. "Thanks for the reminder. I had forgotten I'm a target because someone wants Hank dead and I'm not in Switzerland on vacation. I'm hiding out with a hitman."

His reply was thwarted as a waitress came the table. She was blond and petite with a perfect rack and a tight sweater highlighting the pair. "Back so soon?" She batted her eyes at Emmet and gave Bailey the brusque once over. A sister she probably summed up and dismissed as inconsequential.

"Yes. I wanted to bring my wife."

Her smile withered as Bailey waved at her with the rock on the fourth finger of her left hand. And call her shallow, she did enjoy the moment. "I'll have a rum and coke, please."

"Bring me a beer and two menus, thanks." He dismissed her and relaxed into the seat. Facing the front of the establishment, he had a bird's eye view of the pub. His gaze darted about, touching on everyone. He'd kept his coat on, as did many others in the pub. She knew he was armed, but even sitting, she couldn't spot a telltale bulge. To the patrons and herself, Emmet was just a hot guy chillin', not a man with a body count, a number she suddenly wanted to know.

"You're really good doing this." He arched an eyebrow at her, silent encouragement for her to continue. "No one would guess you're a killer. You sit there seeming like an ordinary guy, but you're not. Were you always a killer or did Hank train you to be one?" She quipped.

"Always a killer?" He snorted and cocked his head to the side. He clammed up as the waitress returned with their drinks and menus. "No one is born a killer, Bailey." He tsked after the waitress had left.

Bailey studied the entrees. "Not what I implied, but thanks for the clarification."

The silence strung out between them. She glanced up to find his eyes locked on her, not the menu, his expression unreadable. "Did you happen to try the food when you were in here? I'm not sure what to order." Silence. She turned back to the menu. "I guess I'll stick with what I know."

The waitress returned. Bailey planted her elbow on the table and dangled her hand and those rings in the air. Yeah, this was all make-believe, but they were the only two in the room who knew it, and she was feeling petty. "I'll have a hamburger and fries."

"Make that two." Emmet chimed in and handed over the menu.

Bailey did the same and took a long sip of her rum and coke. She ignored the awkward tension between them and focused on the patrons. There were a few couples. Some single guys playing darts and women ogling them. The bartender said goodnight to a guy leaving as he wiped down the bar, and the waitress brought an order out to a table three booths down.

"I told you, I was twelve when we met."

His voice startled her, but she had enough sense to keep her mouth shut and not interrupt.

"Dayton, Ohio. Stepfather wasn't a stand-up guy. Got in trouble with the mob. We went on the run." Short, clipped sentences as if they were dragged out of him. "Hank caught up with us."

A gasp caught in her throat and she leaned forward. "Hank killed your father?" she whispered.

Emmet nodded once.

Exasperated, she flopped back in the seat. "And you're his friend? His protégé?" How could he after Hank killed his father?

Emmet's lips pulled back off his teeth, and he snarled, "He killed the man who beat my mother for years. The man who starved us to the point where I had to dumpster dive outside of restaurants or neither of us would've eaten. My mother wouldn't leave him. Fear kept her from escaping and saving us. He broke her. He almost broke me."

The waitress interrupted their conversation. "Do you require anything more?" she asked.

Go away. "No. We're good." Bailey kept her focus on Emmet, his outburst over, and his stoic mask back in place. An arctic front came off him in waves. Regardless, she couldn't let this opportunity pass. Finally, they'd had a real conversation. He volunteered something about him, filled in his mysterious backstory, and wanted more. "Don't stop." Not now.

"Eat your food, Bailey." He grunted.

Damn it. She picked up a French fry and shoved it in her mouth. Pushing him wouldn't get him to spill. He'd clam up, and she'd never get the opportunity again.

"He moved us from Dayton to Colorado, to a town not bigger than this one after my mother overdosed. If that wasn't bad enough, without my mother to beat he started on me." Hands fisted, head buried in his chest, he was a dichotomy of strong man vs broken child, and her heart ached for that child as she strained to hear each word and contain her horror.

"He alternated the beating with the molestation."

"Emmet, I-I..." What she wanted to say got tangled up between her brain and her mouth.

"Then Hank showed up and put a bullet between his eyes at the dinner table. I had a front-row seat from my place on the floor. That's where I took my meals when there was a meal."

The French fry rolled in her stomach. It took everything she had not to gag while Emmet took a bite of his burger, chewed, swallowed, then wiped his mouth. "Hank saw me there. Pointed his gun at me. He weighed whether to kill me. I was a witness, after all. I don't hold a grudge that he needed to think about it."

Appalled, she gasped. She squeezed her hands together in her lap to keep from reaching for him, and hissed, "He pointed his gun at you? You, who was clearly a victim?"

Head bowed, shoulders curled in, lost in memories she forced him to dredge up, he was that battered child again. Then his chin lifted and his flat gaze reached across the distance between them. "Yeah. And then he lowered it. And helped me up. And took me out of that place."

As he should have. As any decent human being should have. Didn't mean he deserved the adulation Emmet had draped him in. "He got you the therapy you needed?" Maybe Hank wasn't the complete monster she'd believed. Maybe he had some redeeming qualities.

Emmet snorted. "Therapy? I got all the therapy I needed learning how to fire an AK-47."

Bailey forced herself to breathe instead of cry for the image of little Emmet, hungry, treated like an animal, abused, training to be a mini-hitman instead of a little boy. He'd take it as pity, not empathy, and would hate her for it. "So, he visited you in foster care? They allowed that?" she murmured.

"I never went to foster care. Hank took me in. Got me tutors. Made sure I had an education. Academic and trade."

Bailey's heart twisted inside her chest. "A-and he never told you he had a daughter?"

His head sliced from side to side. "No. I didn't know you existed."

It wasn't anything she hadn't already known, but God, it still hurt. She thought her father hated children, that's why he didn't love her. Turned out he hated *her*. Just her. He had no problem loving a child. He had a problem loving *her*. What a revelation to have at age twenty-five.

She wasn't jealous. What she felt was way past jealousy. She mourned because deep in a corner of her heart, she held onto a kernel of hope that Hank had a good reason for how he treated her. Loving her was something he wasn't capable of doing because a part of him was missing. It was a physical thing he couldn't control.

Excuses. All of it was an excuse for a father who would never give her what she needed, his love.

And on top of it all, in a strange twist of fate, if she had been a part of Hank's life, raised as his daughter, and if he had brought Emmet home, their relationship would be *completely* different. Funny how fate worked.

"Excuse me, I need to use the ladies' room." She didn't wait for permission to grab her purse, slide out of the booth, and rush past him to the bathrooms at the rear of the building. Once inside, she slammed into the handicapped stall and pressed herself into the corner by the sink.

She thought she was okay with this, okay with Hank parenting Emmet, being a father to someone other than her, his biological child. On a purely non-emotional level, she was okay with it. There was more than enough love to go around. People were capable of loving more than one person. Loving more than one child.

People were. Hank wasn't.

He had enough love for a little boy. Not a little girl. The minute kernel of hope the Daddy's girl buried deep inside her secretly held onto, died. And it was about damn time.

Bailey climbed to her feet. She avoided the mirror until she'd splashed cold water on her face. Then avoided it again when she saw her swollen eyes and red face. Her makeup was ruined. She reached into her purse for her repair kit and brushed against her Samsung. She pulled it out and hit power. While it powered up, she did a quick fix up on the makeup—foundation, fresh mascara, a dab of eyeshadow, and some lipstick. "Never let them see you sweat" applied to more than a brand of deodorant.

She swiped her thumb across the screen and almost shouted. Her phone had connected to the Wi-Fi in the building. Still couldn't make a call, but she didn't need to, not for Google Hangouts. She hadn't used the app in a while, but it was always available whenever she opened her Gmail account, which was her primary account. She logged in and only had to wait a few seconds for access. Her mail came up first. Next, her folders and finally, Google Hangouts. The only person in the contact list was Daisy.

Hey girl. I'm alive. I've finally taken your advice and hooked up with a hottie. I'm enjoying the Alps. Having lots of fun. I'll be back in town in a week.
Hopefully.
And I'll tell you all about it. Miss you. Love you. TTYL.

She turned the phone off, dumped it in her purse and straightened her clothes. She left the bathroom with her emotions intact. With Emmet's back to her, he didn't see her approach. Which was a good thing since he was on the phone.

And she had a good idea who was on the other end.

CHAPTER 13

*E*mmet didn't stop her, and he didn't watch her go. He gave her the privacy she needed to recover. Hell, he needed to recover from the pain carved into her face.

Damn you, Hank! Why? Why did you do this? The need to smash something, *anything, everything,* fired his blood. Been a while since he'd felt this kind of uncontrolled violence, at least fifteen years. Rage killed in his profession. Only those with clear heads survived. To protect Bailey, he needed his head clear. Crystal clear.

He grabbed his beer, drained the glass, and returned with a slam to the tabletop.

"Everything satisfactory?" The waitress returned. "Your wife, she's upset?" she asked with false concern.

"I'll worry about my wife. You worry about bringing me a fresh beer." She flounced away.

My wife. Never had he ever thought those two words would fall out of his mouth. Worse, the horror he should feel wasn't there. He wasn't the marrying kind. Had no desire to be tied down and neutered by one woman. Hell, he alternated between bouts of celibacy when he couldn't stand the human race and sexual feasts when human touch was all he craved.

Before laying eyes on Bailey, he'd been between both states. It had been months since he'd shared more than a handshake with a woman and years since anyone had piqued his interest longer than a weekend. What was it about her? When had loyalty to Hank flipped into…

Fuck! He had to get his head out of his ass and his dick out of Bailey. Treat her as a client until after Rogers took a cement swim, then… What? What then?

His phone vibrated before he came up with an answer. Only one person had the number. He yanked it out of his pocket and braced.

"Report," Hank demanded.

Emmet bit back his sharp reply because this was Hank, the man he respected, the man he owed, the man who'd never asked anything of him, until now. "The house is secured. Cameras inside and outside the property. No activity noted." He glanced around the room to see if anyone was paying undue attention to him and his conversation. "I take it there's nothing new on Rogers since you didn't lead with that."

"No. We're reevaluating the situation."

It wasn't like Hank to be evasive. "Reevaluating it how?"

"The Philippines was a setup."

"No surprise there, but as always, you survived."

"I believe that was the intention. A quick death will not appease his need for vengeance. That's why I've come to a decision."

There was that tone, the one that didn't allow for discussion, not that discussion was ever allowed when Hank made a decision. The fact that he even uttered the sentence and hadn't issued a command spoke volumes of his current situation. Emmet got the sense he wasn't gonna like Hank's decision. "Yeah, what's that?"

The waitress returned with another drink. Beer wasn't gonna cut it. He needed something stronger for this conversation. He stopped her departure and mouthed *vodka, no ice.* Two booths down, someone laughed loudly.

"Where are you?" Hank snapped.

"Bar in the village."

"Is that what you call protecting her? Parading around town?" Hank growled, sounding very much like an overprotective parent. A little late in Emmet's opinion.

"I am protecting her, and there's no parading. She's not a prisoner, and I'm not going to treat her like one."

Hank sighed heavily, totally uncharacteristic for him. "Perhaps it's for the best."

What the hell did that mean? The best for whom?

Silence echoed from the other side of the phone. Emmet gripped his phone certain Hank's next words would irrevocably alter his world. "We're going to use her to draw him out."

Pulse-pounding in his ear, Emmet went deaf for a few precious seconds. "...Repeat." This time with more conviction.

"We're going to use her as bait to draw Rogers out."

Bailey as bait. The back of his neck went tight, along with his vision. Everything narrowed down to those three words. "No."

"It's the only way, Emmet."

"The only way? The only way for what? To save your ass? Or hers?"

"Emmet!" Hank shouted through their connection. "Boy, you have a better way to handle this, then spit it out because we leaked her whereabouts two minutes ago on the dark web and we're fifteen hours out."

Son of a bitch!

"How have you secured the house?"

"Cameras to see them coming and blind spots to stop them

before they get to the house," His voice was layered with the right amount of professional detachment he did not feel.

Another stretch of uncharacteristic silence. "We do this. We end it. Hold down the fort, we're on our way." The phone clicked, and Hank was gone.

The hairs on the back of his neck prickled. He wasn't alone.

Bailey slid onto her seat, her face blank, unreadable, her body tense. He didn't have to ask if she heard. He needed to know how much.

"Tell me."

He dropped some cash on the table and stood. "Not here."

Bailey ignored his outstretched hand and climbed to her feet. Eyes so much like Hank's studied him while he examined her pale skin and grim lips. She moved past him, marching to the exit, her stride no nonsense. He grabbed her coat because she'd either forgotten or didn't give a damn about the cold.

He caught up with her at the door and handed it over. No murmur of thanks. She punched her arms through the sleeves and zipped it up. He stepped in front of her, forcing her to slow her roll as he scanned the street.

Bailey body checked the door and glided around him. He hauled her back, made her slow down for a sedate stroll to the car.

A quick walk around the BMW with a mirror to check the undercarriage, then he unlocked it. She didn't wait for him to be a gentleman and open the door. She plopped her ass in the passenger seat and glared at him as he did the same in the driver's seat.

"Tell me."

He started the car and backed out of the parking lot. "When we get back to the house."

"Goddamnit!" She slapped the dashboard. "What did he say?"

"When we get home."

"That's not home! That's a hideout! My home is in Atlanta. It's a three-bedroom *home* in a gated community. *That's my home.*" Her face twisted in rage as she pointed out the passenger window in a vague direction.

He had wondered where her breaking point was, and he'd just found it. "I'm not doing this in the car." Not while driving one hundred and fifty kph. She flipped back into her chair, seething in her silence.

They pulled up to the house. Emmet had barely coasted to a stop when Bailey yanked the door open and jumped out. He slammed the car into park and snatched her to him before she made it to the first porch step.

"Let me go!"

"No."

"You said you'd tell me when we got *home*," she snarled low. "Well, we're *home!*" She twisted in his arms.

"We are not in the damn house. We're in the damn snow. Sitting fucking ducks."

"Then let's go in the fucking house!"

"After I fucking check it!"

Some of the fight left her, but by her tense body and the glint in her eyes, she was ready to go again.

"Why when you have that house battened down tighter than a submarine?"

"Because I won't take chances with your safety." *Aww, shit. I just lied to her.*

Bailey folded her arms across her chest. "Fine. Get to it. Go protect me." She marched back to the car, back to the passenger seat, but left the door open.

He couldn't leave her there, not because of the inherent danger, but it didn't matter where he told her. The car, the porch, the barn, in the snow, she deserved to know, and he had to be the one to tell her.

His steps deliberate, Emmet advanced, her wary eyes

following him, and crouched in front of her. She reared back as if she wanted no part of him to touch her. "I spoke to your —Hank."

"Glad one of us did," she snapped. "What does he need from me now."

Rip the Band-Aid off and watch her bleed. "He wants to use you as bait to end this."

She blinked, then closed her eyes for ten long seconds. When she opened them, the fire inside her midnight blue eyes had vanished. "I want to go inside now."

"Bailey…" He needed to explain but kept his trap shut. He allowed her to push him out of the way but joined her at the front door with his gun in his hand. "Stay behind me."

Once again, they went room to room, this time twice as thorough as he had when they first arrived. "It's all clear." He told her and was surprised she didn't hightail it to her bedroom.

Eyes locked onto him, she stood in the middle of the living room, coat and hat still on, leading him to believe she had every intention of fleeing for the nearest exit if she didn't like what he had to say. Even if he had to force her to stay, he couldn't let that happen.

That was the last thing Emmet wanted, to force her, to bend her to his will. No! Not his will. He didn't place her—*them*—on this path. The blame lay with Rogers and Hank, yet here they were, Emmet and Bailey, the result of two arrogant bastards whose war would get an innocent woman killed.

"Do you trust me?" It was important to him now when he hadn't given a damn before.

Bailey stiffened. "I did."

But not now was implied. "Guess I deserve that even though everything I've done has been to protect you."

She backed up a step. Her gaze darting to the gun still in his hand. Great, now she was angry and afraid of him. He flipped the safety on and stuffed the gun back in the arm holster. He yanked off his coat and tossed it on the sofa. She didn't do the same.

Wanting a drink, but needing to remain sober, grabbed a bottle of water from the bar in the corner of the room. "I will not let anything happen to you," he said out loud and twisted the cap off.

Her voice stilted. "What is not going to happen to me?"

"Hank leaked our location on the dark web to draw Rogers out. To put an end to all of this so you can have your freedom back." *See, didn't sound so bad. Actually, it sounded horrible.*

Her lips parted, and a strangled sound escaped before she snapped them closed. Her gaze lowered, and she inhaled a long breath. She swayed, and he moved closer to block any exit she may choose.

"Was this your idea?" she asked, then nailed him with a cold glare.

"No, Bailey. It wasn't."

"But you are going along with this." Statement, not a question because she already knew his answer.

He couldn't get the words about because it was wrong. All of it was wrong. "Pack your things. We're leaving."

Her chin lifted, and she faced him with palatable determination and pain she failed to mask. "No."

His head cocked to the side. "What do you mean no?"

Her lips peeled back in a sneer. "This is where my father wants me, a lamb for the slaughter, then this is where I stay. Maybe then I'll finally get a chance to see him, speak to him, if I'm not already dead."

"Don't say that." But the picture was already in his head.

"You want to go?" She pointed at the front door. "I never asked you, nor did I hire you to protect me. You are free to leave. I'll even pay your going rate." Slowly, she turned. Back rigid, not even the merest sway to her hips, she marched away.

Going rate? *Son of a bitch.* "You can't afford me." She kept walking toward her bedroom, in no rush at all. "We leave in ten minutes."

Not even a hitch in her steps. Emmet wasn't having it.

Incensed, he caught up with her in the hallway, shoved her into the wall, and kept her there with a hand to her chest. "You are no one's sacrificial lamb. I won't allow it."

Her sad little smile held all the warmth of an open grave waiting for a fresh body. "This is the best way to save Hank and you. It's the only way. We lure him here and kill him, and you and Hank live happily ever after. Father and son," she said in a low, vicious purr.

He took her by the shoulders, tempted to shake some common sense into her, put the fear of-of God, if she was a believer, into her. By the fury on her face, that wasn't going to happen.

"Let. Me. Go."

Maybe it was the hint of anguish in her voice, the glint in her midnight blue eyes, no, it was the slight quiver of her bottom lip that fractured her fury and broke through his impotent rage. Emmet's hand dropped as if it lost power all on its own. He backed up and kept going until his back touched the opposite wall.

Her gaze locked on him as if he were an animal to be wary of, yet she still wasn't afraid, not of him, not of anything. He didn't think she'd ever been afraid of anything or anyone. Just like her father. "You want to stay. Fine. *We* stay," he growled.

Bailey pushed off from the wall and crossed the short distance to her room. She paused to twist the diamond engagement ring and wedding band off her finger. Both hit the floor with twin clinks as loud as sledgehammers striking an anvil. She disappeared inside the bedroom, the door closing with a soft snick signaling the end to more than just this *conversation*.

For her sake, he had let her leave.

For his sake, he couldn't let her go.

CHAPTER 14

The outrage fueling her in the initial hours after discovering Emmet on the phone with Hank and hearing their plans for her had settled into a low simmer vibrating through her veins. He'd betrayed her. So what if they'd known each other less than a weekend and it shouldn't matter. She felt betrayed and lied to.

She hadn't slept with him because she expected loyalty in return. But because she had slept with him, was it wrong to expect him not to drive a spear through her heart and dangle her bloody body over a shark-infested pool? Apparently, it was.

And that "Johnny come lately" I'm taking you somewhere else bullshit was exactly that, bullshit. From the moment they met, he reminded her of how much danger she was in. Running away from it wouldn't help. So, in some roundabout, fucking up, twisted, karmic, reality, she agreed with Hank. Let's draw the bastard out and kill him, even if meant she happened to be the chum seeding the waters.

It had been forty-eight hours ago and since that eventful evening, and Bailey hadn't uttered a single word to Emmet. It wasn't her style to play the avoidance card. Head-on was how she dealt with things. Not quite true. She buried her head in the sand as well as the next woman.

Not this time.

Because after everything, she still desired him. *There! I admit it.* And he desired her. She wasn't ignorant to the way he looked at her, touched her. They ignited something in each other. Something combustible that turned all their smoldering heat into a passionate explosion. Good or bad, who knows, and at the time, who cared. For once, she lived in the moment. Maybe because tomorrow truly wasn't promised. Someone wanted her dead. Yet, in his arms, she breathed, kissed, fucked, and cried. She lived.

It sucked, especially when he chose her father over her. There was no getting over that.

I should've taken him up on his offer and left with him. Declining in favor of martyrdom was the height of idiocy. Now, it was too late, she realized as she stared out her bedroom window at the activity. No longer was the chalet their private love shack. A guy named Whiskey showed up yesterday with two other men who didn't bother sharing their names.

She didn't like whiskey, the taste of the liquor or the man. He had a hard, roughhewn edge, created by forces she could only guess at. With short brown hair and a clean-shaven jaw, he was all sharp edges from the blade of his nose, the slash of his mouth, and flinty dark eyes. Slighter shorter than Emmet's six feet three inches, he made up for the difference by being broader. Dressed in a simple white shirt and jeans, he tried to appear casual and failed.

He'd greeted her by name. "Hello, Bailey Monroe." Shook her hand and had even offered a friendly grin while Emmet stood close by, features neutral, yet a glint in his cool gaze. He knew who she was, Hank's daughter.

"Mr. Whiskey." Not his given name, no doubt.

A dry sound she assumed was a chuckle had escaped him.

"Whiskey. No title or chaser needed." He stared at her with a smirk on his face, as if he knew something she didn't. He probably did, which further pissed her off.

From her perch on the window seat, she spied one of the unnamed men exiting the barn. He vanished in the tree line. A usual occurrence since the trio had arrived. She wondered about the activity in the woods but doubted she'd get a truthful answer. Also, she couldn't handle another lie, not from Emmet.

A knock sounded at her bedroom door. Bailey didn't move from her curled position, and she didn't answer. The view from her window was better than the person on the other side of the door.

The knob turned, and the door opened with a soft snick. She didn't need to turn around to know who entered. "Lunch."

A little late for lunch at three in the afternoon. She heard the clink of a plate and ignored the rumble her stomach let out. Her last meal was breakfast yesterday. Still, she ignored him and the plate. Talk about not playing the avoidance card.

"Enough already," he grumbled. "You're behaving like a child. You have to eat."

He wasn't wrong. Without looking at him, she uncurled from the seat, moved around him for the plate on the dresser. Swedish meatballs and toasted bread with a salad along with a bottle of water. She took the food back to the window seat and dug in.

"You're welcome."

Her head jerked up, and she gave him the attention he certainly craved to risk even entering her room. "I didn't ask you to bring me food," she said with a mouthful of balls.

"Chew and swallow, argue later." He planted his ass on her bed.

She swallowed and chugged down half the bottle. "You want me to be grateful, well I'm not. Not for the food. Not for you *protecting* me." She speared two meatballs and shoved them in her mouth.

He cocked his head to the side and nodded once. "Understood. But, I never wanted your gratitude."

Hard to miss the husky tone his voice had dipped into. She snorted and side-eyed him as she chewed and swallowed. *Not falling for it, buddy,* was her silent reply.

"That wasn't a line."

She rolled her eyes.

Emmet dragged his hand through his hair and down his face to scratch at his five o'clock shadow. He seemed tired with his bloodshot eyes and grim tilt to his mouth. She hadn't slept much, but she had slept. Feeling something for him wasn't what she wanted, yet she did. "Have you eaten?"

His head jerked up. "Yeah. I had a big breakfast. I thought you would've left your hidey-hole for food by now, but you are stubborn. I've been too busy to notice until now."

She'd seen him marching in and out of the barn into the woods with the other men. "Oh yeah, with what?"

"Finish eating, and I'll show you."

Bailey didn't miss the entreaty in his voice, a plea to break the deadlock they'd fallen into. She liked the deadlock, needed it to keep her walls up because he was her weakness she hadn't expected. Even now, still bruised from his betrayal, she cared whether he'd eaten, slept, how he felt about... All of it was pointless. She had to take care of herself because no one else would. If his guilt pushed him to share information with her, then she'd damn well take it.

"All right. I'll meet you in five." She dipped the bread in sauce and took a satisfying bite.

He rose and stood there as fine as he could be with his thumbs hooked into his belt loops, gun strapped to his side. Her stomach wasn't the only thing that needed feeding. Her libido had just peeled open an eye and had taken a prolonged, leisurely look at him.

"I'll be waiting for you."

She watched him go and had to admit, she liked this softer, contrite version of Emmet. His guilt? *Could be all an act.* But that wasn't his style.

She cleaned her plate, took a quick shower because she'd ignored hygiene while sulking, and dressed in her last pair of clean jeans and fresh underwear. Yoga pants and a Henley were the only items left. Laundry would have to be done after Emmet showed her what he'd been up to.

She opened the bedroom door to find him waiting, already dressed in his coat, holding hers and an iPad tucked under his arm. "Thanks." She pulled on her coat and followed him through the silent house to the back deck.

The sun and fresh air! A deep inhale cleared the cobwebs out of her lungs as she tilted her head up to receive some rays. Staying cooped up inside wasn't her nature. She ran down the short stairs ahead of Emmet eager to hear the crunch of snow beneath her boots.

His hand landed on her shoulder. "Careful. We've been busy." He pulled up a schematic on the iPad laying out the current landscape. "I'm expecting a two-pronged attack, from the front of the house and the rear. The isolated nature of the chalet is conducive to a sneak attack from the rear, especially since that's the logical place to retreat. That's why we've engineered a surprise for Rogers. Landmines."

"Landmines?"

"Small explosives buried under the snowpack."

She glanced at the snow-covered mountain over her shoulder. At three thousand feet, she considered it a baby Alp; however, it could still kill a person. "What about an avalanche?"

"I've factored that in. The explosives we've used are small, but an avalanche could happen. If it does, and we're buried—"

"We?" Her attention snapped back to him.

"Yeah. *We.*"

One word said with implicit intent. Wasn't the first time he'd said in that tone, with that particular glint in his eyes. Also wasn't the first time heat stirred her blood at hearing it.

"I'm glued to your side. You're not going anywhere without me."

That shouldn't give her the warm fuzzies tingling her nipples and creating a slow burn in her groin, not when she was still angry at him and the world in general, but it did.

"If we're buried, I have the local rescue team on speed dial." He tapped the phone sticking out of his left pocket. They'll be able to locate us with GPS, hopefully."

"Hopefully." Better not to dwell on that.

He tilted the screen for her to see. "This is the layout of the explosives. There are two safe paths out of here. The one to the left is only safe for a tenth of a mile.

"It's a trap."

"Yes. The path to the right is the only safe passage out of the woods to the road. I have a couple of snowmobiles camouflaged to get us out to a small town where I have a car parked." He led her down the right path. She noticed he shortened his strides to match hers. Instead of marching ahead, they strolled, leisurely.

"Seems like you've planned everything." She focused on her steps and the surroundings.

He shrugged. "I'm trying."

He was trying, that she couldn't deny. Not only to save her but to include her. She touched his forearm. "I-I haven't said thanks for this. Any of this. Jamaica and..." She thought of their night spent together. "Everything." *I did not just thank him for sex.*

"I should say it's my job, but you're welcome." He smiled, he actually smiled with his mouth and his eyes. Flustered, she dropped her hand and looked away. *Self-preservation, Bailey. You let him get under your skin. You can't let him get that close again.*

"Notice the trees marked with charcoal on the trunk. It's a

roadmap." He pointed to the mark on a series of trees located seven feet above. Not easy to find unless a person knew what to look for.

"Can't see that at night."

"No, you can't, but I'll be with you."

Yeah, but it didn't hurt to memorize the route. In case shit took a bloody turn south. A tenth of a mile later, he showed her the location of the snowmobiles.

"What about the front of the house?" she asked as they headed back.

"Same setup. We've lined the driveway with remote charges that won't detonate unless we want them to."

He had thought of everything, except... "What about afterwards? We can't leave all these bombs around for someone to find. What if it's a kid?"

"Everything will detonate after we leave, including the house."

She frowned and glanced at the structure over her shoulder. "Aww. But I love the house."

"I'll buy you a new one," he murmured, tapping away on the screen.

Emmet buying her a house. She tiptoed away from that topic and tackled the one topic she'd avoided long enough. "Is Hank here?" She concentrated on her footsteps and spotting the charcoaled markings on the trees, not Emmet or his reaction to her question.

"Yes, he was," he said with no hesitation.

She was about to ask where, but it didn't matter. Hank didn't matter. They were almost back to the house when Emmet stopped which caused her to stop.

"I can't speak for Hank—"

"No, you can't." She cut him off. "And I don't want you to speak for him. You shouldn't have too." She marched ahead, but he stopped her.

"I wasn't finished," he growled.

Staring into his eyes, she waited, not ignorant of the concern ebbing from their depths.

"I'm sorry—"

She slashed her hand across her throat. "Don't apologize for him."

"Will you stop cutting me off."

She shook her head. "Not if you're gonna make excuses. I don't want to hear it."

His mouth compressed into a grim line, but he didn't say anything else.

"I do have something to say."

He folded his arms and glared at her. "Shocking, but go ahead."

Bailey ignored his sarcasm. "I said thanks already. I just want you to know...I trust you." It wasn't a lie or even a half-truth. Emmet wasn't perfect—far, far from it—but he was trying and that deserved appreciation. Even if his loyalty to Hank brought him to her doorstep, he didn't have to be here, with her, playing with bombs and putting his life on the line. Whatever the reason, he was here.

The glaring stopped, and something more dangerous entered his gaze. He reached for her, cupped her face in his calloused palms. "I trust you is much better than a thank you." He tilted her chin up, and she didn't fight him because she wanted his lips on hers, his tongue in her mouth, his body pinning her down, merging. She wanted him.

"Sorry for the intrusion, but I need to show you something."

Whiskey's voice was a cold dose of reality. He stood on the right side of the tree line with an iPad in his hand, leering as if he knew something he shouldn't. Cheeks flaming, Bailey yanked away from Emmet and didn't stop until she reached her bedroom.

*E*mmet snatched Whiskey's iPad from him and glanced at the coordinates. "This could've waited."

"Yep. It coulda. You may not thank me now, but I've just saved you a world of hurt."

Emmet looked up from the screen and tracked Whiskey's gaze to Bailey entering the house. "What are you flapping your lips about?"

"Her, and you. Kaboom." He made a mushroom cloud with his hands. "That's what will happen when Hank finds out you got a stiffy over his daughter."

Emmet headed for the house. "Hank doesn't give two shits about his daughter outside of using her to get to his enemy."

Whiskey fell in step with him. "You're wrong, dude. He doesn't show it, but he cares."

Emmet snorted. "If you had a kid would you use them as target practice?"

Whiskey shuddered. "I am never having a kid. *Never*."

Emmet gritted through clenched teeth. "Well, I wouldn't. When I have a kid, dust will be afraid to touch it."

Whiskey held up his hands in surrender. "I don't doubt it, especially since you already have the mother picked out."

Emmet turned on Whiskey. "I don't have anything picked out. I'm here to protect an innocent woman from a madman, and her father." There, he finally spat out what he refused to acknowledge.

"Okay. I hear you." Whiskey gave a toothy grin. "And after this shindig is over, I'll help you pick out a ring."

CHAPTER 15

Bailey entered her bedroom. Halfway to the bathroom, she paused. Call it a sixth sense, woman's intuition, whatever, but suddenly she was certain someone had been here while she was out. The one camera she and Emmet placed was still in position, along with the sensor on the window.

Copying how Emmet did things, she started with the crown molding, then the light fixtures, and found it in the picture frame. A small hole in the corner of the canvas. The tiny camera blended in with a depiction of a cloudless night sky. A middle finger to anyone watching and she yanked it out. So much for trusting Emmet. What a fool!

Furious, she held the camera in the palm of her hand and noticed it was different from the ones Emmet had placed, in size and shape. This wasn't him. He hadn't placed this camera.

Bailey slammed open her bedroom door and marched into the living room. Emmet and Whiskey and the two other men were in a deep huddle in front of a laptop. The whispering ceased as she approached. "Don't stop on my account. I'm here to return some property."

She slapped the camera down on the desk, next to the laptop, studied the gathering fury on Emmet's face and Whiskey's neutral expression, and had her answer. She picked up a paperweight snowball with a little village inside and smashed the surveillance device into a thousand pieces. Then she scooped them up and blew the remains into Whiskey's face.

"You want to see me naked? Ask."

"That wasn't—"

Emmet's fist cut off the rest of his sentence. She leaped back, out of the way of the two men swinging at each other.

"It wasn't me." Whiskey groaned after a gut shot. Emmet flipped Whiskey onto his back and placed him in a chokehold. "I was in the field. You saw me." He gasped.

Whiskey was in the field. He'd met them outside. That brought Bailey's attention to the two who'd never bothered to share their names. One of them had to be the one.

Emmet shoved Whiskey away and stepped over his prone body. "Which one of you snuck into her bedroom and placed that camera?"

The blond with the Fu Manchu goatee spoke. "I was under instructions."

"From who?" Emmet demanded.

Bailey spun away. The man's answer wasn't necessary. She already knew. Reentering her bedroom, she closed the door, blocking out the sounds of Emmet and whatever his name was, fighting. It didn't matter that he placed the camera when he wasn't the one behind the placement.

"I have to get out of here but can't because I'll end up dead." But after this was over… A sharp knock on her door, then it opened and closed behind Emmet.

"Hank told him to place the cameras, but not where. He did that on his own, but he won't be doing that again. Whiskey is getting his replacement."

"Tell me you didn't kill him." She wouldn't be responsible for someone's death over a camera.

"I didn't, but I don't know what Hank will do to him."

Hard to miss the hopeful note in his voice. Bailey wasn't sure she didn't like it.

"I'm going to check out the room, make sure you didn't miss anything."

Once more, she followed behind him, double-checking his search. When they were done, the only cameras remaining were the ones he'd placed. And those, he removed. "It's not enough that I want you safe. You need to feel safe, and cameras won't do that." He pocketed the devices and headed for the bathroom.

"You don't think he put a camera in there?"

"He'd better hope he hadn't."

It didn't take long for him to find a camera hidden in the light fixture in the shower, and a second camera in the large mirror. Both cameras would've had a perfect view of her naked.

"He's dead." Emmet headed for the exit.

Bailey jumped in his path and stopped him with one hand to the center of his chest. "Stay." Why did she do it when the sane, rational side of her demanded she keep her distance? She needed a hug, to be held close to someone's heart and cherished like she mattered, for just a little while, and maybe that would be enough to stave off the cold seeping into her bones, changing her forever.

He started to argue until she wrapped her arms around his waist and buried her head in his chest. She held on tight and pretended she was somewhere warm and sunny with umbrella drinks and suntan lotion. A place where no one wanted her dead because of a father she managed to forget she had. She imagined everything was different, everything except the man she clung to, everything but him.

Back to her senses, she pulled away, ducking her head as she separated their bodies. It would be great if he'd leave now so she could forget she'd made a fool of herself.

Not a chance.

Emmet picked her up and plopped her onto the counter. He caged her with his hands, blocking an escape on either side of her body. "Eyes on me, Bailey." His tone thick with a hunger she recognized. Her nipples pearled, her core clenched and slickened, ready, needy.

Schooling her face to not betray her, she obeyed and raised her chin. Heat blazed from his icy eyes stoking the embers of a blaze that always seemed a breath away from igniting in his presence.

His fingers stroked up from her hips to her waist, over her breasts, her throat, to thread into her hair. His thumbs hooked under her chin, tilting her head at the perfect angle for the first brush of his mouth. She sighed and parted her lips in a blatant invitation for him to take what he wanted.

First, he licked into her, gently teasing his tongue along her bottom lip. Then, in an ever-tightening grip, he fisted her hair and drew her head back. The press of his mouth, the glide of his tongue, the nip of his teeth, she shuddered at the unbridled passion and clung to his arms even as the rest of her went boneless from the pleasure. No one had ever kissed her like this. She was ruined, utterly ruined for any other, just from one kiss.

He broke away to trail kisses down her throat. Panting, she brought him back to her. "I want you so bad, but-but, they're right outside the door." She'd never been shy before, wasn't sure why it mattered now—

He silenced her with another kiss and licked into her mouth. "The shower. Get in the shower."

Shirt and bra, boots, then jeans and panties. Emmet helped with the last part. Finally, naked, she leaped into his embrace and wrapped her body around him while he palmed her ass, kicked off his boots, and made for the glass enclosure.

Back pressed to the cold tiles, Bailey gasped into his mouth. He swallowed the sound and murmured an apology as he traded places. At some point, he reached over and flipped on the hot water, turning the shower into a steam bath.

Water pelted her. Pelted him. His wet clothes plastered to his body. She helped peel the sweater off his chest. It hit the tile with a soggy splat. The jeans required both their efforts but gave way to their passion. Finally naked, steam swirled around their bodies, leaving them covered in mist.

She eased down his body, going onto her knees. Those eyes of his burned into her as she took him in her hand, the first time she held his girth and licked up the warm, steely length of him.

His taste—salty, earthy—had her wet and aching. But she wanted to do this, him in her mouth, at the back of her throat, losing control. Up one side and down the other, there wasn't anything better than watching his abs clench and release with each stroke of her tongue. Even better was his hooded gaze. How could she ever think his gaze was cold? Wrapping her lips around him, she drew him in, circled the flushed crown and the bundle of nerves underneath.

His head hit the tile with a thud, and he hissed sharply, "Bailey."

To the back of her throat, she took him, sucking, licking his erection, loving the smooth, velvety hardness on her tongue. She alternated her feasting while grinding him like a pepper mill between both her hands.

Back arched, he rocked into her mouth, a rhythm they found together. "Don't stop," he growled.

She hummed her agreement and reveled in her mastery, her control, his pleasure. No one else. She popped him out of her mouth and ran her thumb over his slick head, down his veined shaft. His hips jerked violently, and she took him back into her mouth.

Another lick, another swirl of her tongue, another squeeze of his shaft, and finally, a squeeze of his balls. His body tensed, and he barked out a curse over the background hiss of the shower.

His lips peeled back from his teeth. He swelled and convulsed in her mouth. The taste of him swamped her. She took all his orgasm down, sucking deeply as he bucked and trembled.

She released him and licked her way up his body for a kiss. "I'm incredible. I know. You can tell me so when you catch your breath." She nipped his chin and danced under the hot spray, out of his way.

Emmet flicked off the water and snatched her to him. "You are incredible." He swept her off her feet and brought her out of the bathroom to the bed, then backed away. Still, she lay as his smoldering gaze stroked her in a tangible caress. In the cool bedroom, she felt hot, fevered, from her hair follicles to her nipples, to her wet core, to her curled toes.

He yanked open the night table, retrieved a condom, and tore it open.

"You need to get on birth control 'cause I want to feel you, skin to skin, nothing between us." He sheathed himself.

Asking her to get on birth control meant one thing. He planned on sticking around. She bit her lip to keep the burst of joy inside. "I can do that."

With one hand, he twined her hair around his fingers and pulled her head back for a raw kiss as his other hand did a slip-n-slide between her thighs. "I've never said that to anyone."

Right there! At that moment, with that statement, she knew she'd gotten beneath his armor, beneath his *skin,* as he had gotten beneath hers. Maybe she wasn't in this alone, this war that had come to her doorstep, this man she was about to welcome into her body, into her heart.

She blinked and bit back a yelp as he flipped her over and propped her ass up. Spread wide, she cranked her head around to watch him meld their bodies together. Inch by exquisite inch, he buried himself inside her. She groaned long and loud from pleasure almost too much to bear.

"Pillow, babe."

She stretched out, grabbed the nearest pillow, and bit into it as he grabbed her ass and hauled her to him. They crashed together, flesh slapping from the intensity of his thrusts. Lost, utterly lost, in pleasure so intense it bordered on pain, begged him not to stop, sobbed into the pillow as she threw her hips back.

From the corner of her mind, the part clinging to a thread of sanity, the rational Bailey remembered they weren't alone in the house and ordered her to glue her lips together. Whimpering, she tried to obey, until he reached around to rub her clit. Lightning ignited in her veins. Her entire body lit up. Body torqued, toes curled, knees locked together, trapping his cock inside her. Her orgasm consumed her and didn't stop until she was a limp mess.

She came back to herself wrapped in now familiar arms, surrounded by familiar heat, inhaling a familiar masculine scent, feeling loved, even if neither had said the words…yet.

CHAPTER 16

*P*leased, Emmet studied the firs dusted with fresh snow. The forecast called for another kilometer to blanket the area tomorrow. The additional powder would camouflage the area nicely after all their activity and wouldn't hinder the explosives.

How much longer? They'd been here four days, prepared for Armageddon the last two. There wasn't a time limit on these things, yet he sensed Rogers' haste.

He'd had never been a patient man. Collateral damage wasn't something Rogers tended to factor. Quite a few times Hank had to rein him in with a firm set of boundaries or risk mass casualties. He liked to make a mess and leave a statement, even when discretion was warranted.

Emmet had never been a fan, and the feeling was mutual. He needed to die.

The rustle of sheets drew his attention away from his thoughts and the scenery to drink in something more beautiful than the Swiss Alps draped in pristine snow.

On her side, one toned leg peeked from under the down comforter. That's all she gave him, the tease. The rest of her remained hidden. He'd spent all afternoon and a good portion of the night enjoying all her delights, it wasn't enough. He still hungered.

On a primitive level, he accepted the constant craving she'd unexpectedly aroused within him. The rational, self-serving level he usually operated on, waited to be sated. None of his other conquests had lasted longer than a weekend. He was a loner. Bred by a loner, raised by a loner. He didn't need anyone. Not even Hank, to whom he owed his life to.

But Bailey... Man, she was different. Made him *feel* different. Could be because she was a loner too. Two kindred souls.

Whatever the reason, she woke something in him and he wasn't sure he liked it. Wasn't sure at all.

"Emmet?" Her muffled voice came from beneath the comforter, then her head poked out and her midnight gaze found him. Sitting up, she murmured, "What's wrong?"

Hovering over her like a damned ghost, what else could he say? He sat and smoothed her hair away from her face. "Go back to sleep. It's early." He pressed a kiss to her forehead.

Without further resistance, she settled back and yawned. "Come back to bed."

Shit. Warmth curled around the center of his chest causing an unfamiliar ache. "I will in a bit. Going to make sure everything is secure."

A sleepy curl of her lips was her response and damn he wished he could strip and climb in next to her. That wouldn't keep her safe. Another kiss to her forehead and he forced himself away.

He paused at the top of the stairs and absorbed the quiet, though he wasn't alone. Whiskey made himself comfortable in front of a crackling fire in the brick fireplace. Emmet joined him, choosing to stand opposite Whiskey with his back to the flames.

Whiskey picked up a tumbler full of an amber liquid, his namesake would be Emmet's guess. "Sam's out front patrolling.

Tex got *recalled*. I cleared everyone out once we heard the shower come on."

Emmet's hackles rose. "How did you hear the shower?"

"Old pipes."

"Bullshit." He had an image of Whiskey's ear pressed to the bedroom door and fisted his hands to keep from reaching for his gun.

"It's true, and I'm not that much of a pervert. I don't rain on another man's happy happy joy joy." Whiskey drained his glass and rose. "Besides, I don't have to rain on your parade when the Hurricane Hank is waiting for you. By now, he should be a Cat 5."

Emmet's gut clenched, an automatic response. "Where?"

Whiskey tipped his empty glass to the window. "The barn. Been there about three hours now." He headed for the bar.

"Are you drunk?"

Whiskey snorted. "Not even close, unfortunately."

Emmet grabbed his coat off a peg by the back door and was striding across the snow before he had it zipped up. He yanked open the barn door and stepped inside.

Sitting on a stool at the work table, Hank tapped away on a laptop. A single light barely illuminated the area. He didn't turn around when Emmet entered or closed the door behind him. "Have a nice nap?" he asked in a tone that would've rattled a rattlesnake.

No use avoiding the inevitable. "I did."

Hank spun on the stool to face Emmet. "I told you to protect her. Not fuck her!"

That he did, and a tad bit of guilt stabbed Emmet which he promptly shoved away. "Say her name."

Hank's eyes narrowed. "I trusted you with her life, and you used her—"

"Say her name, Hank."

Hank slammed his fist onto the work table. "Why her? Why her when you could've had any other wom—"

"Do you even remember her name, or have you said *her* for so long that's all you know *her* by?"

Hank stood. Emmet had an inch on him, but it didn't matter, and they both knew it. "Bailey Michela Murray."

Wrong. "You mean Monroe, not Murray."

"She was born Murray. I had it changed after her mother died." The last sentence seemed to take the wind out of Hank's sails. He looked away, his chin dipping into his chest.

Emmet took a moment allowing Hank to breathe, but only a moment. "Car bomb." Hank's head jerked up, surprise on his face. "Bailey told me. That's what you told her on her eighteenth birthday."

Hank moved away to grab a thermos off the work table. He screwed off the cap and took a swig of what smelled like strong black coffee. "Constance had a doctor's appointment with her OB. Prenatal care. She was seven months pregnant with our sons. Twins."

Oh, Jesus. Now Emmet had to look away. The pain on Hank's face was too raw, too fresh, too real.

"I had bought her a minivan, and she hated it. Took my Porsche Turbo, probably to spite me because I joked she was too big to fit behind the wheel. I'd gone to all her appointments, but I was on a mission. Diplomat's kid went hiking in Turkey too close to the Iraqi border and got kidnapped. Once the CIA was called in, they sent in the Seals. We got the kid out cleanly. Third extraction in a year. The team was on a high. I came back home to SoCal to find the police, firefighters, and an ambulance in my driveway."

Emmet knew about Hank's time as a Seal, but staring at the man in front of him, the man who'd raised him to be ruthless, efficient, and emotionless, Emmet had difficulty reconciling the image of Hank at an obstetric appointment with the killer he'd become.

"Constance and her sister, who helped out when I was gone, both were dead, and Bailey was missing. The guy was sloppy. Radical wannabe recruited by Jihadists learned how to make a bomb off the internet. Son of captain on base, you believe that shit. That's how the fucker knew who we were and how to find us."

"I didn't wait for the investigation. I tracked down the piece of shit and tortured the information about Bailey's whereabouts out of him, then peeled the skin off his hide. I arrived in Nebraska before the traffickers handed her off to the buyer and I took my child back."

"You didn't take her back. You let her go." Easy to understand now that Hank had explained it. "And stayed on the periphery of her life."

"I got her to safety." He continued as if Emmet hadn't said a word. "And prepared to face a court-martial until the agency made me an offer I accepted. I handed her over to Theresa, an operative who needed an out outside of the USA, and I spent the next four years in moving between Syria, Iran, and Iraq."

Honing his skills, Emmet added.

"I made sure Bailey was safe, and all these years she was safe until Rogers broke into my house and stole her file."

Emmet had heard parts of the story before, but not the entirety. It explained a lot. "Did he know it was there? Someone tip him off?"

Hank sighed. "I tipped him off." He threw the thermos against the opposite wall. "On our last mission, I had a top secret file on Delgado I needed in the safe. I went up to get it and didn't realize he was behind me. A slip that shouldn't have happened."

"Damn right, it shouldn't have." Emmet rubbed the back of his neck and circled the room. He needed to move, do something, kill something. Stagnant water soon became polluted, and that's what was happening to him, to them. This waiting would be the death of them. If this didn't work, they'd have to go on the offensive, only do it better than Rogers, but how? What hadn't they thought of?

"You know why there are no old hitmen? Because they're all dead. One mistake is all it takes, Rogers and Veronica, that was mine."

Hank's cryptic tone had Emmet jerking around to study his mentor.

"What are you glaring at?" Hank grumbled and picked up a flask.

"Just checking if there was a shovel near you."

He grunted, his version of a laugh. "Not ready to dig my grave."

"So why can't you see her now? Why haven't you talked to her? Hell, why are you here in the barn and not in the house talking to your kid?" Emmet demanded.

Hank opened his mouth, and nothing came out. For the first time, Hank had nothing to say. It was painful to see his mentor flounder.

"She thinks you don't love her. I know that's not true, but me telling her doesn't matter. She has to hear it from you."

Hank sighed and shook his head. "Too little. Too late. It's best she hates me. Hating me has kept her safe." He inhaled a sharp breath and refocused. "Back to what you're doing with my daughter."

Emmet dragged his hand down his face. He'd let him change the subject...for now. "What we're doing is none of your business. She's a grown woman, not a child."

"She's my child." His tone nothing but menace.

Emmet cocked his head to the side and sneered. "A little late to start parenting especially since you ignored her for the last seven years."

"You know that's not true. I didn't ignore her." He gritted out through clenched teeth.

"You neglected her, which is as bad as ignoring her."

Hank got in his face. "I kept her safe!"

Emmet didn't back down. "From a distance! Someone could've stolen her, *again*."

"Not possible when I've erased all traces of Bailey Murray. She is Bailey Monroe. Mother: Theresa Monroe. Father: unknown."

Emmet threw up his hands. "Yet here we are."

Hank moved away, putting much-needed space between them. "You're not good enough for her, as I wasn't good enough for Constance."

Bullshit on the comparison. They were nothing like Hank and Constance.

Hank flipped open the laptop and tapped in his password. "I love you like a son, Streets. You hurt her, say goodbye to your nuts." He cranked his head around and gave Emmet a bared teeth smile colder than the artic. "I'm fucking serious. I'll cut them off and burn them in front of you. Like I did Tex."

Emmet's only reaction was a sharp intake of breath that caused a humorless grin to stretch across Hank's face. "Exactly where is Tex?"

Hank tipped his head to the shuttered window on the side of the barn. "He's enjoying the view, permanently. I told him to plant extra cameras. Not plant them in her bedroom, and definitely not in her fucking bathroom, which he admitted to after we had an intimate conversation."

One less thing Emmet had to take care of, but he couldn't let it go. "Whiskey had no right to tell you. That was my kill." *Because she's my woman.*

Hank spun on the stool and raised a single brow. They stared each other down. No need to threaten when the unspoken was sufficient. His laptop chimed, and slowly Hank shifted to the computer. "When this is all over, I'm gonna ask you a question, and you better have the right answer."

Emmet didn't need a crystal ball to guess at the question. He didn't need a crystal ball to see what his answer would be either. Walking out of Bailey's life had to be the result because in the end, after Rogers was dead and buried, she would return to her world, safe and sound, and he would return to his. They would never meet again. It's what was best, regardless of how his body clenched at the thought.

"The decoy site is set up. Once Rogers enters the building, it will blow, taking him with it," Hank said. Emmet squinted over Hank's shoulder to the laptop screen showing the chalet a half a mile away. The house was similar in design to their current location with no surrounding neighbors. Wired with cameras and for sound, Hank and Co. had laid enough explosives to make sure Rogers would leave in pieces.

Hank pressed a button, and the lights and tv came on. They even fitted the fireplace with timed smoke canisters, to appear to be in use. It didn't take much arm-twisting to agree to the alternate play and fortify their current location. In fact, Hank seemed relieved at an alternate location. So much so, Emmet wondered why Hank hadn't thought of it on his own.

"We'll know soon enough if it worked," Hank muttered.

True enough.

Emmet spotted Tex's phone on the workbench and picked it up. A swipe of his thumb activated the screen but didn't unlock the device. That wasn't what gave Emmet pause. The Wi-Fi signal had his balls drawing up. "Any chance you had Tex unlock his phone before burying him?"

Hank spun on the stool. "Why?"

Emmet pointed at Hank's laptop. "Tap your Wi-Fi icon," he ordered and didn't need to explain. Hank dragged the cursor over to the icon and tapped. Two networks were available. The laptop was already connected to one, their secure network.

Hank clicked on the other network. It should've asked for a password.

It didn't.

Tex's network was open and traceable. He was more than a perve. He was a traitor. And he was lucky he was already dead.

An alert chimed on Hank's laptop. "He's here, Emmet." The cryptic tone returned to Hank's voice, this time mixed with anticipation.

"What do you mean 'He's here'?"

Hank pointed to the translated police alert flashing on the screen. "Three border guards were found dead. One at Tägerwilen, Switzerland, the other two at Margrethen, Switzerland. The border of Germany and Austria. Fifty-one miles apart."

"Where we *had* connections," Emmet murmured.

"The bodies were found an hour ago but were missing for *two* days. Fuck!" Hank leaped to his feet. "He could be—"

An explosion rocked the barn.

CHAPTER 17

*E*mmet told her to go back to sleep, but the bed was cold without him warming her back. Soon after he left, she shoved the comforter off and propped herself up. The clock read one a.m. Wide awake with a stomach that rumbled for nourishment, she headed for the bathroom first. One whiff and anyone could tell what she'd been doing all evening. She smelled like him, not that she minded, but what was the point of advertising when it wasn't a secret anymore.

Dressed in her last pair of yoga pants and Henley with no panties, she reused her bra and socks and laced up her boots. She pulled her phone out from between the mattress and surprise! Surprise! She had a Wi-Fi signal. And a response from Daisy.

Finally getting you some dick! Sweeet! Shower or grower?! I want deets when you get stateside. In London w Mom. Be back in the ATL in a week. TTYS.

A week. Hopefully, all this would be wrapped up by then. She missed her friend. She missed her life. *Wonder if Emmet would like Atlanta?* "Horse before the cart, Bailey."

A lot to tell you. Have fun in London.

A quiet house greeted her. Carefully, she eased to the staircase and peered over the railing into the open living room. No one was there. She jogged down the stairs, wondering where Emmet and everyone else had gone. So much for protecting her.

She rounded the corner to the kitchen and bumped into Whiskey. "So sorry." He steadied her with a hand to her shoulder.

"No harm done." He stepped aside and let her enter. He had bread and slices of carved turkey and some other meat she couldn't readily name on the counter. "Late night snack. Care for some?" He asked layering mustard on the bread.

She wasn't sure about that.

He pressed a hand to his chest. "It wasn't me placing cameras in your bedroom. That was Tex. I'm a freak, but I'm not a pervert." He winked at her.

This was the most time she'd spent in his presence and wasn't quite comfortable around him, another killer, though he was charming. "Okay. Where's he at?" 'Cause she had a chunk of her mind to give him with her fist.

"Oh..." He waved vaguely at nothing and in no particular direction. "He's around here, somewhere."

"Where's Emmet?"

"In the barn going over last minute details. Mustard? The mayo is strange, not Hellmann's at all." He screwed up his face.

"A little bit of mustard, please." She went to the refrigerator for bottled water and pulled up a chair while he served up the food. "How long have you known Emmet?"

"Oh, about ten years. I've been in the game longer than that though, if that's what you wanted to know." He took a large bite of his sandwich.

She nibbled on hers. "Thanks for the intel."

"You two got cozy quite fast."

Under his speculative gaze, she took her time chewing. "Protecting his virtue or mine, are you?"

"Both, actually. Don't want to see anyone hurt."

"That's…sweet of you. I didn't get the impression you two were friends."

"We are not friendly, but there aren't a lot of us in this field, so we are friends when it necessitates."

"And it necessitates now?" She didn't hide her skepticism.

"Things could get messy and bloody, and I'm not talking about the tiff with Rogers. You understand me. You are the boss's daughter. Even the most pacifist of men would have a problem with his employee having carnal relations with their kid? Hank's never been a pacifist if you had any doubt."

She didn't. "Hank's temperament would concern me if he were the typical father, but he's not. He doesn't give a damn about me. He never did."

His head sliced left, then right. "You're wrong about that. Completely wrong. He's…" Whiskey's brow furrowed, and his voice lowered as a whistling noise filled the air. "Run!"

She hesitated, a natural response until the house rocked and a ball of fire rolled down the staircase. Her feet took flight, she ran straight out the back door as the blast lifted her off her feet and pitched her into a snowbank.

Muffled voices reached her as if her ears were stuffed with cotton. Heat baked her back. She pushed up, and the house exploded behind her, raining chunks of debris. Something flattened her, a body she realized through a haze of pain. "Stay down." She deciphered and couldn't agree more.

Head to the side, she breathed in the scent of smoke, charred wood, propane, all mixed with pine and wet snow stuffed up her nose. Hands roamed her body and lit on a tender spot on the back of her head. She cried out.

"Shhh, it's okay. I'm here. I'm here, and I'm so sorry." Emmet rolled her onto her back.

His form swam in front of her. A few blinks brought him into focus and the flames behind him.

"Get her out of here!" A deep voice shouted, one she recognized.

Emmet lifted her into his arms, but she fought him. "I'm fine." Even she recognized she slurred her words.

"Shhh!" Emmet cradled her, and she nestled into his chest. She drew in his comfort and was desperate for more. Shots came from somewhere. Everyone ducked. "Let's go."

"I'm staying."

There was that voice again, familiar, yet distant. She pushed away from Emmet's chest to see her father standing defiantly in front of the smoldering remains of the chalet.

"We've overstayed our welcome. Let's go."

"He's here! I'm not leaving without his head." Hank started toward the house with Whiskey next to him.

"Hank," she called out, only to have him ignore her. "Hank!" She shoved off from Emmet, forcing him to let her stand.

Without her to carry, Emmet palmed a gun. "Damn it, Hank, answer her."

"Dad!"

He stopped and turned a quarter. Their gazes locked. And for a precious moment, he saw her. Then continued on his way. She'd waited years for him to see her again, he did exactly what she'd expected, he turned away. Damn, if it was a dull knife in her heart.

Emmet grabbed her hand and yanked her away. She stumbled but caught herself before landing in the snow. Gunfire whizzed past them. She ducked but kept moving with Emmet leading the way.

He returned fire until an explosion lit up the trees. And another one. And another one. Screams filled the air and more gunfire. "Keep running! The landmines are working," Emmet ordered.

Her stomach heaved, and she gagged on the vomit crawling up her throat.

"We can't stop."

She hadn't realized she had stopped till Emmet threw her over his shoulder. She spewed but thank God, she didn't have much in her stomach. Someone came out of the woods behind them. No time for a warning, she pulled the gun tucked into the small of Emmet's back and fired. She got two rounds off when Emmet spun and followed up with two more.

A blur in her peripheral caught her attention too late to shout a warning. A body slammed into them. Bailey went flying. At the last second, she tucked her knees into her chest and landed in a snowbank at the base of a tree.

She rolled out of the snow in time to see Emmet, his arm wrapped around a man's neck in an unbreakable headlock. One brutal twist and the snap reverberated until another explosion rocked the house.

He flung his assailant away and, breathing heavily, stalked over to her and pulled her to her feet. He studied her as she wobbled on her feet, then hoisted her onto his shoulder again.

Bouncing along, the dry heave returned. By the time he dropped her to her feet, she was groggy, and her head wanted to come off her shoulders and walk away. She reached up, trying to keep it on her shoulders. Her hands came away bloody.

She couldn't breathe, there wasn't enough air.

She was on her feet only for a few seconds while he yanked the camouflage off the snowmobile and dumped her on the seat. A shot echoed, and Emmet grunted. He leaned heavily into her yet gunned the engine of the snowmobile and took off.

Behind her, the sounds of gunfire and explosions continued. All that planning and they were running away, leaving carnage, and leaving Hank to his death.

CHAPTER 18

*B*link.

The dim interior of a trailer lit by the neon blue of a lot of electronics swam into focus. Men shouting, their voices heated, yet Bailey shivered from the cold. Their identities she couldn't discern. The fog clouding her mind prevented it, and when she tried to force it, darkness swallowed her.

Blink.

Same trailer, but they were moving, bumping along a pitted road. Emmet sat on a stool, back bowed and crimson from the blood covering his tanned skin. Elbows braced on his knees, someone stitched up a wound on his back, a large wound that needed a doctor and a hospital, not someone with passing knowledge and a spare sewing kit.

Muscles tense, his face tight from the pain, he gritted his teeth, yet uttered not a single sound, until she groaned. His head whipped around and those blue eyes of his landed on her with the force of a freight train. He pushed away from the man stitching him up and came to her, but she couldn't hold on. Darkness was a cool, comfortable blanket she couldn't fight.

Blink.

A light pierced the soothing cocoon surrounding her and stabbed deep into her brain. She flinched and tried to pull away but had nowhere to go.

"What's your name?" a man said, elderly by the tone, Swiss by the accent.

"Bail—"

"Ask another question. Her name, you don't need to know," Emmet demanded with no room for argument.

Bailey managed to open her eyes and focus on the short, gray-haired gentleman in front of her. But she wanted to see Emmet.

"Yes, of course." His jowls trembled as his head bobbed up and down. "Miss, what month is it?"

"February," she said through a dry throat.

"Good. What color are your eyes?"

"Blue." Dizzy, she forced a quick glance at her surroundings. They were in a small hotel room. White walls, functional furniture, it was clean and neat. No frills.

"How old are you?"

"Twenty-five." She forced through a bout of nausea.

"And, where are you?"

Not quite sure, she paused. How much time had passed since the explosion? "I was in Switzerland."

"Good." He took her hands. "Now, squeeze as hard as you can." She did as she was told and earned a grin and another "Good." He looked over her shoulder. "She has a concussion, but her pupils are reactive, and she's cognizant of herself and her surroundings. Standard procedure dictates a CAT scan and an overnight hospital stay—"

"Unless she is dying, that's not happening."

The doctor's—Bailey took a guess that was his title—eyes widened. "S-she's not dying; however, without a CAT scan I cannot guarantee that won't happen."

"We'll take the risk." Emmet came into view. Dressed in

jeans and a white tee, he grabbed the elderly man by the back of his button-down shirt, shoved a thick stack of bills into the man's hand, and bodily led him to the door.

"We'll take the risk?" she echoed, her vision blurry again as he rushed back to her. "I want to go to a hospital."

"We can't, at least not a hospital in Switzerland." He helped her into a seated position.

"Why?" She winced from the throbbing pain in her head and instinctively reached to soothe the ache. Her fingers brushed against gauze tapped near the back of her head. "W-what —why?"

He took her hand and moved it away. "It's not as bad as it feels."

He should know since he had his own scar on his back. "Why can't we go to a hospital?"

"Because Rogers is still out there, babe, and I have to get you away." His hand rubbed her back in calming circles.

She closed her eyes and buried her head in his chest. "I'm tired of running."

His lips brushed her temple. "I know, babe. I'm tired of running too." He lifted her chin and met her gaze. "We won't have to run for much longer. I swear it won't be much longer. You—*we*—will be free of Rogers and Hank."

And Hank? That gave her hope. "You promise?"

His lips whispered across hers. "I promise." He slanted his lips over hers, and his familiar taste filled her mouth, then it was gone in a too-brief kiss and, oh, how she missed it.

"We're getting out of Switzerland. I'm taking the backroads, which are gonna be brutal on you."

Propped up under her own power, she watched Emmet reach for a bottle of pills and a bottle of water on the bedside table. He shook out two and twisted the cap off the water. "These are the same pills I slipped you on the plane. They'll make you sleep, get the rest you need."

Bailey reared back and shook her head, which made stars danced before her eyes.

He took her in his arms again. "Breathe through it. Slow and easy. I've had a few concussions in my life. All you can do is rest and sleep it off. The pills will help you do that."

Her head hurt like a sonofabitch, but…

"You said you trusted me. If you do, then trust me now." He placed the pills in her lap. "I won't force you to take them or trick you, Bailey. It's up to you." He rose and went to the window. Body slanted to present a smaller target, he peeked between the blinds.

Bailey shoved the pills into her pocket and pushed to her feet. "Shouldn't we be on our way?"

He picked up a coat off a chair in the corner and held it open. "It's from lost and found."

She shoved her hands in the sleeves. "I'm not picky." Then stood still as he played nursemaid and zipped it up.

"Stay here. I'll get a wheelchair."

"I can walk."

"Not fast enough." He hefted a familiar duffle bag onto his shoulder and left. It didn't take long for him to return with a chair. Bailey parked her butt in the cushioned seat and didn't complain as he sped through the hotel, even though her stomach rolled from the motion.

He got her to a blue Mercedes, strapped her into the passenger seat, tossed the bag onto the back seat, and drove out of the hotel parking lot at a sedate pace. She flipped down the visor, shielding her from the blinding sun making like an icepick behind her eyes.

"This isn't so bad. European roads are light years better than American roads." The pills were unnecessary. She closed her eyes and settled into the plush, heated seat for a comfortable ride.

Which lasted exactly ten minutes by the dashboard clock.

"I warned you we were going off-road," he murmured.

"Don't be an ass." She moaned and opened her eyes. She lasted another ten minutes then gave in and reached into her pocket for the pills. They bounced off the back of her throat and went down with a gulp of water. He spared a moment to glance away from the road to study her. "I trust you."

His smile was quick, then he was all business.

"What happened? I know the house exploded, but I don't know what happened."

"Rocket launcher is my best guess," he said dryly. "Not much defense against one of those.

They were all lucky to be alive. She settled deeper into the passenger seat. "You didn't tell me where we're going?"

"Not far. Germany. Plan B is in effect." He checked the mirrors.

"Plan B?" she gritted her teeth through the pain. He nodded once and gave her nothing else. "I suppose there's a Plan C and D?"

"One plan at a time."

She didn't like the way he said that. "Is this your Plan B or Hank's?"

"It's *our* plan."

She took that to mean Hank's plan, and she had run out of faith on any plan he created. "You keep putting your faith in Hank," she said through a yawn.

A muscle flexed in his jaw. "This isn't faith. It's a plan."

She reclined the seat and found a comfortable spot. "It better work this time, Emmet. I refuse to be blown up again. Understand me." She mimicked his deep voice, which earned her a chuckle.

"Yeah, I understand. Now, stop talking and go to sleep."

Not a problem when sleep crept at the corners of her mind. But she had one last question. "Is Hank alive?"

"Yes. He's alive and fine."

And he wasn't here, with his daughter, checking to make sure *she* was alive.

CHAPTER 19

The briny sting of the sea had Bailey stretching and peeling open her eyes. She glanced at the clock. Nine hours ago, they'd cleared the border between Switzerland and Germany. One pitstop for food, petrol, and the bathroom, and they were back in the car. Except for the one stop, she slept the entire time. It was the best thing she ever did. While not one hundred percent better, her head had stopped ringing and her stomach no longer heaved every time she moved.

"Where are we?" She adjusted the seat and peered out of the windshield at a postcard picture of a town dusted with a fresh coating of snow, in the distance, a river. He turned down a cobbled street as a church bell rang.

"Hamburg, Germany."

Hamburg, three hours from Berlin, approximately six and a half hours from Prague. She spent some time tooling around Germany when she was nineteen with Daisy. God, they had a blast.

"We have to dump the car."

"The university is a mile away. We can dump the car there."

She didn't ask why they needed to dump their ride. It had to be part of the mysterious Plan B.

His gaze narrowed on her, sharp and assessing. "How do you know about the university?"

"Spent a summer here with Daisy. Not here, but all over Germany and England."

He snorted which digressed into a dry chuckle. "You and your bestie are trouble magnets. So how much did you get into?"

She tossed him a sly "I'll never tell" smirk. "A lot. Daisy is the best kind of friend. She's a ride-or-die bad influence with a heart of gold."

"I found your phone and the messages you sent her."

Damn, she thought she'd lost it in the Swiss woods. Now, he had the sly smile. "So, can I have my phone?"

"No." He pulled into a parking spot and cut the engine.

Not that she expected a different reply, still it irked her.

"Calling her places her in danger. Rogers won't hesitate to use your friend to get to you. Think about that the next time you want to contact her." He exited the car, and she didn't wait for him to be a gentleman. She climbed out under her own steam and took in the bustling streets even on a cold wintry day. Goosebumps ran down her spine and spread outward. They crawled across the front of her body and leeched all the warmth from her body. The thin, donated winter coat wasn't cutting it.

Wrapping her arms tight around her shivering body, she joined him on the sidewalk. "Where to now?"

He slung the duffle bag over his shoulder and said, "Shopping and food. We have some time to kill."

Time to kill for what, she didn't ask. Instead, she wedged herself to his side and hustled down the road.

He wrapped his arm around her and pulled her closer. "I'd give you my coat, but I'm armed."

She felt the steel between their bodies. "I'm good. The shopping district is up ahead." Two more blocks and they struck gold.

"Oh! H&M." Her favorite store during her college days. She grabbed his hand and dragged him inside.

A blast of hot air hit her the moment the sliding doors opened, thawing her frozen bones. She wanted to linger but dare not give in to the temptation. "I'll be quick and grab a coat."

He grinned into her upturned face. "I told you we have the time. Plus, you need everything, and so do I." His gaze skimmed the half-empty store. "Do your thing, I'm heading to the men's section."

"Y-you're leaving me alone?" She didn't hide her surprise.

"We're safe, for now. And by the time it's not safe, we'll be gone." He kissed her temple and headed away.

She didn't buy it. He was up to something, probably had to check in with Hank. She gritted her teeth and forced all her ugly thoughts away. He told her to go shopping, and that's exactly what she planned on doing. Shop.

She snatched up the warmest coat in the store, a reversible blue/red down jacket. Three pairs of fleece-lined jeans and a bunch of sweaters, and socks. She was headed to the lingerie section when she caught a glimpse of herself in the full-length mirror. It took concerted effort to avoid all the other mirrors in the store. By the few stares she'd caught, she had a good idea of the hot mess she presented to the world.

Well, you go on the run and get blown up and see how presentable you are to the world.

Ignoring the nosy busybodies, she rounded a corner, and the mirror practically leaped out at her. That may have been an exaggeration. She may have been the only one doing the leaping.

The person staring back at her wasn't the person who vacationed in Jamaica ten days ago. She'd lost weight, weight she couldn't afford. Dark smudges under her eyes gave her a gaunt, haunted appearance. The bruise on her jaw made her the poster victim of a domestic abuse flyer. And her hair, let's just say the white bandage on the side of her head, in the middle of a shaved patch of her black hair, wasn't a fashion statement.

Emmet came up behind her. He had her by a full head. Their eyes met in the mirror, his questioning. "What are you doing? You've been standing here for three minutes."

Him surveilling her should've been disconcerting, not comforting. Also, it wasn't fair that he was Mr. Rugged with his bruises and scrapes while she doubled as a punching bag. "Should I thank you for not telling me how ragged I look, or slap you for letting me out in public like this?"

His brow furrowed, and his head dropped down to rest on her shoulder. "What are you talking about? You're beautiful. A scar, a bald spot, a bruise, doesn't mean shit. You survived an explosion meant to kill you. A bath, a couple of hot meals, and some rest, and you'll be fine."

A quick kiss to the side of her neck and he took her hand. "Let's finish up and get you out of here."

She pulled him back and brought him down for a lip lock. Sometimes, all it takes is the right words from the right person to see yourself in a new light. He may or may not get how those four sentences propped her up, which made them matter more, because they were sincere, and precisely what she needed. "Thanks."

"For what?"

Bailey shook her head. "Just thanks." She handed him her mesh shopping bag. "I need a few more things, and I'll meet you at the cash register." She headed to the lingerie section and grabbed a pack of functional bikinis when she caught him studying a pretty lacy thong on display. He winked at her and strolled away.

Bailey tossed the bikinis away and headed for the thongs.

"Where to now?" She asked as they headed back into the cold loaded down with packages. Her strength waned, and a fresh headache teased her temples.

Emmet pulled his phone out of his pocket. Someone had sent him a text. He tapped a reply and shoved the phone back into his pocket. A cab waited, whether for them or there by chance, she didn't ask as he held the door open and she slipped inside.

Emmet gave an address, in German she might add, to the driver and off they went. "Can you tell me now where you're taking me?" Snug in her new coat, she peered at him over the rim of her collar.

He wrapped an arm loosely around her shoulders and whispered, "We are going on a cruise."

"We are not." A cruise? Them, around a thousand people, while targeted by a killer.

The skepticism on her face must've tipped him off because he whispered again, "Trust me. You have so far, don't stop now."

More and more, she found that easier to do. "I hope you know what you're doing."

He reached inside his coat, fished around for something and pulled out her pretend engagement and wedding rings. "I know what I'm doing, Mrs. Reynolds."

"Famous last words." She snatched the rings out of his hand and shoved them on her finger.

The cab coasted to a stop. "Wir sind hier," the driver said.

"We're here." She translated, though Emmet didn't need it.

He paid in Euros and climbed out of the car, his hand tucked into his jacket on his gun, his gaze on everything. He blocked the door, preventing her from exiting the cab and joining him.

What if Rogers was out there, in broad daylight, sighting him with a laser. A single round to the head would end whatever this was between them.

Hell, it would end him.

She lifted the back of his coat, ran her hand up his ass, earning her a questioning glance over his shoulder, but he didn't pull away. She reached the small of his back and pulled a gun free. All under his appraisal.

She tucked the gun into her pocket as he moved aside and helped her out of the cab. They were at the harbor on the commercial side of the Elbe River, where all the tankers lined up to load and unload their containers. "Where's the cruise ship?"

She had visions of Carnival, Royal Caribbean, Celebrity. Nothing close to those ships were moored. They hiked half a mile, passing tanker after tanker until he veered toward one named Mercury Star.

Emmet pushed her in front of him, and they jogged up the gangplank and shook hands with a man in dark blue pants and a pale blue shirt with insignias on the collars who waited for them at the top. "Mr. and Mrs. Reynolds, welcome. Nice to have you on board. I am Jasof. Let me show you to your cabin," he said in a heavy German accent.

Hand to the small of her back, Emmet kept her close as they navigated the containers to the command tower.

Through narrow hallways, they were shown to a cabin with a bed slightly larger than a twin bolted to the wall, a metal table and chair, a single lamp, and a single tiny porthole window. There was a minuscule shower and toilet with a steel basin on the wall outside the door.

"Thank you for the accommodations."

"Bitte," he said and tipped his head to Emmet. "Now that you are on board, we will leave. Expect departure in twenty minutes."

"Radio the captain, I need to speak to him as soon as possible."

The man pulled a radio off his waist and relayed the message. The reply was, "Bring him now."

Emmet studied her, concern flickering in his eyes, and she couldn't deny the flutter in her heart. "Go. I'm going to take a shower."

"Is there food in the galley?"

"The hour is between lunch and dinner, but I'll bring your wife something. Come. I'll take you to the captain."

"Umm, Jasof. Give me thirty minutes to freshen up."

Jasof tipped his head to her. "Yes, Mrs. Reynolds."

Mrs. Reynolds and Mrs. Jeffrey. Strange hearing those names associated with her.

"Thanks."

"I'll be back," Emmet said.

She stopped him with a hand to his chest. "Come back soon."

"Absolutely, Mrs. Reynolds."

CHAPTER 20

*E*mmet didn't hurry back. Bailey had enough time to remove the bandage from her scalp and assess the damage. Located a few inches behind her ear, she didn't have a clear view, but someone had closed an inch-long gash. Probably the doctor who'd questioned her. The bags under her eyes demanded attention, along with the black and blue area on her jaw. Hell, she looked as if she'd gone several rounds in the ring and had lost.

"Should've bought makeup along with the clothes." Staring in the mirror wouldn't make any of it better.

Carefully, she washed her hair and body under the tepid spray of water in the tiny shower. Tepid or not, clean beat dirty.

Dressed, she packed her new duds, and Emmet's in a worn garment bag Jasof brought her, along with a meal. After all that, she had time to snoop through Emmet's duffle bag, which he hadn't taken with him and hadn't tried to hide. He left it on the counter, out in the open.

Cash, passports, and credit cards. All the ones she'd seen before with her picture. He must've packed and hidden the bag with the snowmobile. Always thinking ahead. She loved that about him.

She loved a lot of things about Emmet. That was part of the problem. Ten days into this misadventure and she'd fallen in...

She parked her ass on the narrow bed. Holding the passports and credit cards in her hands stripped away whatever romantic notions swirled in her head. "I am not in love," she said to an empty room. Then what was she?

Leave it alone, Bailey. Unfortunately, she wasn't the type to "leave it alone."

What was this, the thing taking root between them? It may be stupid, but she needed to name it, give it a label, so her expectations had hard limits.

"We are not in a relationship." A week and a half on the run does not qualify as a relationship. A laugh ripped from her throat as Daisy's voice filled her head. *"Girl! You are in a situationship. You're stuck together because a psycho is after you, but once that is over..."*

Yeah, once the situation was over, they'd go their own way. Yeah. Because did she really think when all this was over they'd play boyfriend and girlfriend? Set up house? He'd mow the lawn on Saturdays while she pulled weeds in the garden. Have three kids, two dogs, and one cat. A mortgage and a minivan?

"He's not a keeper, Bailey. The bad boys never are." *And he's a fucking hitman!* The ache in her chest was acid reflux, not her heartbreaking.

She had enough time to return the passports and credit cards to the duffle bag before the door opened and in strolled the object of her soul-searching. "Good, you're dressed."

"Why?" she asked as he grabbed the duffle bag off the counter and the garment bag off the lone chair. "We just got here." *Just* being a few hours ago.

"And it's time to leave." He tossed her coat at her.

Panicked, she asked, "Is Rogers here? Did he find us?" He shook his head. "Then what is it?"

"Plan B."

The mysterious Plan B. "Where are we going, Emmet?"

He ignored her.

Coat half on, she stepped in front of him. "I'm not leaving until you tell me where."

Posture rigid, voice sharp, he snapped, "A little too late to not trust me."

Which had her bent. My, his attitude had flipped faster than a gymnast in the Olympics. "Who said anything about not trusting you? I want to know where we're going. I'm tired of being a yo-yo, not knowing anything that's going on in my life."

He got in her face, way too close. "Your life is my responsibility, that's what's going on. Questioning my every move is getting old fast."

She didn't back down, because hell if any of this fucking situation was her fault. She didn't ask to be hunted, or be the daughter of a killer or fall hard for a hitman.

Damn it!

She was no one's pet project. Not now. Not ever. "I didn't ask you to take this responsibility. You don't like it anymore?" She pointed at the door. "Leave."

Sharper than a razor, his voice cut into her. "I leave. You die."

The finality of his statement rang millimeters from the truth. She didn't want to die. That didn't mean she had to put up with his bullshit. "Maybe. Right now, that's a better option than staying with you."

His gaze dipped to her mouth. A few inches and they'd be locked together. His tongue would be in her mouth, and his hands would be on her body.

Situationship.

Bailey moved to the porthole to stare at the calm moonlit waters, which was better than looking at him.

"Melodramatic much?"

She couldn't disagree, however, the entire argument was melodramatic.

He came up behind her. "We are moving to another boat. A private yacht. Plan B is us sailing up and down the Elbe. Constant motion. A moving target with the benefit of access to several major cities where we can get lost. Any further questions?"

"No." She spun away to finish yanking on her coat and grab the garment bag he'd tossed down during their argument. She didn't wait for him to step into the hallway or join her as she headed back the way they'd entered a few hours ago.

"Wrong direction. We're not going up. We're going down."

So much for a dramatic exit. A quick pivot and she followed him to an elevator at the end of the hall. Ten decks below, they emerged onto a lower deck off of the engine room where Jasof waited. That's when she noticed the ship had stopped. It probably had been stopped for a while, since a ship this size couldn't brake on the dime.

"Mrs. Reynolds. Mr. Reynolds. Follow me, please."

He guided them to a pressure sealed emergency hatch. An alarm sounded when he pressed a button, and the hatch swung open.

"From here, it is a short climb down."

"Down to where?" She took a few hesitant steps forward and peered out of the hatch to one hell of a yacht waiting in the distance and a speedboat bobbing one hundred feet below with a crewman at the controls.

"I'll go first." Emmet stepped up and tossed his duffle and garment bag out the hatch, then studied her with those cold blue eyes of his. "Are you afraid of heights?"

Until this moment, she would've said no. She leaned out of the hatch and peered at the boat bobbing below.

"You'll be fine. Most of the ladder is caged. Let's get going."

Bailey zipped her coat and nodded more to herself than to Emmet or Jasof. "I can do this," she mumbled. "I survived an explosion. I can climb down a ladder." A few deep breaths, two quick snaps of her head to relieve the tension, then… "I'm ready."

Emmet disappeared out of the hatch. One tentative step brought her to the handrails and damn, they were cold. A pair of gloves would've come in handy. Hopefully, she wouldn't be here, hanging over the side of the ship, long.

Three rungs into this fucked up adventure, she made the mistake of looking down at the inky ocean spread out like an oil spill. Instantly dizzy, she clung to the ladder.

"Bailey."

"Gimme a sec," she said through chattering teeth. Beneath the layer of clothing, sweat collected on her clammy skin.

His hands circled her waist, and Emmet crawled over her. Now she was caged by his warm body instead of cold metal.

"I'm here. Right here with you and I'm not going anywhere. We'll go as slow as you need."

His voice in her ear, his breath on her cheek, both grounded her. She swallowed down the lump in her throat along with the fear. One rung at a time, with Emmet's steady hands on her, she descended. As she got the hang of it, he descended faster, and she heard him land on the speedboat.

"Five more to go," he said.

She counted them off, and next she was in his arms.

"I got you."

Pressed up against his body, he certainly did have her. "Thank you. I'm fine, now." She pushed away from him and failed to ignore how she slid down the length of his body.

The hatch slammed closed with a resounding ring at the same

time the engine of the speedboat kicked on. She stood for the short ride to the yacht and asked over the roar of the speedboat, "Whose yacht is it?"

"An industrialist who owes us a favor."

"His bank account must be huge and his dick very small." That got a chuckle out of the crewman.

With a steadying hand on her back, Emmet stood next to her. "He's a billionaire, so the size of his bank account is enormous. I don't know anything about the size of his dick."

She laughed, couldn't help it. "Well, that's a relief."

The speedboat docked inside the yacht. The steward met them. "Mr. and Mrs. Fredericks, welcome to the maiden voyage of *Chrysalis*," he said and took them on a winding course through the ship to the staterooms.

Now they were the Fredericks, Bailey noted as Emmet took the bag of clothes she'd packed from the crewman. "Thanks. We got it from here. I'll be sure to tell Mr. Morgan how great you've been."

"Morgan?" she whispered when the crewman walked away. There was only one Morgan that came to mind who could possibly own a boat this lavish. "Julius Morgan?"

His half smile gave his non-answer.

Bailey opened the door and entered the most beautiful suite she'd ever seen. Private office, next to a private conference room, living room done in tan suede with blue trim, and mini-kitchen with all the accouterments for extra private meals. Then they entered the bedroom.

Circular and situated at the front of the boat, it gave the occupants nearly a panoramic view of the wide river. Done in dark wood with amber accents. The carpet plush and beige, the lighting recessed. Behind the California king-size bed, a walk-in closet stocked with clothes, the tags still attached, and a full bathroom with a marble sunken bath and shower big enough for an orgy.

This was how the other half lived. *Damn!*

Living here would not be a problem, ever.

"Should we be staying here when the suite is clearly meant for the owner?"

Emmet tossed their bags down. "He'll get over it."

Bailey eyed the bed. No way would they share it tonight, or any night. Nope, not happening. Time to make sure he understood.

"Which room are you…"

He stood in the middle of the room, shoulders drooped, face tense but not from anger. Brow pinched between his thumb and forefinger, he was exhausted.

And that's when it hit her. The blast happened, then the escape and the tanker, now the yacht. Through it all, Emmet had taken care of her at the expense of himself. Every second, he was with her, protecting her while she slept, without a break.

When was the last time he'd slept? Ate?

Bailey shoved him to the edge of the bed. Elbow on knees, he sat there while she tugged off his boots and socks, then tackled his shirt. Through it all, he offered no resistance.

She got a good look at the bandage on his shoulder. Dried blood colored the white rectangular barrier a deep burgundy. Carefully, she pried an edge free and peeled the rest away revealing a neat row of stitches. A lot of stitches.

"What hit you?"

He shrugged, and she focused on the way the stitches pulled tight with each flex of his muscles. "Felt it. Didn't see it. Pulled it out and kept going."

Weariness edged each word. "Lie down, and I'll take your pants off."

"Now that's how I like a woman to proposition me. Get to the fucking and cut the preamble. Unfortunately, the spirit is willing, but the flesh is weak."

"That's not what I meant, and you know that." She scoffed.

"Yeah, but I couldn't resist."

She slapped the back of his head.

He snickered. "One day you will mean it. One day soon," he murmured.

Arrogant man, but maybe he wasn't entirely wrong. She pushed at his shoulders to get him to comply. Emmet didn't budge.

"Shower first. Too dirty for bed," he complained and shoved to his feet. By the time he circled the bed to the bathroom, he was naked. Gloriously naked. Every muscle on display for her pleasure alone, a view she'd never tire of seeing.

She picked up the phone on the desk and called for a turkey sandwich with lettuce and tomato, mustard and mayo on the side —everyone liked a turkey sandwich—and a first aid kit. By the time he exited the bathroom, a towel draped around his hips, hair slicked to his skull, beaded water clinging to his skin, and steam chasing him, both items had arrived.

Seated at the desk, he wolfed down the sandwich while she spread antiseptic cream on his wound and re-bandaged it. When he finished, she helped him the few feet to the bed. He collapsed in stages, like an accordion folding badly. But once his body hit the bed, he was done. He flopped back, dead to the world at the wrong angle.

It wasn't easy, took a good amount of tugging, but she managed to get him stretched out. At her mercy, she studied his relaxed features. Without the scowl, he had an innocent baby face. It was easy to imagine him as a child, rambunctious and fearless. The exact opposite of her.

She took Taekwondo and karate, not because she had an affinity for martial arts, but because she wanted to impress Hank. It didn't work. He still ignored her.

"It's too late to take a trip down memory lane." She moved away from the temptation of stretching out next to him and snuggling into his side.

Situationship had her bed of choice, not the California king, but the sectional under the windows. An extra blanket and pillow she ferreted out of a closet were all she needed to fall asleep as soon as she was horizontal.

Sometime during the night, she opened her eyes to find herself cradled against his chest. She didn't question it, didn't fight it when he lay her on the opposite side of the bed. And she didn't protest when he tugged off her yoga pants and sweatshirt, leaving her in panties and bra.

Something about sleeping in the arms of the man you want puts your soul at peace and your worry to rest. For the moment, all was right in her world, and she was where she wanted to be. Maybe that would change tomorrow. Maybe with the light of day, she'd have the clarity to block the emotion taking root in her heart. Right now, in the dead of night, with his body cocooning hers, he felt like home, and sleep was as warm as the blanket he pulled over them.

CHAPTER 21

Make me no promises and tell me no lies. A personal mantra that had always worked. No promises meant no expectations. No lies meant a clean getaway.

But what if the promises are implied and the lies are ones you told yourself?

Bundled in a sheepskin jacket Bailey had found in a walk-in closet off the bathroom, she stretched out on a lounge chair, a fur throw over her lap. The German countryside eked by. The yacht had to be traveling no more than six knots per hour, and that was into a stiff wind. Basically, they were going nowhere fast. Hell, she could walk faster than the boat's current speed, which suited her fine. For the first time in what seemed like a year, she felt rested.

A crewman brought a fresh thermos of cinnamon apple cider, and she hadn't asked for a refill. Her gaze cut to her silent companion in the chair next to her. Collar pulled up, only the top of Emmet's head was visible. "Did you—?"

"Morgan's staff is exceptional." His muffled words misted in the frigid air.

The staff and the boat. The yacht was a work of art. Anything they wanted was a few taps on a monitor positioned in every room on the boat. They even had a private kitchen in the improbable occasion one of them decided to skip the gourmet meals provided by a Michelin chef and wing it. Breakfast, lunch, and dinner, he was at their beck and call while snacks were just a tap away on the kitchen monitor. This was definitely the way to survive protective custody.

Also, this wasn't the first time Emmet's comments hinted at a closer than cursory knowledge of the reclusive billionaire, Julius Morgan. How did the two meet? She wondered. Was it professional or personal? None of it was her business which didn't stop her rampant speculation especially after the last three days they'd spent tooling down the river.

Emmet hadn't left her side for more than an hour. They'd slept a lot, caught up on much-needed downtime, and spent hours in the gym—some of that time she studied the sweat rolling down his chiseled body. They watched movies in the custom movie theatre and lingered over gourmet meals at each sitting. They talked about sports, politics, religion, Atlanta, favorite countries, Android versus Apple, DC versus Marvel, favorite countries, favorite holidays, outdoor or indoor, morning person or sleep in 'til noon, and exes. She had three. He had none. He'd never stayed around long enough to have an ex, and he didn't have a current fuckbuddy.

As much as they talked, they spent an equal amount of time in silent companionship, kind of like testing the waters to see if one could spend time with someone in quiet reflection, without wanting to stab each other because they breathed too loudly, or chewed with their mouth open, or picked their noses and flicked the boogers away. Thankfully, he did none of those things. On the Richter scale of annoying, he was a comfortable three point five.

Still, she couldn't ignore what he did for a living. Plus, she'd seen him kill a man, and he had pushed her at the chalet. He apologized, and the horror on his face at his actions wasn't a lie. Regardless of what this budding thing between them was, Bailey refused to be that woman, that abused woman, whose violent lover kept promising not to beat her anymore.

"Have you ever killed a woman?" Her voice broke the comfortable silence between them.

His movements deliberate, Emmet angled his body toward her. "No." One word, clipped.

The question was too general. "Ever beat a woman?" She pressed.

"I have never laid hands on a woman in any way she didn't consent to and enjoy. Next question." He sounded insulted. She didn't care.

Bailey had one more question, a peek into his character. She met his intent gaze. "Ever cheat on a woman?"

Emmet rolled his eyes. "I've never been in a committed relationship where monogamy was expected. Is that what you want, monogamy?" His gruff voice raised her hackles.

"No, not at all," she lied, completely refocused on the snowy landscape. "I love having the freedom to choose who I'll sleep with at any given moment. There are so many men in the world, so many choices. Why should I limit myself to one dick?"

From the corner of her eye, she saw his head drop, and he muttered something she didn't catch, but then his head shot up. He scratched at the dusting of whiskers on his jaw. Several days' worth of growth darkened his jawline and mouth. Didn't make a difference, he was sexy with and sexy without. "Ready to go inside?" His tone light, as if she hadn't mentioned her desire to screw other men.

Fine. Bailey didn't buy it yet kept her opinion to herself. She picked up the thermos and sipped. Warmth spread throughout her chest and landed in her stomach. "Wimping out on me? It's only been an hour."

"Not trying to get frostbite on my dick, babe," he grumbled, and she had to laugh, which earned her a slight lift to the corner of his mouth.

"We haven't tried the sauna or the indoor pool." His gaze stayed focused on the winter-white landscape.

Her pulse quickened. Three days they'd slept in the same bed and hadn't shared so much as a kiss. She didn't doubt he wanted her. The evidence was the hard length against her ass when he spooned her each night. Yet neither of them made the move to take the pleasure they'd already tasted.

"I don't have a bathing suit."

His head cranked her way, and something sensual and mischievous entered his eyes. "You won't need one." Emmet stood and pulled the fur off her lap, took her hand and pulled her to her feet. "Come on."

He led the way to the second level where the pool, sauna, and gym were located. Along the way, they stripped off their outer gear. They passed a crewman. Emmet handed over their coats to the man and whispered something as she continued.

Pushing open the frosted glass doors, she paused in the doorway and let the humid air wash over her. Emmet nudged her further inside and let the door swing closed behind them. Her back to his front, his hands settled on her hips, and his head dipped to the crux of her neck. He inhaled deeply. A low growl rumbled from his throat, and his hands tightened on her hips before slipping under the edge of her sweater. "You smell wintry as if Jack Frost kissed your skin." Cool fingers stroked her waist, sending shivers across her skin while sparks ignited an inferno between her thighs. "FYI. I don't share."

"Good to know, 'cause neither do I."

He flicked his tongue along her collarbone and left a wet trail to her earlobe while his hands coasted up her abdomen to knead her breasts, still encased in her bra. She moaned and leaned against him, rubbed her ass into the hard-on trapped in his jeans, and angled her head for more. He groaned and mumbled something unintelligible, then yanked the cups of her bra down and folded the material under. The results freed her rigid nipples and propped up her small breasts for his complete access.

His calloused palms brushed over the peaks. She cried out and reached between them to unzip his jeans and—

The door to the pool swung open. Simultaneously, Bailey yanked away and fixed her clothes. Embarrassed, she couldn't even look at the man, even as he offered an apology for interrupting.

"Not your fault," Emmet said, and she listened as the glass door swooshed open and closed with a soft thud.

A quick glance over her shoulder confirmed they were alone again with an open bottle of Ace of Spades waiting in a silver bucket of ice.

"My fault," he murmured behind her once again. "I thought I'd have you naked, and in the sauna before he returned with the champagne." His hands settled on her waist again.

Bailey moved out of his embrace and faced him. Arms folded across her chest, body on lockdown and not liking it one bit, she snapped, "What do you think you're doing?"

One side of his lip curled, and he gave her a look that made her panties go up in flames. "If I have to explain then I'm doing something wrong."

Oh, he wasn't doing anything wrong, at least not according to the moisture pooling below. "We've slept in the same bed three nights in a row, and there was none of…this." She waved at him because she couldn't find the words after he'd pulled off his sweater and Henley in one hard tug.

"I had to make sure." He bent to unlace his boots.

She fought the mesmerizing pull of his of muscles rippling as he stripped down to his birthday suit, and said, "Make sure of what?"

Free of his boots and socks, he unzipped his pants. "Make sure I liked you."

That got her head cocked to the side, and her brow knit tighter than a wool sweater. "What?"

He sighed and shot her a droll look. "It's easy to feel lust for someone. To want to be inside them and stay there. That works for a while until it doesn't. Lust burns away, and if you don't have something more all it leaves is ashes. But if you like a person, like having them around, talking to them, listening to their voice and if you care about what they have to say, when the lust burns away, you have something that will endure."

A giddy bubble of light expanded in her chest and she struggled to contain it. "Like a diamond?" she whispered.

He took her face in his hands and brought her in. His gaze roamed her face and that light she struggled to contain entered his eyes. In that instant, she knew. He didn't have to say, not yet, if he didn't want to, because it was there written all over his face. "Yeah. Like a diamond."

She bit her lip to keep the light from exploding. "Didn't know you were romantic."

He shrugged. "I'm not. I'm just speaking the truth."

"So, you like me?"

He snorted. "I more than like you, Bailey. I more than like you a lot."

He slanted his lips over hers before she could tell him she more than liked him too. But it didn't matter, not at that moment when his fingers stroked her cheeks, and he had that look in his eyes. That dangerously sexy twinkle meant she was in trouble, the very best kind of trouble. The kind of trouble that happened when two bodies came together in the heat of blistering passion. She pulled back to get the sweater out of the way. He helped, roughly yanking it off, and tossing it aside.

She reached behind her, unsnapped her bra and let the straps slide down her arms. His breath hitched and then his hands were on her body, and his mouth was on her flesh. He laved one nipple with long strokes of his tongue while working the other between his thumb and forefinger.

"Off." He tugged at her pants. "Naked. Get naked."

She tugged at his pants. "You. Get naked."

He worked fast and got her pants and panties down to her knees before she got any further than his zipper. Dropping to his haunches, he unlaced her boots and tugged them off her feet followed by her clothing. Without pause, he licked up the center of her body. Her pleasured moan at the sensation of his tongue gliding over her changed to a gasp when he swept her off her feet to carry her and the champagne into the sauna.

Standing on a wooden bench, steam swirling around their bodies, Emmet pushed her against the wall. He lifted one leg and rubbed his whiskers against the tender flesh of her inner thigh. She giggled and squirmed to get away. A nip to the same area and a soothing lick caused a different reaction. She needed him to lick a little to the right.

Emmet grabbed the champagne and took a swig. Then, he hooked her leg over his shoulder. As if he'd read her mind, he locked eyes with her, right before his cool, liquor-laced tongue split her wet folds. She shuddered hard, the pleasure was sharp enough to wrest a deep groan from her throat. She grabbed onto a fistful of his hair, anchoring him to the spot.

He palmed her ass, dug his fingers into her flesh and feasted. His tongue, now warm, circled her clit and lapped at her opening, then returned to suck on the bundle of nerves at the top of her sex. No rush to his torture. He latched onto her core and sucked her into him as he brought his nose up to nudge her clit.

"Emmet," she cried, trying to stave off the inevitable, but her limbs already trembled.

"Come," he commanded, his voice guttural and tight, as he rubbed his stubble against her sensitive flesh.

Bailey tumbled into an abyss filled with stars. Boneless, she slid into a heap on the bench hypnotized by the swipe of Emmet's tongue licking his lips clean. God, she'd never tire of looking at him.

Corded muscles defined his tall frame. Naturally tanned skin was marred by a faded scar across his left pec and another along his left flank. Not the first time she'd seen them and not the first time she wondered who'd slipped beneath his guard.

"How did that happen?" She pointed to the longer of the two scars on the front of his body.

He touched his flank and traced a finger over the raised flesh. "An Algerian in Morocco. Accused me of improper thoughts after helping a woman who'd fallen in the street. She happened to be in a burqa."

She was aghast for him and the poor woman while he shrugged. "I was young and ignorant of the region's customs. My fault."

"And the other?" She wanted to know.

He glanced at the faded scar on his chest. "Hank," he said and laughed at her expression. "Training exercise when I was sixteen."

He pulled his pants off his muscular legs, ending the conversation. From its bulbous head, slick with pre-cum, to its thick shaft, his cock was a thing of beauty. He took himself in his hand, stroking his length. From a pocket of his discarded pants, he freed a condom. "We're running low," he grumbled, sheathing his cock in latex.

"Shouldn't be difficult to park the boat at the next CVS." Her eyes still locked on his cock.

He cracked a smile, which broke into a chuckle and he picked up the champagne.

She dragged her gaze away from her new obsession to watch him take a long pull on the Ace of Spades. He leaned over her, caged her with his body and merged their lips. Champagne trickled from his mouth into hers. In little sips, she drank quickly, until it was just his tongue in her mouth, licking, sucking, driving her mad.

He broke away to grab the bottle for another mouthful. This time, he covered a nipple. Cold bubbly and a hot mouth, both on her overly sensitive flesh had her arching into the sensation. She grabbed at him, desperate to make contact with all that hard muscle.

Finally, he gave in and stretched out on top of her. Their bodies touching, his stubble teased her cheek when he came in close to wrap one arm behind her back, the other around her hips. Her legs came up to his waist, opening herself for him, yet all he did was tease her by sliding his length between her wet folds, riding her clit. She arched her pelvis in a mission to get him inside her. He pulled away in a cat-and-mouse game she couldn't win with him controlling her movements.

He kissed her, his tongue gliding in and out of her mouth, his need as raw as hers.

"Gimme," she pleaded when the wait became too much. He slid home in a single thrust. Arching at the abrupt intrusion, her muscles clenched around his shaft and cried out in relief. The wounded emptiness was gone.

"Fuck." His strokes languid, effortless as if they'd done this for years. He eased in and out with a rhythm designed to drive her insane. "Being inside you is…" His sentence died on a strangled growl as he ground into her. She bucked and tightened her legs around his waist.

What? She wanted to ask but that slip of clarity unraveled at the sparks firing her bloodstream. "Emmet." She wailed. "Don't stop."

"Not going to." He cupped her breasts, kneading the peaks and brought her in for another kiss, unhurried, like the hands on her breasts and the cock buried inside her depths.

"Please." She reared up to suck on his nipple, earning a strangled, garbled sound from him.

He shifted and split her legs further apart; he went at her hard with deep, powerful strokes. Each stroke an affirmation of who she belonged to. She whimpered. He swallowed the sound down and suddenly pulled back. His cold eyes blazing from an internal heat she got lost in. Lips peeled back in a half grimace, half smile, nostrils flaring, he watched their bodies merge.

In a move she didn't see coming, he flipped her on top of him and lowered to the step below the bench. Each movement brought him deeper inside her until she could scarcely breathe. He clasped her hips and murmured, "Ride me."

Using the bench as leverage, Bailey planted her feet on the wooden surface and her hands on his shoulders. She rose, her inner muscles gripping him tightly, as if afraid to lose him, and slid back down. She repeated the motion until his eyes rolled back in his head, and his mouth fell open. He gasped, the most erotic sound, the most erotic sight she'd ever seen.

"Fuck me, Bailey," he commanded and met her down stroke with his upstroke. Grunting, snarling, sweaty bodies slapping together, the sounds they made heightened the pleasure.

"Now you come. You come for me," she ordered.

Emmet took over. He gripped her hips and slammed into her over and over again. Caught in a net of desire, pleasure so intense it paralyzed her, Bailey leaned back. Legs raised and braced on the edge of the bench, she came apart. Her orgasm blinded her to anything except Emmet climaxing beneath her.

CHAPTER 22

Sated in more ways than he could count, Emmet ran a lazy hand down Bailey's sleek back. Naked and absolutely loving how she used him as a pillow, he ignored whatever movie she'd chosen on the seventy-inch flat screen that popped up out of the cabinet at the foot of the bed, and checked his emails on his iPad. The only one of importance came from Whiskey. Hank had gone his own way. Two whole days ago. His choice. After Switzerland and the explosion, after losing Rogers again, he took to the road and cut contact with everyone.

The agency may be able to track him, but letting them know Hank was in the wind like Rogers would plant a target on the remaining members of which there weren't many left. One of them on the run, out of contact and possibly off the rails was enough.

Emmet loved traveling the world, but not as much as he loved his own soil in the USA. If the agency turned their backs on them, life on the run would be permanent. That's not what he wanted for Bailey. She deserved better, and he would be the one to give it to her.

Find Rogers. Find Hank. That's what he had to do. Both had priority, but only one wanted Bailey dead. If Hank had gone to ground, that left him alone to protect her *and* find Rogers. He couldn't leave her on her own, and he couldn't take her into the field with him. Also, he trusted no one except himself to do either job. Not even Whiskey, who was looking like Emmet's only option for either job.

A message popped up on the screen.

In the conference room. NOW.

Only one person spoke to him like that.

Emmet kissed Bailey's forehead. "I'm gonna get us something to snack on. Want anything in particular?"

She stretched that body he'd loved several times in the last few hours and tilted her face for another kiss, which he obliged. "Some fruit would be nice."

He tossed the iPad aside, climbed out of bed and pulled on a pair of sweats, bottom, and top, and made his way through the suite to the private conference room. He heard the low, angry rumble of Hank's voice first and wondered who'd pissed him off now?

Sliding open the conference door, Emmet found the man seated in a black leather chair, a squat glass in his hand full of a clear liquid, most likely vodka, his go-to liquor.

He'd looked better than he did after the explosion. Running back into the house had been a colossal act of stupidity, not bravery by any hallucination. His left hand remained bandaged, but he shot with his right. He'd taken the time to shave the singed hair off the back of his head. Now bald, Hank took menacing to a whole other level, especially as he cursed into the phone pressed to his ear.

"It's your call if that's how you want to play it." He paused, listening to whoever was on the other end of the conversation, his expression darkening by the second. "I will not stand down and let someone else kill him or play forgive and forget. He dies, or I do. The when and where are the only things negotiable."

Emmet didn't like where this was headed. Their dealings had always been straightforward and orderly. They provided the target information and the payment, and occasionally a time frame. Nothing else. There were no meetings, no time cards to punch, and no Christmas parties. Categorized as contract employees, they answered to no one.

Until now.

The war had brought unwanted attention. Not good in this line of work. Attention brought the authorities. Journalists tagged along with the authorities, which with time and persistence could lead to congressional hearings and jail time.

"You do what you have to do." Hank ended the conversation and tossed his phone onto the table in front of him.

"How bad is it?" Emmet remained on his feet. He preferred to take bad news standing.

"They want me to stand down. I told them to fuck off. They told me to fuck off and now they're pulling out until the dust settles."

Which meant no more toys, no more bombs. Got it. Emmet could tell Hank wasn't pleased. Fuck, neither was he. "All of this could've been shared over the phone. Why are you here?"

"I've been summoned by your patron, Mr. Julius Morgan."

Another surprise. "For?"

Hank shrugged. "Seemed important enough for me to come since my daughter is here. He arrives in a few hours. The boat will be docking at—"

"Julius said he wasn't using the yacht for the next month, so why is he coming?" Emmet asked.

"I suspect he's gonna tell us what we owe him in return for this little cruise."

Again, something that could be shared over a conference call. "How long have you been on board?"

"Long enough for a shower and some food."

Long enough to find out that Emmet and Bailey shared the same room, the same bed. "Whiskey thinks you're missing."

"I am missing," Hank snapped, then added, "Where is he?"

"Tracking a lead in the Philippines. He checked in yesterday since you weren't answering your phone or emails."

No comment from Hank. Not shocking. He had a habit of cutting ties and hunkering down when shit went bad. They couldn't do that anymore.

"He wants out, you know."

That was news. "When?" Emmet asked.

"Not up to me."

Getting out? Was such a thing possible? Emmet filed that thought away for another time and plopped into a chair. "You missing may not be a bad thing. It'll give us time to regroup. Come up with a new plan. Bring in fresh blood. Blood that's off the books." Blood Rogers isn't privy to. Their community was an intimate gathering of people with similar skills and few outliers, though with a cast of second-string players waiting in the wings for an invitation to the big league. All Hank had to do was send the invites.

"Fresh blood," Hank said as if he rolled the two words on his tongue and didn't like the taste. "Fresh blood leaves us vulnerable. People we don't know leaves us vulnerable. I have enough *vulnerabilities*."

Emmet didn't miss the not-so-subtle hint and ignored it. "Consider them cannon fodder. We distract him with extra bodies thrown his way. He'll slip, and we'll slip in and kill him."

Hank drummed the table, his fingers tapping a familiar tune. "Cannon fodder, huh. When did you become so jaded?"

"A father who starved me and a killer who raised me, that's when."

"Ah." Hank nodded. "Seems like you've been with me from the beginning. Sometimes I forget how we met."

It wasn't the first time Hank had uttered that statement, and the words never failed to stir Emmet's heart. His life began when Hank took him out of that hovel. He owed Hank everything.

"It has been a long seven months, Emmet. I've seen all I've built teeter."

Voice low, pained, Emmet had never seen his mentor like this. Hank wasn't known for deep reflection. A man of action, he didn't do stalled. "Teeter, but not topple."

"Doesn't feel like it, my man."

They were silent, each man in his own world. Hank's full of regret. Emmet rethinking the plan and coming up with nothing new. "My plan is good. Workable. I'll call it in and get more men."

"Admit we need help? Weakness is weeded out, not praised." His tone graveyard quiet. "It's too late for that, anyway."

"What do you mean?"

"The agency has removed their support. Rogers is no longer rogue. Now they're waiting to see who is the victor, and guess where that leaves us."

Emmet sat back in the leather chair. "That leaves us screwed."

"With no foreplay and no KY."

"Damn."

A heavy beat of silence stretched out. Then, "Where is she?"

The she, Emmet didn't have to question as to who Hank could possibly be referring to. The fact that "Where is she?" followed Hank's no foreplay and no KY, well, that was a bit disturbing. "She's in bed, asleep." The only reason he didn't tag on *my bed* was because he didn't own the boat.

Hank sighed and nodded slowly. "So, this is happening, huh?"

Emmet mimicked Hank's head bobbing up and down. "Yes."

"You and my daughter."

Emmet nodded.

Hank planted his elbows on the table, folded one hand over the other and stared Emmet down. "And afterwards? If we survive?"

If we survive. Emmet didn't like those odds. "When we survive." He corrected.

Hank conceded the point with a careless shrug.

Emmet had already thought this far ahead. The past few days as they'd drawn closer in mind and spirit. They moved together as a unit, inside and out of the bedroom. They clicked, two puzzle pieces that fit. She calmed him while making him crazy. Satisfied him, yet he still hungered. Made him consider the future when he'd lived second to second for so long it was his default setting.

Hitmen didn't retire, Hank reminded him. The thing is, Emmet had more than enough cash squirreled away to start anew. After Rogers was in several thousand pieces, he'd see what his options were with his life—the agency—and with Bailey.

And none of this was Hank's business.

"She and I will decide."

"Is that right?" Hank grunted.

"I told you before, Hank, she's not your little girl anymore."

"Wrong. She's my daughter. *Mine*. And I won't have her hurt."

Emmet took exception. "Who says I'm going to hurt her?"

"I say." Hank pushed his thumb into his chest. "Because that's who we are. We hurt people for a living. Many of them permanently. We place a target on people and do what's necessary until, one day, a target is placed on our backs and the backs of those we love."

Emmet didn't have to be a psychic to know where Hank was headed, and he didn't fucking like it, not one bit. "Don't compare me to you." A vision of Hank burying his pregnant wife popped into Emmet's head. He closed that train of thought, hard. "I'm not you, Hank."

Hank shook his head. "Wrong, Streets. You could be my twin. Never told you how I met Constance."

He hadn't and right now, that's the last thing Emmet wanted cluttering his mind. "I don't want to know."

"She worked for the Defense Department. I met her by accident, then I met her on purpose."

Damn it, I said I didn't want to know.

"She was a secretary in Human Resources and pretty clueless to what I did. And I never told her the truth. She thought she married a run of the mill Marine. Maybe if I had fessed up, she could've protected herself better, that's what chewed me up inside for half a decade. Took that long to catch all the bastards involved."

"Bailey isn't Constance," Emmet barked.

Hank pounded the desk. "She is. Not only in image. Constance was an innocent. She was clean, full of life. She had no part of our world until I dragged her inside. And she left bloodied and dead. I'm the best in the business and couldn't protect my woman. But I've protected my child."

"By throwing her away?"

Hank slammed both fists onto the table. "She's alive, ain't she?"

"And she hates you."

Hank drained his glass and crossed to the bar in the corner of the room and poured another. "It's a price I accepted and was willing to pay; otherwise I wouldn't have done it."

And what a steep price it was. Could Emmet have been that strong? He prayed he'd never have to find out. "But it's a price you didn't have to pay. You said you found her in Nebraska. A couple had adopted her. You could've left her there. Made sure the couple was nice. You didn't. Why?"

Hank tossed himself back into his chair as if the weight he carried was suddenly too much to bear. "She was a piece of my Constance. I couldn't let her go. Still can't, truth be told."

Yet he kept her at arm's length.

"Do you love her?" Hank spat as if the word had left a bad taste in his mouth.

Emmet knew what lay in his heart. Yet to say the words, words he'd never uttered to another person, words he hadn't spoken to Bailey, to say them to Hank?

"Don't answer that. I don't need the answer when it's written all over your damn face. And that's why you will do the right thing and walk away. Right, Streets?"

The right thing. What exactly was, "The right thing"? The right thing for Hank? The right thing for Bailey? The right thing for him? Doing the *right thing* wouldn't make everyone happy, definitely wouldn't make him happy if the right thing was to walk away from Bailey.

An image of him holding her charred body in his arms exploded in his brain. That's what Hank went through. What he could possibly go through if he stayed with Bailey. They had enemies, and that fact would never change. She'd be in danger, doubly so because of the man who sired her and the man who loved her.

Damn, he didn't think he'd ever understand how Hank walked away. Now he did because to save the one you loved, nothing was impossible. Not even leaving and never looking back. If it kept Bailey safe from men like himself, Rogers, and Hank, then he'd be as ruthless as his mentor. He had no other choice. Emmet looked at his mentor and matched the grim countenance and fierce determination in his blue eyes. Eyes the exact color of Bailey's.

He nodded once, in silent agreement. Then he affirmed his decision by saying aloud, "Yeah. When the time comes, I'll do the right thing… And walk away." But it wouldn't come to that. He wouldn't let it.

Hank's gaze cut to a spot above Emmet's head and his face went neutral, even though the hand reaching for the glass of liquor trembled.

Ah, fuck!

CHAPTER 23

"Did he have to go to Mexico and pick the fruit?" Bailey shoved the blanket away and scooted out of bed. She didn't have to go find him, but her bladder demanded attention. That taken care of, she freshened up and couldn't help noticing the circles under her eyes had faded. She'd also added a few pounds to her lean frame. There was a jiggle to her boobs that weren't there before and a hickey to the underside of the right one. It was close in size to the hickey he placed on her left boob, right in her cleavage. The memory of him doing it had her pulse quickening.

She ran a hand through her hair, touched the area where her stitches were slowly dissolving, and her hair had started to regrow. Time for a new haircut, maybe even a new color. *What would Emmet like?* Funny thing, she'd hacked off her long hair without a care of what Richard thought.

There were bruises on her inner thighs, she remembered how that happened too and bit her lip at the throb that kicked off in her core. Addiction, that's what this was, and she wasn't at all upset about it.

Yet her mind kept going to the day when all the running was over. Nothing was promised. How could he promise anything when the situation was fluid? They may be dead tomorrow. She'd finally found the person she wanted to be with and could lose him before they'd begun.

What did she have to do to prevent that from happening? From what she understood, Rogers wanted Hank dead, not Emmet. She hadn't cared for the reason before. Now, she wondered why. She didn't buy Emmet's procedural differences bullshit explanation. The feud went deeper than that. Bone deep. Protecting Hank was bad for Emmet's health, and hers. They had to leave, disappear into the ether. She had enough money to make that happen, at least for a few years, until Hank was dead, and Rogers was appeased.

The thought knocked the air from her lungs. Doubled over, she had to catch her breath and to keep from screaming. Her father had to die to save her lover and herself.

She and Emmet had to talk, make a decision other than blindly following Hank onto Plan C because Plan B had been all about hiding, which couldn't last. Eventually, Julius Morgan would want his yacht back. Eventually, they'd be kicked off the Love Boat at the nearest port.

Ugh! Her brain kept churning, and she wanted it to stop, get Emmet and go back to bed. And talk. In the morning. Talk and make plans for the future. Make plans for him to leave this life. Would he do that? Leave the life of a hitman behind. For her? And how do you ask a man to leave the only thing he's known behind? For her.

A walk through the walk-in closet for a silk robe then she went to find Emmet. There was no sign he'd been in the private kitchen, which was fully stocked with fresh watermelon, grapes, mango, papaya, coconut, and pineapple. The menu icon on the tablet mounted on a counter linking all the all the ship's systems for easy customer usage, blinked. It was a message from the head chef about tomorrow's options. Surf and turf was never a bad choice.

"Do you love her?"

Bailey heard the sentence and thought, *Who the fuck is he talking to?* She exited the kitchen and paused in the entrance to the private dining room. The room was empty. Her attention switched to the slight opening in the double doors of the adjacent conference room.

"Don't answer that. I don't need the answer when it's written all over your damn face."

The voice, *that voice*, struck a chord within her and she knew, without a doubt, knew *he* was here. Her father was here, on the boat. How long? How long had he been here? Did he just arrive? Or was he here the whole time and didn't care enough to even see her? And was Emmet a part of it?

Her knees jellied, and she took a step back, prepared to flee to the bedroom and never leave. *No*, a voice whispered in her head, and she marched forward, determined to have the confrontation that was long overdue.

She crossed the dining room, careful to stay in the shadows of the room. Carefully, she peered through the part in the double doors for a view of the back of Emmet's head, and locked eyes on the man sitting across the table from him.

He'd changed a lot in seven years. Bald now, though by his pale dome, that seemed recent. A bit heavier around the jowls, gray in his eyebrows, all new. The intensity in his eyes, the grim set of his face, the same.

His appearances always terrified her. Truth be told, her racing heart wasn't from excitement. He still frightened her.

"And that's why you will do the right thing and walk away. Right, Streets?" Hank said.

The right thing? Streets? Emmet Streeter. Streets had to be *his nickname.* She glanced at Emmet, his back still to her as he sat in front of Hank.

"Yeah. When the time comes, I'll do the right thing and walk away."

Acid poured over her at the sound of Emmet's voice dumping her at the behest of her father. Up in a puff of smoke went any plans for a future with the man who'd stolen her heart. She could admit that now as her heart turned to ash in her chest and she bit back a sob.

Hank shows up, and she gets dumped. Once again, he pulled the rug out from under her, seemed to take pleasure in doing so. But Emmet... That pain she'd have to deal with later because right now, she had a few choice words to share with her sperm donor.

"Hello, Bailey." Hank's gruff voice was a quick dip in an icy pond.

She wanted to see him. Well, here he was. The little girl in her wanted to run into his arms and beg for the love she was denied. The woman in her wanted him to hurt, badly. She wanted blood. Maybe they were more alike than she was willing to admit.

She pushed open the door and entered the room, total focus on the man in front of her. "Hello, Henry."

That wasn't what she really wanted to say. He didn't deserve the respect she gave him by using his given name, but nothing else came to mind at that moment. It was Theresa's fault Bailey had manners.

He held up a hand. "Call me Hank. Everyone does. I prefer it."

Everyone does. *So, I'm everyone.* She gave herself a mental slap. *Be grateful he didn't say call me Dad. Thank God.* She pushed open the door and entered the room. "What are you doing here, Hank?"

His forehead puckered, drawing his brows into angry salt and pepper slashes. "You're angry. That's expected." He scratched at his temple and flexed his fingers until he dropped both hands to his lap. "How are you, Bailey?"

What the fuck type of question was that? And how should she answer it? "I'm..." *Not fine!* She sat at the head of the table between the two men, because long or short, this conversation was overdue and beyond necessary. Hands folded in her lap, she didn't take her eyes off Hank. Not that she wasn't aware of Emmet's gaze locked on her. She just refused to acknowledge it.

"Strange question." She wanted to sound strong, in control, untouchable. Not like the broken little girl caged inside her chest. "I'm on the run because a killer *you* trained is after me to hurt you. I've been shot at, coerced, kidnapped, blown up, stitched up, and now I'm on a yacht talking to the man who caused all this. Does that give you an inkling of how I'm doing?" The last sentence was barely a whisper, which pissed her off. So much for being untouchable.

"I'd say I'm sorry, but a sorry is worth as much as a three dollar bill." He studied the glass in his hand.

She'd waited a lifetime to hear two words, *I'm sorry*, and would keep waiting. Which was as pathetic as Hank not being able to say them.

Hank's mouth, puckered into a tight asshole, mimicking his not so secret identity. "I'm sorry," he spat as if she should be grateful.

Wow, that had to shave a decade off his life. Too bad it was seven years too late. But, she'd roll with it and use it to her advantage because that's all she had. This moment. In front of her father.

"What exactly are you sorry about? And why should I care?"

A muscle ticked in his jaw. *Oh look, he's pissed. Good.*

"You didn't deserve this." A nonchalant wave of the hand not holding the glass of liquor summed up...nothing.

"This? Do you mean my presence on the yacht? Or maybe

you mean the scar on the side of my head." She angled her head so he could see the healing wound. "Maybe you mean the explosion?" His lips flattened into a grim line, but she wasn't done. "Could be you meant your protégé kidnapping me from my vacation." She pointed at Emmet. "I'm sure one of those things were what you were referring too, right, Hank?"

Features glacial. "Like I said, a sorry is worthless."

Tears pricked the backs of her eyes. Yep. It was confirmed. Hank was an asshole, and she was an idiot for holding onto a sliver of hope. Her gaze cut to Emmet whose gaze drilled into her. Her idiocy stretched to both men. Now, she didn't know who she wanted to cry over.

I can't do this. She gave into the little girl crying in the corner of her mind and bolted.

Bailey rose, felt a cool draft shoot up the robe, and realized she was naked beneath a thin layer of silk. She snatched the two halves together over her exposed cleavage and spun. Emmet blocked her path.

And she was grateful. Blocking her path gave her a second to catch her breath and realize her mistake. Leaving wouldn't solve anything. She entered the room for answers, and by God, she would get them.

"Bailey, let me—"

She held up a hand, cutting off whatever trivial nonsense Emmet was about to spew. She didn't need his help, not ever again.

Adjusting her robe, she planted her ass, again and locked eyes with Hank. "Tell me about my mother. Not Theresa. I want to know about the woman who birthed me."

She expected him to shut her down, was prepared for a brutal rebuttal per his M.O. Nothing surprised her more than when he reached into his suit pocket and withdrew his wallet. From the leather billfold came a single 2x3 photo. He held it up, studied it as if he'd never see it again. And he wouldn't. Regardless of the sadness plainly visible on his face, that picture now belonged to her.

His gaze met hers, and he slid the photo across the table. She stopped it from going off the edge of the table with a finger to the center of the picture. Trembling, she flipped it over and brought it close.

Yellow around the edges and a watermark in the right corner discolored the side of her head. The rest of the picture…

Her hair was jet black and fell in waves around her shoulders, similar to how Bailey kept her hair before the pixie cut. Their features were also identical, oval faces with strong jawlines, wide-set eyes. The color, a soft baby blue. In her lap, a chubby baby, dressed in pink and white. She looked radiant, her head thrown back in laughter, her eyes twinkling. Whoever held the camera captured a moment of pure happiness.

"Did you take this picture?" She managed to say through a throat constricted by a swell of emotions.

Hank cleared this throat. "You had turned a year old a week earlier, last warm day of the year. I was leaving for a trip and wanted something to take with me, though I didn't get it developed until I returned."

"She loved you." Bailey could tell in every line of her mother's body. A woman in love can't hide it, and her mother clearly loved Hank.

"I loved her."

Why did he sound dead inside, like a gutted fish left to rot, but he didn't rot. Instead, he let his grief consume him and any potential relationship he could've had with his daughter. Bailey clutched the picture to her. She wouldn't cry, not in front of them. There were more questions she had but didn't care anymore. The answers were irrelevant when the questions didn't matter.

"Her name. Give me her name," she growled.

"Constance Michela."

That was a knife in Bailey's heart. It took everything she had not to sob.

With the picture in hand, she rose.

"Is that it?" He seemed confused. "Nothing else you want to ask me?"

She kept moving toward the door, ignoring him as he ignored her.

"Are you sure, babe? This is your chance?" Emmet touched her shoulder as she walked by.

She knocked his hand away. "My chance? To do what? Connect with a man who hates me?"

"I don't hate you," Hank murmured. "I regret you believe that."

She refused to look at him. Instead, she focused her contempt on Emmet. "I don't care what you regret. I got what I came for, and I need nothing else." She waved the picture of her mother and walked around Emmet.

Back through the dining room, the private kitchen, to the master suite, she moved as quickly as her feet would carry her. She didn't stop until she was staring the window at the bow of the ship gliding along the surface of the water.

"You should feel complete because Hank is here now." She met Emmet's gaze in his reflection on the window.

"Bailey."

"Don't bother. Whatever you have to say, tell it to Hank. He cares. I don't."

He cut the distance between them and paused only a few paces behind her rigid back. "How much did you hear?"

She looked over her shoulder at him, couldn't help it. "This conversation is unnecessary. Get what you need and get out. Go bunk with Hank."

"I want to know what you're thinking." Stubbornly, he stood

in the middle of the room, legs spread, arms folded, looking irresistible.

"Thinking?" She shook her head. "I'm not thinking."

"Your opinion then," he gritted out the words between clenched teeth.

"I have no opinion."

"A woman without an opinion is an oxymoron," Emmet snorted. "When Rogers has been caught, and you go back to your life, I will walk away, and you will have the life you want."

"Aww." She wheeled around. Now, he deserved her attention. With her hand pressed to her chest, she gave him her brightest smile instead of planting something sharp in his chest. "You're such a gentleman. Thank you for agreeing to walk away from me. I'm so lucky. Very, very lucky to have spent quality time with you. Was the seduction Plan A.2, Plan B.1?"

"I didn't seduce you. *We* seduced each other."

God, she wished she could call him a liar.

"And it wasn't a plan, Bailey." He came closer.

She backed up, but there was no place to go. She couldn't ghost through the bulkhead to avoid him but suspected even if she could, she wouldn't escape his presence unless he allowed her to. Yet, there had to be a way. Had to.

"There wasn't a plan to end up in bed with you. What happened between us was…"

He stumbled over the words, and she supplied them. "A mistake." And that's why he could walk away. "One we don't need to repeat." She swallowed down the hurt and focused on what was important. "What's Plan C, or am I still not allowed to know how you and Hank will use me next?"

A vein pulsed in his temple and she found herself fascinated by each throb. "We haven't gotten that far yet. Hank was too busy interrogating me about our relationship and no one is using you."

That was a surprise. Not the "no one is using you" part, but

Hank questioning Emmet about their relationship. "What relationship? We had sex. Now, we're not having sex." Especially after he promised to walk away. *Think of something else, anything else.* "After all this is over, and Rogers is in his grave, you go back to working with Hank where? In America? In Europe?" He opened his mouth to answer, but she wasn't done. "The only reason I care is because I don't need your super-secret agency coming after me because I know too much."

With measured steps and open arms, Emmet came to her. "No one will come after you. I won't let them, babe."

She allowed him to wrap his arms around her and draw her into his body. She allowed his warmth to seep beneath her skin and sink all the way to her bones. Yet, she remained cold, as if her soul had walked into a freezer. "You won't let them. Unless, Hank yanks your chain. Or is there someone higher than Hank who yanks his chain?"

His face gave nothing away, but everybody had a boss. Everybody had to answer to someone.

She drew back and met his gaze. "I'm not your babe."

Carefully, she extricated herself from his arms and headed for the bathroom. She ran a bath. It filled quickly from two faucets at opposite ends of the sunken tub. She added bath oil for some much-needed aromatherapy. All the while, he stood there. Arms folded again as he leaned against the jamb, body a tense wall of muscle, watching her strip and lower herself into the hot water.

Eyes closed, she leaned back and let the water soothe what it could. Which wasn't much as she listened to his footsteps draw near. She couldn't ignore him, not when his presence was hotter than the bath water which had yet to thaw her soul.

He was there, on his haunches, inches away. It took everything she had not to reach for him. She did it. She resisted even when he scooped up a handful of water and poured it over her exposed shoulder. "You're angry. I get it. You want to hate me. I get that too. But know this..." He gripped her chin and angled her head toward him, forcing her to meet his gaze. "I regret nothing."

His free hand entered the water and slipped between her thighs. "Go ahead. Tell me you regret what happened between us."

He parted her flesh with a single finger and circled her clit, then he dipped deep inside her. She could've stopped him, grabbed his hand, pulled away, told him to stop, not to touch her, *leave me alone*. All that came out of her mouth was a strangled sob bordering on a plea for more. Why? Because it wasn't over, not in her heart. Not in her soul which melted at his touch.

So close they shared a breath, he breathed into her and said, "That slickness I feel, it's not the water. Lie if you can, but, *babe*, your body doesn't lie. And neither will I. I will protect you with my life and—"

"Walk away at the first opportunity."

His icy gaze dipped into her soul, and it wasn't cold she felt, but a blazing inferno of desire. "Not the first." He pumped his finger into her depths and rubbed his stubble against her cheek. Her head fell back, and her knees fell open, granted him complete access to everything he wanted. "But if it keeps you safe, away from our world, then yeah, I will walk away and never look back."

Tears pricked her eyes, and she took his face in her hands while his fingers plied her body. He was right, she could lie to him and herself...tomorrow. "Then give me tonight."

Just one more night of make-believe where she wasn't hunted, and he was there because he wanted to be not out of loyalty to Hank. One more night where they had a future in the morning. One more night to feel loved, even if it was all a lie.

Bailey kissed him, poured everything she felt for him into their joined lips. She didn't know how he did it, but he stripped down to his birthday suit without breaking contact, or maybe she was lost in the ecstasy as he brought her to a swift release, then joined her in the tub. Water poured over the rim, soaking everything, though neither cared.

CHAPTER 24

A phone ringing pulled Bailey out of the light sleep she had succumbed to after a long night exhausting night. She didn't move as the bed shifted and the ringing silenced.

"What?" Emmet said to whoever was on the opposite end. "All right. I'll be there in a few." Then his lips were on her throat. "I have to go meet Julius Morgan. Want to join?"

She stifled her shock. He included her? Why now, her jaded half wondered even as she wallowed in the warmth his body provided. "I didn't hear a helicopter."

"We're docked in Magdeburg. Have been for about an hour. He'll be here in a moment."

She snuggled deeper under the covers. "No." She would've loved to meet the billionaire. "No. I'm gonna stay in bed most of the morning and catch up on sleep."

"Okay. I'll be back when I can." He pressed a quick kiss to the side of her throat and then he was gone. She listened to the muffled sound of water striking his body in the shower, followed by him in the dressing room, and then the sound of the bedroom doors opening and closing.

Bailey whipped back the covers and went for the duffle bag

in the closet first. She got out all the credit cards and passports and took them into the private kitchen to the tablet. Windows based, a few clicks got her into Programs and onto Internet Explorer. She considered doing this earlier in the week to check her emails and voicemails but knew what Emmet would say. Already conditioned to his wants and desires, she automatically deferred to his unspoken wishes. What an idiot. But that's what women did. They put their desires, their best interests, on the back burner because of love, regardless of whether it was reciprocated.

Not anymore.

They had their final passionate night, one she would remember forever, but she had to go. It took all night to come up with her plan, while snuggled against his naked body, absorbing the indelible feel and smell of him into her mind, but she had one. And it was a good plan. She lived her life with the threat of Hank around her neck for two and a half decades and had taken a few things to heart.

Hank claimed to be the only one protecting her from all the bad in the world even though he was nowhere to be seen and probably lived thousands of miles in the opposite direction of her little enclave in suburban Atlanta. She'd never truly believed that and had taken precautions. Emmet wasn't the only one with a g-to bag. All she had to do was get to Atlanta, get her stuff and no one would ever find her again, she hoped. A lot of things could go wrong; still, she had to make an effort to reclaim her life.

It took a precious thirty minutes to book all the flights. Quickly, she showered, dressed in a bathing suit and a plush robe with the name of the yacht emblazoned across the left breast. In the deep pockets, she hid the passports and cash. In a large towel, she rolled up her underwear, socks, and sneakers. Inside one of the sneakers, a nine-millimeter. She couldn't get it on an airplane, but it would help get her to the airport in one piece.

Through the deck, she strolled, dodging crewmen as they

hustled by. The owner was about to arrive. "Is there anything I can get you, ma'am?" one harried crewman stopped and asked.

"Oh, no. I'm just on my way to the sauna." Which wasn't far from the linen closet, a fact she discovered early on during her stay when she knocked a stack of towels into the pool. Fortunately, the linen closet held more than sheets and towels. It also contained the crew's uniforms, including outerwear.

She pushed open the frosted glass doors to the pool and sauna and pressed against the wall, waiting for the tide of crewmen to die down. Three bells sounded over the intercom, and all the crewmen headed for the stairs.

Bailey bolted for the closet. Once inside, she locked the door and stripped out of the bathing suit. Within two minutes she had changed into the navy blue pants, light blue button-down shirt, and navy blue sweater. The hooded down jacket matched the uniform along with the knit hats and scarfs. Julius Morgan cared about his crew's warmth. She stared into her blurry image reflected off the shiny side of a metal cabinet. The only thing that gave her away were her white sneakers.

Nothing could be done about that.

Pockets full of cash, credit cards, and passports, Bailey inhaled a deep breath to steady her nerves and headed for the top deck. She emerged into the bitter cold and waited at the end of a long line of crewmen as Julius Morgan and two women arrived with him. One on his arm, the other holding a briefcase. As expected, he shook the captain's and the steward's hands. She didn't expect the man to go down the line shaking everyone's hand, including hers.

A glimpse of his brown eyes and blond mustache was all she got, then he spun and walked back to the head of the line where he, his guests, and the captain entered the bridge. She wondered about Emmet and Hank but didn't have time to dwell. The crew broke into a flurry of activity, all of it seemed orchestrated. Half went below deck, the other half headed down the gangplank. She headed with the latter half who divided their efforts between unloading the limo and restocking the ship with food and other goods, along with dock workers.

Bailey kept walking, her pace steady as if she knew exactly where to go when in truth, she winged it. However, no one stopped her. She made it outside of the docks and through the terminal and onto the street. The first person she saw—a woman —she stopped and asked in German for the nearest taxi stand. The woman directed her to the main thoroughfare where she found a taxi idling at the curb.

Logic dictated she'd head for the nearest airport. Bailey did the opposite, because in this situation, on the run from a killer and her ex-lover, also a killer, being predictable was sure to get her caught and possibly dead. "Take me to the train station."

CHAPTER 25

"Where is he?" Hank grumbled from his seat on the sofa. "The boat docked almost two hours ago."

Across the room, Emmet poured two cups of black coffee and delivered one to Hank. "Not enough sleep?"

Hank grunted, a combination of thanks for the coffee and an agreement to his lack of sleep. Emmet sympathized over the absence of shut-eye, though his reasons were completely different.

Bailey...

Warmth flooded his chest at the same time his gut clenched.

"You all right over there?" Hank studied Emmet over the rim of his cup.

Staring into the black brew cradled in his hands, Emmet realized he wasn't *all right*. However, the reason for his disquiet, that he couldn't share. There wasn't a way to explain after a night of making love to Hank's daughter, leaving her on her doorstep when all the killing was over, wasn't going to happen.

He wanted her. Period. She'd seeped beneath his skin, got into his bloodstream.

Emmet cranked his head around and locked eyes on Hank. "I'm keeping her."

A single eyebrow arched as steam curled from Hank's cup. "You sure about that, boy?"

Emmet placed his cup on the coffee table and climbed to his feet. He was nobody's boy. He faced his mentor without taking offense at the slight. After all, regardless of Hank not being father of the year, he was still her father.

"Yes, sir. I am."

"She feel the same way?" Hank demanded through lips that barely moved.

After last night... "Yes, sir."

A grimace crossed Hank's face, then settled into a wary acceptance. "You better be serious about this, Emmet. Being with my daughter means you're not in the agency anymore. You can't have it both ways. Understand me?"

"Yes, sir."

He shook his head and gave his signature sigh, meaning he was resigned to Emmet and his daughter as a couple. "And don't think you're gonna shack up with her without a ring." He glared.

Him, a married man? The thought terrified him, though didn't make him want to run. "All in due time."

"There's a reason why they call it a shotgun wedding."

"Someone getting married?" Julius entered the room with an assistant trailing behind him—a tall, full-figured African American woman in her mid-twenties with a no-nonsense demeanor whose neutral features seemed cast in granite. He wondered if she'd ever played poker.

"Yes," Hank said, rising to shake Julius' hand.

"No." Emmet countered, annoyed at having to defend himself.

"He's in love with my daughter. So, yes. He will be getting married in the near future if he wants to make it to thirty-three."

Julius turned to Emmet. They slapped palms and met for a

bro-hug. Friends since Hank mistakenly dropped fifteen-year-old Emmet off at a boarding school in Massachusetts. Their friendship had made that year bearable. "She better be worth it to have you in Hank's crosshairs and using my master suite before I've even had a chance to see it," Julius murmured in Emmet's ear.

"She's worth it," Emmet replied loudly, then whispered, "We've enjoyed every inch of your suite."

Julius snorted. "Well, make sure I get an invite." He lowered himself into a leather chair on the other side of the coffee table. He held out his hand, and his assistant whipped out a document from a manila folder and passed it over. "Thank you, Miss Coleman. You may leave."

The assistant tipped her head in her boss's direction, spun on her sensible heels, and headed for the exit. Julius waited until the door closed behind her to give Emmet and Hank his undivided attention. "I need a favor."

Both Emmet and Hank waited for Julius to continue.

"I can't tell you what it is because things are…fluid. This is the type of favor where I can't allow you to refuse, that's why I've bought a contract."

Emmet shrugged. "Anything you need, Julius, ask, contract or not, it's yours. However, we are in the middle of a war right now."

Hank interrupted with, "Who do you want dead, boy?"

Julius' gaze cut to Hank. "No one, *yet*, old man. But when I do need someone killed, there will be no questions asked. I want it done immediately without discussion."

"And you think a contract will guarantee my compliance, boy?" Hank mocked Julius and leaned forward.

Ever the gentleman, Julius crossed his legs, but Emmet wasn't fooled. While he was no operative, Julius was no lightweight.

"The contract isn't for you, *old man*." Julius' gaze cut back to Emmet. "It's for you."

Emmet opened his hand for the document with the pen clipped to the edge. He flipped to the back page. Julius had already scribbled his signature on the top line next to his printed name. Miss Calico Coleman and her notary stamp occupied a space near the bottom of the page. A blank line next to his name waited. Emmet didn't hesitate. He scribbled his signature.

Hank leaped to his feet. "What are you doing? You're not going to sign that without reading it," he shouted though it was too late.

Emmet closed the document, dropped the Montblanc on top, and slid everything back to Julius. "Of course I'm going to sign it. First,"— he held up a finger—"Julius is my friend." He held a second finger. "He has billions, so stealing from me is absurd." A third finger popped up. "Whatever he needs it must be important for him to go to this length to secure my absolute cooperation when he could've just asked." A fourth finger joined the rest. "If he betrays me, the friendship is over, and he knows what I do to my enemies." Emmet ended with an indulgent chuckle.

A knock sounded at the closed doors to the lounge and then opened with a slight swoosh. The assistant had returned, followed by the chef with a cart laden with everything a person could want for breakfast. Julius' gaze followed her as she helped lay out a morning feast and didn't stop until she delivered him a steaming mug of coffee. Apparently, Emmet wasn't the only one who had it bad.

"Is there anything else you may need, Mr. Morgan?" For a woman, she had a deep, slightly husky voice.

"No, Miss Coleman. You may leave."

With a signal to the chef, they both departed, the signed paperwork in her hand.

"I'm not your enemy, and I value our friendship." Julius continued as if they hadn't been interrupted. "You're one of the few friends I have. I could've gone to someone else, but I came to you because I trust you. As you trust me, otherwise you wouldn't be here. Besides, it may not come to me needing you to kill anyone. I like having the option."

Emmet was onboard while Hank kept his opinion to himself, which was as close to a seal of approval Julius would get.

"Now, how goes your war against your former associates?" Julius switched subjects smoothly.

"We're hiding on your yacht; how do you think it goes?" Hank growled.

Emmet ignored him. "We've killed almost everyone helping him. Only Ivan is left. I snapped Jerrod's neck at the chalet in Switzerland."

"Unless he recruited more, as we had planned." Hank headed for the buffet.

"I'd forgotten what a ray of sunshine Hank is." Julius chuckled.

"I'm too old to change." Hank groused and returned with a plate of pancakes and bacon for Emmet, and a plate with an egg white omelet and turkey sausage for himself. He had a slight cholesterol issue. His one concession to his advanced age.

"How is your daughter handling it?" Julius questioned.

"Ask him." He tipped his head to Emmet.

"Handling it? She's amazing." And she wasn't here where he needed her to be, at his side, meeting his best friend. "I want you to meet her."

He was on his feet and striding through the ship without a second thought, the need to see her driving him forward to the master suite.

"Bailey." He expected to find her still beneath the covers. She wasn't there. Neither was she in the bathroom, though a discarded towel lay in a pile on the floor. Maybe she was in the kitchen making breakfast? But she wasn't there either, and nor in the dining room. A sense of urgency propelled him out of the suite and back through the ship. He had to find her, now.

"May I be of help, sir?" The steward stepped out of his private office and into Emmet's path.

"Yeah. Have you seen Bailey?"

"She was on her way to the pool and sauna roughly an hour ago."

Emmet headed that way with the steward trailing him. He threw open the door and marched over to the empty pool, noticing not a towel out of place, not even a wet spot on the tile indicating someone had taken a dip. And the sauna, it wasn't even on.

"Security cameras," he said more to himself than the steward. He ran there and shoved the security guard out of his seat. He didn't need help manipulating the camera and looping through the day's video.

Bailey appeared outside of the suite dressed in a robe with a towel bundled under her arm. A towel she didn't need since there were plenty already at the pool. She did enter the pool, where there were no cameras, and exited when the passageway cleared. She darted down the passageway, to a door he'd never paid attention to before."

"What is that room?" He pointed to it on the screen.

The steward leaned over Emmet's shoulder. "The linen closet, sir. All the staff were upstairs awaiting Mr. Morgan's arrival; otherwise, someone would have seen her enter the room."

He didn't have long to wait for Bailey to exit, except now, she was dressed in the navy and sky blue colors of the crewmen's uniform, right down to the down jacket and skull cap. She blended perfectly with the crew, except for her sneakers.

Through a series of cameras, he observed her winding her way through the ship and emerge topside where she met Julius, and then mingled with the crew and walked off the boat.

Emmet pushed back from the monitor and rose.

"Sir, is there anything I can do to—"

The rest of his question was drowned out by distance and the drum of his heartbeat in his ears. That's what hurt the most, she planned all of it. While he was inside her, she planned to leave. He pulled his cell out of his back pocket and called Bailey's cell, because though she didn't have her phone, at some point she'd check her voicemails and reconnect with her world.

"Hi, you've reached me, but I'm not available. Leave a message." The longest ten seconds of his life passed, then

"I will find you, Bailey. Understand me. All you've done is stick your neck out for a garrote." He slammed his fist into the nearest wall. It was either that or crumble the phone in his hand, and he needed the phone. "I can't believe you could be this stupid. If you have any sense at all, you will find a hole to crawl into and stay there 'till I find you. Do you understand me, Bailey? Get someplace safe. I'm on my way." *And whatever caused you to run, I'll fix it.*

Back through the boat he traveled passing Hank and Julius who'd come to find him. "Where's Bailey?" Hank demanded.

Bursting back into the master suite, Emmet headed straight for the walk-in closet and the duffle bag beneath the satin bench. He snatched up the duffle bag with the passports and money. The damn thing felt light. *Do not tell me she—*

Yanking it open confirmed what he'd already guessed. *All* the passports and credit cards were gone, along with a brick of cash. She'd cut him off at the knees. If he weren't so enraged, he'd be impressed. If she weren't in danger, he'd be laughing his ass off at how she played him.

But she was in danger, now more than ever, because of him. Not Hank. Emmet couldn't lay this at Hank's feet. Emmet pushed her away. Last night, he thought the energy between them felt different, even as they made love all night long. Turned out, he wasn't wrong. For her, it was a goodbye screw while for him, he was holding onto the best thing in his life. What a piss-poor time to find that tidbit out that she'd meant it when she said, "Give me tonight."

That was not their last night. He refused to have them end it this way.

"I'm coming for you, babe, and you'd better be alive when I find you or I will seriously be pissed off, more than I already am," he murmured and took a deep breath as he tore through the room, packing only the essentials.

"Emmet. I asked you a question. Where is Bailey?" Hank demanded. He stood in the middle of the suite with Julius by his side.

Lost in his own world, Emmet hadn't realized they were there. "Gone."

"Gone?" Hank shouted but couldn't hide the fear in his voice, a fear taking root in the center of Emmet's chest. She was out there, unprotected. "Gone where?"

That, Emmet, had no answer for…yet.

CHAPTER 26

"Ticket, please."

Absorbed in the passing scenery from her seat on the train, Bailey dropped her phone onto her lap and fumbled handing over her ticket. "Sorry," she murmured in German.

"Danke!" The agent moved on.

She reached for her newly bought phone and noticed it hadn't disconnected from her messages. Bailey's finger hovered over the number seven. One quick touch and Emmet's two messages would be deleted.

She saved the messages and ended the call. Why couldn't she do it? The man threatened her with bodily harm, and she couldn't even delete his damn messages because she cherished the sound of his voice.

Bailey flung the phone onto the empty seat next to her. Buying the phone was stupid. She did it out of the instinct to connect with the world, call Daisy and bawl on her preverbal shoulder, but she couldn't place anyone other than herself in harm's way. Calling into her voicemail, listening to Daisy prattle on about her latest conquest, her latest shopping spree, her latest argument with her father, was as close to normal as she could get.

She hadn't expected to hear his voice. Fury made it huskier, which shouldn't be a turn on, but damn it was.

"I'm coming for you," he said.

A threat... And a promise.

Focus on the threat. The promise is a lie meant to hurt you. Good thing he had no idea where she was heading because she had no idea.

She bought fifteen plane tickets to random destinations all leaving at different times. Emmet and Hank had a lot of resources, but the two of them couldn't be everywhere. And if they couldn't find her, neither could Rogers.

Men! Two running around to protect her. One hunting her down on a mission of revenge. And she'd evaded them all. So much for needing to be protected. She did it herself.

"I'm not going to second-guess my decision," she murmured. And it was a good decision. It was a good plan. A quick pit stop in ATL for her own stash of credit cards, cash, a fresh passport, and she'd be in the wind.

"To where?" What happens after Atlanta?

Good thing she had a full day of travel to find out.

∽

*B*ribery only got so far. This time it got Emmet far enough with the help of Julius' influence. One call to a friend in the German government and all of Bailey's aliases were on a no-fly list. She would be detained when she checked in.

All Emmet had to do was collect her from security, which he was about to do right now.

With Hank on his heels, Emmet pushed open the door to the airport security and rattled off the list of Bailey's aliases.

"She has not checked in for any of her flights yet. However, the next flight leaves in ninety minutes. Gate D12. The one after that leaves two hours later at Gate A9," the guard said in German.

"I'll take Gate D. You take Gate A," Emmet said to Hank and headed out without waiting for an agreement. He was running this show.

He walked through the airport with purpose, searching. Every short-haired brunette caught his eye, but it wasn't her. None of them were her. Not even at the gate.

He stood there, waiting in the shadow of a column, staring in the only direction she could travel. Frustration gnawed at his bones, a deep ache only getting his hands on her would quench. First, he'd wring her neck.

And afterward, he just wanted to hold her.

Minutes ticked by as he waited for Bailey to show up. The plane began boarding. Emmet kept his position. Hank called twice. She hadn't shown at Gate A either. A nervous buzzing started in his ears, background noise to the chatter of too many anxious humans trying to get to their destinations. The buzzing reached a crescendo when the agent closed the gate behind the last boarding passenger.

Calmly, Emmet strode through the airport and joined Hank at Gate A. Two hours they waited, silent sentinels watching the minutes tick away, analyzing the ebb and flow of the foot traffic, studying each slimly built female regardless of the hair, because that was changeable. When the gate closed behind the last passenger, they had to acknowledge the truth they'd kept at bay. She'd bested them.

"We have to find her, Emmet. I won't lose my daughter." Determination and fear, a father's fear for his child, warped his words. A fear Emmet shared for the woman he loved. They'd underestimated her at every turn, treated her as if she were some fragile hothouse flower and not a tenacious weed that refused to be tamed. "If there is one thing I know, Bailey will be fine."

"What the fuck do you mean she'll be fine?" Hank's face beet red from his fury, his voice brittle. "Rogers could have her right now."

"No. Rogers doesn't have her." Of that Emmet was certain. "This wasn't some harebrained scheme to hit the road and hope to get away. Bailey has a plan. We must figure out what that plan is."

Hank sat there. The gears in his brain churning so fast, any second smoke would curl from his ears. Emmet was already ahead of him.

"Have Whiskey track down her friend, Daisy. See if she's heard anything from her and have him stay with her in case Bailey shows up." Emmet didn't think that was likely. Bailey wasn't the type to put another person in danger, but he had to cover that base.

Hank whipped out his phone and started dialing.

Emmet did the same with his phone, only he called a different person. "Dave, do not hang up."

"You are not supposed to be calling me, not until everything blows over," Dave whispered. In the background, Emmet heard the sounds of utensils hitting plates and the murmur of people ordering.

It was evening back in the States. Dinnertime for Dave, probably at his favorite sushi spot. He had a taste for sashimi and kimchi and the oriental waitresses.

"Don't hand me that bullshit." Dave was lucky Emmet couldn't reach through the phone and strangle him. "Remember that scuffle you got into last March over bitcoin that I took care of? Wrong place, wrong time, wrong girl with a boyfriend connected to the mafia? I smoothed everything over so you didn't dine with the fishes *and* end up fired, and homeless."

Dave groaned, and his voice dropped a few octaves. "Don't remind me. You said we'd never speak of that night again."

"And we won't." Emmet's tone now conciliatory. "After I get what I need. So, put down your fork and head back to work. I need information, and you're gonna get it for me."

"You're gonna get me killed." The background chatter receded, replaced with the sound of cars and horns. He was already heading back to the office. "What is it you need?"

"Information. I need a person tracked."

"Easy enough," he boasted.

"She has four aliases." Emmet rattled off the names. "I doubt she'll use her real name, she's too smart for that. But in case she did, it's Bailey Michela Monroe."

"I know it." Dave snickered. "So, you lost Hank's daughter. Man is he gonna kill you."

"Glad you're concerned about my welfare. Now, use your hacking skills, and find her. Start with Magdeburg and widen the circle from there. Keep widening it. Airports are a priority, trains, and buses secondary. Check cameras. CCTV feeds—"

An irritated scoff came through the phone. "I know how to do a search. I'll pull her picture from her passport. Leave me alone to work, and I'll call you when I have something."

The call ended. Emmet glanced at Hank, striding to his side. "Did you contact Whiskey?"

"He's on the way to Daisy in London in case Bailey shows up there."

Excellent. They'd done everything they could, yet it didn't seem enough. Not by a long shot.

Good thing he was feeling lucky, which proved to be prophetic when his phone chimed three times—Dave's ringtone —eighteen minutes later.

"What do you have for me?"

CHAPTER 27

"Hi, Bailey. It's, umm, Theresa. I haven't, I mean, we haven't spoken in a few months, and I just wanted to check in. See how you were doing. I'm fine. Posted in Turkey. If you ever want to visit, I have a spare room, and it would be great to see you again. It's been so long... Anyway, I love you."

Bailey saved the message as she did with all of Theresa's messages. She made a mental promise to call her as soon as things calmed down but had no idea when that would be. A day? A week? A year? Never? It wasn't right how she treated Theresa. She did the best she could with what she had, and for it, she was shunned by the child she'd raised as her own.

She rubbed away the tears gathering in her eyes. "I've been such a bitch."

A stewardess stopped by her seat. "Seatbelt buckled?" she questioned with a slight Greek accent.

Bailey made quick work of clicking and tightening the belt.

"Phone off, please." The stewardess waited for Bailey to obey, then continued down the aisle.

The next stop on her tour of the world...Brazil.

She pulled the photo of her mother out of her pants pocket and traced the lines of her face, a face so similar to her own.

What would it have been like to grow up with Constance in her life? Not the first time she pondered the question, except this time she had a face and a name. She looked kind, nurturing. She looked happy. Loved. There was an undeniable joy to her the camera captured.

This is what a woman in love looks like. Her mother had that with Hank. Bailey dragged her arm across her now wet cheeks.

It must've been hard for Hank to bury her and have a mini doppelganger running around needing attention. *So what! A good parent would've stepped the fuck up and not abandon their child.*

Hank wasn't able to do that. He loved her mother so much it broke something in him. What did love as deep as that feel like? When she and Emmet were together her emotions raged like a river tumbling over a cliff. Free, yet anchored was how she described it. Being that consumed with one person, obsessed enough that nothing else mattered, not even the child your love created... She wanted no part of.

Good thing she didn't have to worry about that anymore.

∽

Elbows on knees, hands folded under his chin, Hank paid minimal attention to Emmet and Julius. Both men were on their respective computers and phones, pooling all their resources to track down Bailey.

While he sat, revisiting all his mistakes. Damn, there were many, the list miles long. It would take years to document them all. So, he concentrated on the mistakes he made with his only child. Wasn't the first time he cataloged everything. However, the truth wasn't something he often visited and could only take in minuscule doses.

The last thirty-six hours had been eye-opening. He was the

reason for all of this—which he already knew and had shoved to the rear of his soul. Avoidance instead of confrontation. Not his forte, but what else could a man do when peering into his daughter's eyes and seeing not an ounce of love?

She didn't hate him. It was much worse than that. Indifference. She didn't care whether he lived or died. And neither did he. He stopped caring after the car explosion took his wife and unborn children. Then Rogers threatened the only thing he had left—the daughter he'd discarded.

How many times had Constance come to him in his dreams? Sometimes angry, sometimes pleading, her silence a damning condemnation. He ignored her. She was gone, and he was here with a child that reminded him of all he'd lost, a child nearly the twin of her mother.

He was a horrible father. He let his paycheck do his parenting and stayed away for years, fostering her hate as if that would keep her safe. It had, yet the price…the price was so high. Too high.

Everything he did and none of it mattered because one of his own had a knife at his throat.

And it was all his fault.

He had to fix it, and there was only one way to do it. A simple text message and he rose. Emmet and Julius didn't even see him leave, which was exactly the way he liked it.

Except, he paused and gave the kid he had raised one final glance, and then he was on his way.

"Hank!" Emmet's shout halted him, and he turned to face him.

Emmet ran up to him. "I think I've figured out her pattern. At each stop, she doesn't take the first available flight. Each flight is a smokescreen designed to make us think she is running scared, but she's not. At least not yet. She used her last alias for the flight to Brazil. She must figure we're following her, and we're hours behind. She can't know we're still in

Germany, tracking her movements until we decide to make a move."

A humorless grin stretched across Emmet's face. Hank had seen that look before, and it didn't bode well for his daughter. It was the same expression he imagined Emmet had witnessed on his face, excitement for the hunt. Hank had no doubt Emmet wouldn't hurt her, but he would make her pay for this foolishness.

"Luck has been on her side," Emmet said. "She's had no delays. Her flight gets into Brazil at eleven a.m. We can't beat her there. *But*, there are three flights from Brazil to Atlanta. I think that's where she's going."

Not buying it, Hank shook his head. "That doesn't make sense. Why go back to her home?"

"The money she took wasn't much. Five thousand dollars will only get you so far." Emmet gripped Hank's arm. "She's your daughter, with plenty of income inherited from her mother. Who's to say she doesn't have her own to-go bag with cash, credit cards, and passports in a different name. Give her some credit, Hank. She's known who you are almost all her life. She knows how to defend herself and knows how to fire a weapon because you made sure your daughter wouldn't be an easy target. You told her you're the only thing keeping her safe, but that's not true. Right now, she is proving she doesn't need any of us to guard her ass. It's misguided but put yourself in her shoes. What would you have done in her position?"

He would've vanished into the ether a long damn time ago.

"I'd bet my left nut she's taken precautions," Emmet continued, the urgency in his voice notching up. "Bailey's returning to Atlanta to collect her shit and vanish. This time, it'll be a lot harder to track her."

Hank's gut clenched. Everything had fallen into place in the worst possible way. He had to salvage it before his daughter paid the price. "Julius, we need to borrow your jet."

CHAPTER 28

"Just my damn luck!" The flight was delayed. Something was wrong with one of the engines. Granted, when flying, having all engines in working order was important, but so was getting to her destination. Bailey had been lucky. Each layover had only been a few hours, and each last-minute booking had gone through without a hitch. Buying first class tickets helped.

She searched the outgoing flight display. There was a flight leaving for L.A. in five hours. That blew her timeline and wouldn't work. Nervous, she chewed on her thumbnail. Her eyes were gritty, and she'd give anything for a shower. Eighteen hours into her mad dash and exhaustion had set in. She hadn't eaten, had barely slept, her nerves were shot. She needed to set foot on American soil, grab the necessities, and hit the road again. Canada was the final destination. Toronto for a few days in an out-of-the-way hostel. Then, she'd throw a dart at a map of the world and travel the world, again.

With no other choice but to wait out the repairs, she found a small bathroom and freshened up as best she could. An overpriced restaurant for some Brazilian cuisine took the edge off her hunger. She told herself not to recheck her voicemails. There really was no point, yet she couldn't stop her fingers from dialing the number.

"*Call me, please.*" Clear and strong, Emmet's voice reached through the connection. "*I want to make sure you're okay. I'm going insane worrying if you're all right. Just let me hear your voice, babe. Please.*" He rattled off his number and ended the call.

It was the "please" that did her in when she knew deleting the call was her best response. Against all logic, without her usual overthinking, she dialed his number.

"Yeah," he barked on the first ring.

That one furious word sent a chill down her spine. All she had to do was hang up, yet she didn't. She hung on listening to him breathe, imagining his fierce expression, and the glint in his frigid eyes.

"Bailey?" The fury in his voice lowered along with his voice. "Don't hang up," he ordered in typical Emmet fashion. "I know it's you. Babe, say something."

She would if she knew what to say. This conversation was never supposed to happen. A clean break was her objective. So, why had she given in and called?

"Fine. Then listen. I'm an idiot. That's what I should have said last night, but I was, um—"

"Arrogant." She supplied.

He snorted, and she imagined a sneer twisting his lips. "That is my default."

The line went silent again, a void filled with the unspoken. Her finger hovered over the red phone icon. A quick touch and—

"I fucked up with you. You know it, and I know it."

She couldn't deny the ego boost his admission provided, but too little. Too late. "That's nice. I can go now."

"Do not hang up!" An implicit threat accompanied his command.

A threat she ignored. "Do not order me. I don't owe you anything, especially not my time."

"Okay! Okay." He backed down. "You're right. You owe me nothing," he spat, and she sensed it took a lot for the admission. "I lied to you."

"Oh yeah?" She deadpanned though her heart lurched. "Should I be honored you admit it?"

His voice low, threatening. "When I said I would walk away and let you live your life, it was a lie. I can't walk away. I'm not strong enough."

A sob crawled up her throat, which she bit back. This was just another lie. "You don't have to walk away because *I* already did."

"And there's a hole in my heart because of it." His voice cracked as if he'd given up the fight. "I love you, Bailey."

"Don't you dare!" she hissed, cried, sobbed, all three at once from the shock of hearing those words exit his mouth.

"I love you, babe," he shouted into the phone.

Hot and cold all at once, goosebumps flashed over her skin.

"And I'm coming for you. Whatever rock you crawl under, I'm crawling under it with you. Understand me?"

A shiver jolted her as she sniffed, refusing to shed a single tear. She knew what those last two words meant, but she couldn't accept it. Wouldn't accept what he'd offered.

"You don't love me. You don't know me. We've been together for what? Two weeks? Less than two weeks?" God, she couldn't string a coherent thought together all because he said, "I love you."

In a voice threaded with passion she had to concentrate not to go up in flames, he said, "I think I've loved you my entire life. I just hadn't met you yet."

Her ovaries exploded, taking whatever common sense she had with it. "That's such bullshit! You're just trying to get in my head." Every head in the restaurant turned her way, drawing attention she didn't need. She threw some cash, U.S. currency, on the table and left.

"You've been in my head from the moment Hank told me he had a daughter."

"I'm a job for you, nothing more. You were hired to protect me and walk away when the job ended." She powered down the mezzanine, people darted out of her way or risked getting run over. "Well, the job is over."

"The job is not over!" he snarled.

"Then you're fired."

"Tell me that in person...while I'm inside you." He tacked on.

Her steps faltered because she felt him, thrusting deep inside her, the need sharp enough to draw blood. Her core throbbed. Leaning against a pillar to catch her breath, she halted short of her gate. The passengers were all lined up, waiting to board the plane. The conversation was over, except she pressed the phone closer to her ear, afraid she might miss a single word he said.

"What do you want, Bailey? Tell me what you want, and it's yours," he purred in that rough voice she adored.

That was easy. She wanted to be happy, wanted to believe every ridiculous word he'd spewed. She wanted to be happy, safe. To be loved. Loved by him.

"I want Rogers dead and you in my arms, in my bed, in my life, because that's where you belong. With me. We are not done. You know it. I know it."

Standing in the middle of the mezzanine, her eyes slipped closed, and she imagined that life he'd laid out. A life where they woke up every morning in the same bed. A life where she wasn't unwanted. A life where someone belonged to her as she belonged to him. A life with Emmet.

"Where are you, Bailey? Tell me, and I'll meet you anywhere in the world. Anywhere, babe."

God, dare she believe him?

"You trusted me once with your body and your heart. Trust me one more time. I swear you will not regret it."

"I'm in Brazil," she blurted and listened to his sigh of relief.

"Are you safe?"

"Yeah. I'm safe." Even though she'd handed herself over to the man she'd sworn to escape. An announcement came over the PA system. "I have to go. My plane is boarding."

"Where are you going, Bailey? Where can I meet you?" he said in a tone meant to whittle her resolve.

She chewed her lip, stalling, even though she knew it was too late to pretend he couldn't figure out where she was headed. It was also too late to deny what was in her heart. "Atlanta. Flight 3005."

"I'll be waiting for you in Atlanta."

"Okay," she squeaked out and ended the call before more insanity slipped out. "What have I done?" Horrified, her knees gave out, and she plopped into a chair while the plane boarded.

Just because you said you'd meet him in Atlanta doesn't mean you have to. Head for the exit and keep walking. Brazil is a vast country to get lost in.

Except, she wasn't a coward…and she couldn't live with herself not knowing if what he said was the truth or all a huge lie.

She climbed to her feet and got to the back of the dwindling line.

CHAPTER 29

Bailey stepped off the plane a raw bundle of nerves mixed with utter exhaustion. She never wanted to see another airplane, especially not the coach section.

"Excuse me. Excuse me."

People pushed ahead of her on the gangway. Hartsfield-Jackson was one of the busiest airports in the country, a hub for connections all over the country. But this late in the afternoon, most probably wanted to go home, or the next hotel to rest. She wanted the latter. A full night's sleep in her own bed. Didn't mean she'd get it.

She'd come to a decision on her long flight from Brazil. When she saw him, regardless of how her heart skipped a beat or how desire spilled into her bloodstream, the ball was in his court. Everything depended on what he had to say—and it had better be fucking epic because she didn't have two shits to spare.

He said he loved her, well he'd damn well had better prove it or get the hell out of her way. She was done running, and she had not a single tear to spare.

Love shouldn't make you cry.

Love shouldn't make you run.

She exited the gangway and panned the semi-empty waiting area. Her gaze tripped over Emmet waiting next to a metal column. Dark gray suit, white shirt, and silver tie, beneath a leather duster, did little to hide the hard body hidden beneath the clothing, and every woman that glanced his way wanted a taste.

He'd shaved since she'd seen him and as she suspected, his square jaw only added to his rugged handsomeness. And yeah, her heart did skip a stupid beat. And desire had her slick and achy.

She moseyed up to him, raked her gaze from the top of his fresh haircut to the laces on his leather shoes, and kept going. He could stop her, or he could join her, which one he chose, she didn't have the energy to care.

"I deserved that," Emmet murmured when he fell in line beside her. He took her carry-on and together, they moved through the airport to an Aston Martin parked illegally at the curb. The perfect gentleman, he opened the passenger door for her. She paused. Not wanting to be blindsided, she asked, "Where's Hank?"

"He's home."

Good. That meant he was far, far away, probably on the other side of the world. Dealing with Hank would wait for another day if that day ever came. She dropped into the passenger seat, allowing Emmet to close the door. He turned to the airport security guard hovering near the trunk of the car.

In the side mirror, she watched a slick pay off as they shook hands. Emmet deposited her luggage in the trunk, circled to the driver's seat, and lowered his body inside.

He did not start the car. White knuckling the steering wheel, he sat while she stared ahead at the speeding cars on the highway off in the distance. Two minutes passed with his deep breathing the only sound in the car. She didn't want to deal with this, was too damn wasted for the brewing argument. So much for his declaration of love. Her bullshit meter was never wrong.

His head cranked around, and the heat of his gaze drilled into her. Unafraid, she met that heat and braced for his anger. And he had plenty, yet along with his anger came concern and relief, and…

Emmet reached for her at the same time she reached for him. Not sure who kissed who, she absorbed the feel of his mouth on hers, taking what she willingly gave. Tongues snaking against each other. He gripped a handful of her hair, angled her head, and thrust his tongue deeper, rougher. She groaned, clawed at him, not for air because she didn't need to breathe, didn't need anything except for him to never stop.

He eased back, breaking their connection in increments, then came back for another blistering kiss. Gradually, he retreated with a final nip to her bottom lip, and a lick to soothe the sting.

Rough fingers gently stroked her face as if he missed her as much as she missed him.

"Had to do that. Couldn't think straight until I touched you." He licked into her mouth a last time. "And before I drag you over my knee and spank you."

With that husky voice of his, a spanking didn't sound too bad. He swept her hair behind her ears and gripped her head in both of his hands. Foreheads pressed together, those eyes of his glittered like spotlights. She couldn't look away. "All right. You proved your point. I'm an idiot," he griped.

"You said that already and I completely agree. You are an idiot."

"This has been the longest thirty-six hours of my life. No one is walking away from anyone. Understand me."

He said he loved her. Tracked her down from across the globe to prove it. Well, she had no intention of laying down and spreading her legs. "You threatened to walk away first. I beat you to it."

"Like I said, I was an idiot."

"And now you're not?"

Emmet snorted and nipped her chin. He released her, and she plopped back into her seat as the car purred to life and Emmet peeled away from the curb. "Shouldn't have done that there." He checked the mirrors, his game face—a blank slate completely unreadable—was in place. "Should've waited," said more to himself than to her.

"Glad you didn't." She settled into the chair and closed her eyes. "Technically, this is called kidnapping."

"Yes. It. Is." That note in his voice was pleasure and not the good kind where they both got off.

"How angry at me are you?"

He merged onto the highway and opened her up. The V12 engine ate up the road. "I'm not angry. I'm furious."

She side-eyed him. "You always kiss the people you're furious at?"

A muscle flexed in his very attractive jaw. "You are not people."

Pleased, she stared at his arrogant profile. "Good to know I'm not *people*." A smile flitted around his not so neutral mouth. "Are there levels to this furious?"

He swerved around a mustang loitering in the left lane. "Are you asking if I have a temper?" He spared her a glance. "I'm a hitman, Bailey."

The roar of the engine drowned out whatever he mumbled under his breath. She settled into the heated leather seat. "I want a pizza, a shower, and to sleep for a week." She let him drive a while then noticed they were headed in the opposite direction of her house. "Where are you taking me?"

"Hotel."

She groaned, too weary to do much else. "I don't want to go to another hotel, or another chalet, or another fucking cruise. I want to go home."

"Not happening."

"It is happening," she said calmly. "I'm tired of running. I want to go home."

"I said no." Menace oozed from him.

Unafraid, she sighed. "Give in. I'm just going to run again."

"Wrong thing to say to me. Give in." He snorted. "I've never *given in* to anything. And I won't start now. "

"Fine. You have to sleep sometime."

"And so do you."

"I am quite rested," she lied. "How about you? I think I see some bags under your eyes. She tucked her legs under her and shifted all the way around in the seat, then sat up sharply. "Actually, you're exhausted. Pull over and let me drive."

"To the hotel?" He snickered, ignoring her order.

She snorted and let him get away with it. "Sure. The one closest to my house."

He barked out a dry laugh and slowed to turn into a Motel 6. He parked under the awning, made a pit stop at the trunk, then walked around the car to help her out. "Really? We're staying here?"

His answer was to take her hand and guide her inside.

"May I help you?" The desk clerk asked as soon as the glass doors opened.

"We have a reservation under Smith." In no time at all, they were on the way to the hotel room where Emmet placed a camera with a view of the door. "We can leave now."

Well, that confused her. She did a double take between him, the door, and the camera, but in the end, she didn't resist him guiding her back to the car.

Three more times they repeated the process at Best Western, Holiday Inn, and The Radisson. "Where to now? High-end hotels on the other side of town, now that we've covered the lower end of the spectrum?" She yawned.

"And I have bags under my eyes?" he said with a 'pot calling the kettle black' tone, then he handed her his unlocked phone. "Call for a pizza."

Her grin hurt her face as she dialed the family-owned pizza restaurant a few miles from her house. He took I-285. Traffic was the usual nightmare, but he handled it like he handled everything, with skill. In half the time it would've taken her, he got off at her exit.

Familiar streets rolled by, streets with no hotels in the area, streets that led to her home. She glanced at him and noted the slight smirk on his mouth. "You planned on bringing me here all along."

"You left me and flew across the world to get back home. Far be it from me to keep you from your goal. For now." He stressed the last two words.

Bailey folded her arms. "So, all that bitching about me going home was for show? You wanted to piss me off."

His lips twitched. "Not at all."

Her gated community came into view. Emmet pulled in and nodded at the security guard, who opened the gate much faster than he ever had for her.

Shocked and annoyed, she asked, "You've been here before?"

"Yes. Once I figured out your destination. I beat you here by a few hours. I had a chance to check out your house."

She glared at him. "Check out my house? You mean break into my house."

"Semantics. My objective was to secure your home."

Thank God she cleaned it before leaving for Jamaica, and she couldn't fault him for going into protective mode when she skipped out of Germany. "And did you?"

"Tight as a drum, though a rocket to the front door won't make a difference." He coasted down the quiet streets at a sedate pace.

"Does Rogers have access to those kinds of weapons stateside?"

"Of course he does."

Damn it. So much for spending the night in her own bed.

"Doubtful he'd use it. A kill like that on US soil would draw too much attention."

Interesting. "What's too much attention?"

"FBI, CIA, NSA, White House. The trickle up effect would be massive. The damage control would take all of us out."

Her blood ran cold. "Take all of you out?"

He parked alongside her curb, short of her driveway, and turned to face her. "We work for the government, which branch, I'm not sure of. We're not sanctioned. We do what is asked, and we are paid extremely well. There are rules, not many, but rules we must live by. Primary rule: draw no attention. Do what we do in secret. The world is not supposed to know we exist. Discovery means—"

"Death." She finished for him.

"Worse. Congressional hearings and prosecution. Understand me?"

That wasn't worse than death, yet she nodded anyway. It's not like she didn't know that already, on some barely submerged level, she knew. But hearing it... "Yes. I understand."

Emmet pulled out a tablet from the door panel. A few taps brought up the interior of her house and a readout.

"Anything interesting?" she asked. He ignored her and kept scanning. "It's unnerving having someone rifle through your home without your presence or permission."

"You'll get over it." He closed the tablet and hit the garage door opener, *her* garage door opener.

"My car too, huh?"

He pulled into the garage and parked next to her Escape. Ever the gentleman, he circled the car to open her door. "Welcome home."

He stood close, inside her bubble. She caught his scent, the slightly musky, piney scent of him, and breathed him in.

"I missed you," he murmured.

All of her went loose, and she swayed. His arms circled her waist, pulling her into his body, where she wanted to be. Yeah, she was home, in more ways than the obvious.

An old Honda Civic rolled to a stop, blocking the driveway. Emmet had his gun in his hand and shoved her behind him within a blink.

Bailey grabbed his gun hand. "Do not kill my pizza guy!" she hissed in Emmet's ear and moved around him to intercept the seventeen-year-old driver.

"Thanks, Mikey." She took the box from him. "Tell your grandmother I said hi and put it on my tab with a thirty percent tip for you."

"Oh, thank you, Miss Monroe." His braces on full display.

"That won't be necessary." Emmet handed over a hundred dollar bill and took the pizza from Bailey and headed inside.

His jaw unhinged, and he fingered the bill like it was his first girlfriend. "All of this is for me?"

She slapped Mikey on the shoulder. "You earned it. Now, drive safely."

Mikey skipped back to his car while Bailey caught up with Emmet in the kitchen. She opened the box and shoved a warm bit of saucy, cheesy, heaven into her mouth.

"You make that same sound when I'm inside you. Only deeper."

She sputtered and nearly choked, but he was there with a bottle of water from her fridge and a pat to her back. "You are so bad." She managed to say once she could breathe again.

With pizza in hand, she kicked off her sneakers in the kitchen, shucked off her coat in the living room. Her socks didn't make it to the stairs, and her pants didn't survive the climb. By the time she entered her bedroom, with her brass bed and floral duvet, she had a quarter of the crust left and only her bra and panties on.

She downed the rest of her food, got naked, and stepped into her shower. "Holy!" she shouted when frigid water pelted her body but heated quickly. A squirt of Butterfly Flower shower gel into her shower puff and she checked off the second box on her Want List.

On the other side of the wet glass door, Emmet stood in the middle of the room, watching, the heat in his eyes as palpable as the lust arcing between them from across the room. She hadn't invited him to join her, yet. She wanted his lust as she soaped her body with languid strokes emulating what she wanted him to do to her. So much for him proving anything. An 'I love you' and an 'I missed you' and getting him naked was all she could think about. Damn, she really was a pushover when it came to him.

He shucked his jacket off, folded it neatly and laid it on the countertop. Next came his tie and then he started on the buttons of his shirt. One button at a time, pale skin and hard pecs came into view.

Her hands slipped from her nipples down her stomach to part her folds and slipped inside.

Three chimes sounded, and they both froze. The chimes repeated. She realized it was his phone before he stopped his striptease and reached into an inner pocket of his folded jacket.

"Are you serious?" The foreplay stopped, and she glared, dumbfounded at being bypassed for a phone call.

Eyes still smoldering, the crotch of his pants straining against the bulge beneath the fine fabric, Emmet held up a finger. "One minute. Dave shouldn't be calling me. If he is, it has to be important." He swiped his thumb across the screen. "Better be good, Dave," he spat with his gaze locked on her.

Who the hell is Dave?

The spray of the water striking the tile and her body drowned out Dave's precise words, but not the urgency. That and the sudden non-sexual tension filling the air.

"He did what?" Emmet shouted. "Is he still at his house?" Pause. "Well, find out." Pause. "I swear to God, Dave, I will gut you if you don't spit it out!"

Bailey stepped back under the spray, quickly washing away the suds and all lingering desire.

"Where is Rogers? If you know where Hank is, you know where Rogers is."

Bailey opened the glass door and snatched a towel from the rack. That one went around her body, while a second towel went around her wet hair as Emmet buttoned his shirt and snatched up his jacket.

She followed him out of the bathroom to her walk-in closet, shocked to see two unknown hard-shell suitcases in the rear right corner. He grabbed the larger of the two and dragged it into the bedroom.

"He cleared customs? How long ago?"

Bailey pulled on some underwear.

"Two hours ago!"

A pair of black leggings with a matching long-sleeved hoodie.

"He could be there already!" Hank opened the case, revealing a wide array of weaponry.

Sneakers and socks. Black socks, and she opted for the black sneakers over the white and black Adidas.

"Where's Whiskey?" Pause.

Bailey took the opportunity to shake out her wet hair. It would have to dry on the plane. God, where were they flying to now? So much for wanting her own bed.

"Fine," Emmet spat while picking up a Glock. "I got this." He ended the call and dialed another number. "What the fuck, Hank!"

Tense pause, then, his voice low, promising pain, he said, "I'm going to kill you and enjoy every moment of your agony."

He wasn't talking to Hank. Was Hank even alive?

"Oh, I'll be there. I'm getting in the car right now. I'll see you soon." He tossed the phone on the bed.

She touched his shoulder. "Is he still alive?"

A muscle ticked in his jaw. "There was a shout in the background. It could've been him, I don't know. Doesn't matter, I'm going in."

Of course, he was, she never had a doubt. "Where are we flying to now?" she asked, mainly to know what she needed to pack, cold or tropical gear. Or should she wait to buy what she needed when they arrived at their destination?

"*We* are not flying anywhere." He shrugged on a shoulder holster and filled both sides with Glocks and spare ammo.

"I'm going with you." She double knotted her laces.

"No. You're not."

Her wet hair went into a topknot. "I don't know what's going on. You can tell me on the plane." Her coat was downstairs. She could pick it up on the way to the garage.

Emmet snatched her to him. His grip on her forearms unbreakable. "Hank is in deep shit."

She tried not to snort and failed. "I figured. He's the only reason you'd drop everything and take off."

His grip loosened, and he stroked up and down her arms. "He's not the only person I'd drop everything for, Bailey. You know that."

She cupped his face and brought their foreheads together. "I do know that, and I understand. I will never see him as my father, but you see him as yours. And that's okay. At least he was a father to someone, even if it wasn't me."

He slanted his mouth across hers in a hard, fierce kiss, which was much too brief. "Time is short, and I have to go."

"*We* have to go." He opened his mouth to argue, and she didn't want to hear it. "I'll stay on the plane until you both return. Now, where are we going and is Whiskey meeting us there?"

"There is no plane, Bailey."

"How are we going to get to Hank in time without a plane?" Then it dawned on her that he must be within driving distance. "Okay. Let's get in the car, and you can fill me in on the details."

She pulled away, but he held fast. "*I* don't need a car."

What the hell? That makes no sense. Except... She lived in a gated community, which surrounded a more affluent gated community. A community she'd never visited because she didn't know anyone who lived on the other side of those hallowed walls. Fuck! She lived half a block away from the manned gate. She could see the brick wall keeping her out from her backyard.

"Hank lives six blocks in that direction." He pointed out her bedroom window. "He bought his house one month after you purchased your house. You two used the same realtor."

Her jaw unhinged, and her mouth dropped open. "You have got to be fucking kidding me," she snarled and wrenched free.

"He was never far from you, Bailey. He loves you, always has."

"Yeah, loved me so much he drove past my house every day, on the way to Casa Murray." She pressed her thumbs to her temples to ease a budding migraine.

"It's not like that, babe."

"How is it not like that? How can you possibly not see how that's exactly how it is?"

Her heart ached. Her father was so close, yet still a thousand miles away. It didn't have to be that way, but it was what it was and hating Hank was draining. "Forget it. Let's stick to what we have to do." Plus, this wasn't about Hank. It was about Emmet. That's who she risked her life for because he'd risked his life for her.

Emmet let her go and returned to his case full of weapons.

"Sometime after you ran, Hank sent a message to Rogers on the dark web. It was an invitation to meet him at his home and settle things. Whiskey is in London where we sent him in case you showed up at Daisy's house. I have no backup and no idea who else Rogers has with him. I'm alone, but I'm going in there, and I'm going to bring him back alive because I have to. He's the only father I've ever known."

She nodded slowly, her heartbreaking for him, and Hank. Strange how things come full circle. "You are not alone." She picked up an H&K, checked the magazine, and chambered a round. "Let's go save your father."

CHAPTER 30

"You are not going!" Towering over her, in a useless attempt at intimidation, Emmet pointed a finger in her face.

Hands on hips, Bailey weathered Hurricane Emmet. "You've wasted five minutes we don't have with this tirade."

"I didn't waste anything. In the five minutes since you dropped this idiocy, the sun has set." He flung a hand at the bedroom window while raking the other hand through his hair.

She glanced out the window, and he was right. The late afternoon had turned into early evening. "Oh. Well, let's get going." She headed to the bedroom door only to be hauled back, again.

"Put this on." He shoved a bulletproof vest into her arms, clearly not pleased, yet giving into her.

That was easy. Almost too easy, though instead of bringing attention to how quickly he caved, she followed his instructions. Over her head, arms through the opening, the vest was too big, but that didn't stop him from tightening the Velcro tabs as best he could. She didn't stop him as he obsessed over it. She studied his eyelashes, envious of their length, and his furrowed brow. Did he know he had a single gray hair at his temple or was it so new, he hadn't seen it? Then there was his mouth. It was an angry slash, slightly fuller on the bottom and tasted utterly amazing. She hadn't paused to appreciate his smooth, angular jaw, and did so now. However, she missed his beard.

Maybe I can coax him to grow it back.

He handed her another gun, wrapped his arms around her to slip one into the small of her back. A shiver went up her spine at the touch of the cold metal on her warm skin.

"All right. Let's go." Without another word, he was out the bedroom door.

"Wait." She ran to keep up with him. "Where's your bulletproof vest?"

"Only had the one." He stopped in the living room to retrieve their coats.

One vest and he gave it to her.

"This isn't Texas, so we can't walk the streets armed to the teeth." He pulled on his leather duster and waited for her to do the same with a long wool coat from the hall closet, then ushered her out the front door.

Early evening, the neighborhood was busy with families arriving. A few of her neighbors waved to her, and they both waved back. Just two people taking an evening stroll with six guns between the two of them. Even with skin to metal contact warming the gun, she'd swear she had a Popsicle shoved down her ass.

They approached the security hut situated in the middle of the road in front of two black iron gates. One for entry. One for egress.

"Must be nice," she grumbled, earning a laugh from Emmet.

"Good evening, Lee," Emmet said to the guard, who seemed pleased at his presence.

"Mr. Streeter. How are you, sir?" Lee stretched out a hand.

Emmet seemed all too happy to give the guy a shake. "Good, and you?"

"Fine. Can't complain. Thanks again for the reservations at the Crown Plaza. My wife loved the anniversary surprise."

"It was my pleasure," Emmet said with a nonchalant shrug.

Lee glanced at Bailey and back at Emmet. "Umm? No car, sir?"

Emmet hitched a thumb in the direction they'd come from. "My girlfriend lives around the corner. I want to introduce her to Mr. Murray."

"Oh, that's nice. I'll let you in." He punched in a code, and the gate opened slowly.

"Anyone else come calling on Mr. Murray?"

"Yes. Two gentlemen passed through about ten minutes ago. Mr. Murray was expecting them. Want me to call and let him know you're coming," Lee asked as they walked through the open gate.

"Don't, I want to surprise him."

"All right. Well, you two have a nice evening," Lee shouted and closed the gate.

"Four blocks straight and two blocks to the left. It's the only house at the end of the cul-de-sac." They took off at a steady pace.

The night was balmy for late February in the Atlanta suburbs. A comfortable fifty degrees. A great evening to walk the dog as a few people were doing. With plenty of witnesses, it was a great way to be arrested if things went sideways.

"Stupid question. Are these weapons registered?" Meaning, are they legal?

The asinine glare he threw her way questioned her sanity. "Go back home, Bailey."

She ignored him and asked, "Where do you live?"

"I have a condo downtown, but I visit here often."

"Bachelor pad, huh? Am I gonna have to have a bonfire with your bed as the centerpiece?"

He scoffed. "Quid pro quo, babe."

"No problem. I wanted to redecorate." Her heart was in her throat, and not because of the fast pace. "I'm thinking four posts. Sturdy wood you can tie me to."

His steps faltered, but he kept his attention focused on the road ahead. "We can do that."

"Tomorrow, okay?"

His steps slowed, then stopped, and he captured her face between his cold palms. "Tomorrow we'll get up in the morning, have a big breakfast, and I will take you shopping for anything you want."

Tomorrow. They were going to have a tomorrow. "You promise." Not a question, but a plea.

A glint she could only label as menacing flared in the depths of his brilliant eyes. "I swear to you. We *will* have a tomorrow," he said fiercely, and she believed him.

It may be nothing more than spun sugar sprinkled with fairy dust during a thunderstorm, but it was all she had to hold onto.

"Excuse me."

Hands on her weapons, she spun, only to have Emmet haul her back and block her with his body from a skinny teen with a red mohawk holding up a cell phone.

"Are you Emmet?" The teen asked.

"Who's asking?"

"Someone paid me a grand to call and let them know when you showed up. Pay me more, and I'll tell them you showed up alone, without your friend." He tipped his head at Bailey.

The soft click of his safety releasing alerted her to the gun in Emmet's hand, at his side. That smooth, she hadn't even realized he slipped one of his Glocks free.

"What's to stop me from venting your head and leaving you in the bushes?"

"I check in every ten minutes. My next check-in is forty seconds away."

Emmet took out his wallet and handed him all his cash and a

debit card. "Pin number is 4534. You tell your contact I'm not here and everything in the account is yours."

"Can't do that in thirty seconds, man."

"True, but you don't make that call, you'll be dead in thirty seconds, so which one will it be? Enough cash to set you for life or death in twenty seconds? Your decision."

The teen dialed a number, thus ending the shortest standoff in history. "No sign of him. Yeah. Call you in ten." The teen ran down the street.

"How much money is in that account?"

"Fifty K, give or take. This is where we part ways, babe."

Her muscles locked onto her bones and she couldn't move, couldn't breathe.

"Hank's is two houses down and around the around the corner, but he has cameras blanketing the area starting past this point all the way to his house. Cut between these two houses to the backyard, then veer left for three more houses to the stone colonial on the left. There's a shed in the backyard. Enter through the rear of the shed. Code 25958 for the lock. Under the table is another lock. Code 19393 will give you access to the offsite weapon cache, and a tunnel leading to the laundry room in the house. I want you to stay there and guard the escape route."

Her head bobbed up and down. "Okay." His plan seemed semi-decent. She could get with it, except— "You're coming with me."

His blank face gave nothing away. "I'm going through the front door."

The man had a death wish. "Oh, no, you're not."

"He thinks I'm at my condo, downtown. A half an hour away, and that's with good traffic. That gives us some time to work. They won't expect us early."

She gripped his lapels and went up on her tiptoes. "That means you have enough time to come with me through the damn tunnel." He opened his mouth to utter more nonsense, and she covered his mouth with her hand. "Cut the crap. The only reason you're doing this is to protect me. You are not going to walk through the front door so they can use you as target practice," she yelled. "We are going through the tunnel, Emmet."

He sighed, defeated, and pried her hand off his mouth and off his lapel. "All right. Follow me."

Ducking low, they cut between two houses, one occupied, the other dark, they circled around to the back gate where he punched in a code to a cipher lock. Soundlessly, the high gate swung open.

"No cameras back here?" she asked, darting around a covered pool.

"The house is in my name. We have a retired couple that lives in Ecuador during the winter and pretends to own the house during the summer. There are cameras, but they're on a separate system, so if one system were compromised, the other system wouldn't be."

The red and white wooden shed came into view. Another cipher lock and they were inside. Lawn mower, hedge trimmer, along with an assortment of gardening tools. It was an ordinary shed until Emmet pressed a panel next to the light switch and a hidden steel door appeared at the rear.

"This is very James Bondesque," she whispered.

"Tip of the iceberg, babe." He punched in 19393, and the door retracted into the wall, revealing metal stairs leading to a basement. Light flickered on as they descended into a room filled with an array of weaponry and ammo lining the walls. Glocks, Smith and Wesson, H&K, an assortment of AR-15s, and knives captured her attention. She had no idea what everything was—some looked downright wicked—and made a slow turn to take it all in.

"Should we take any of—"

The clank of a door opening and quickly closing spun her

around. Emmet was gone like he was never there. *Son of a bitch!* Bailey raised her fists to pound on the door and stopped. She couldn't risk making a racket, attracting attention that could get Emmet killed.

"Damn you!" she muttered, the hopelessness of the situation choking her.

She returned to the rows of shelves lining the walls of the basement. She was in a candy shop, but she had no idea what half of them could do or how to use them. She did recognize the missile launcher. That would get the door open and probably kill her, not to mention alert Rogers to Emmet's presence.

She went back upstairs and tried the door at the top. It opened easy enough. He hadn't completely trapped her. He'd prevented her from following him through the tunnel and into the house. It was two against one, with Hank probably injured, if not dead.

Emmet counted on her staying put, but she had to do something. Something to help. *Anything.* Nothing came to her. Until her gaze skipped over the grenades, and the stupidest idea in the entire world lodged in her brain.

CHAPTER 31

The objective was to never bring the job home. What one did outside the four walls of their castle should never affect those inside the castle. That being said, if danger foolishly followed you home, destroy it with immense prejudice.

Exactly what Emmet planned.

Seven billion people on the globe and he cared about two. Bailey was trapped safe and sound in the weapons locker. *Not looking forward to that conversation when I let her out, but she'd be alive.* As would Hank be once Emmet killed Rogers and Ivan. If Hank survived.

That was the real reason he couldn't bring her with him. The real reason Hank drew Rogers back to his home, where Hank would end Rogers, even if it meant ending himself.

"Precaution my ass." That's how he sold the insane idea to Emmet. At which he moved out. Being a hitman was dangerous without adding explosive devices to the mix.

Never thought Hank would be one for self-sacrifice.

The panel next to the washer swung open with a soft squeak. A quick scan of the room confirmed what he already knew. It was empty. Zelda and her cleaning crew came three days a week and today wasn't one of those days. Without them bustling around the house, cleaning everything, no one had a reason to be in the basement at the washer and dryer. He paused outside of the room and took in the silence.

Hank had spent a lot of money soundproofing the house for a scenario exactly like this. One didn't need a hostage screaming their head off, bringing the cops to the party. Never imagined Hank would be the hostage.

Soundproofing was great to keep the outside world from encroaching. Not great when the same soundproofing isolated him inside the house. A house Rogers had been inside of.

Quietly, he climbed the basement stairs and emerged inside of the empty kitchen. Flattened against the side of the refrigerator, he waited for the camera discreetly mounted in the light fixture to circle away from him.

He ducked on the other side of the island, peered into the breakfast nook, and peered into the empty great room with a panoramic view of the backyard until he timed his movements to the camera focused on the parts of the room the camera in the kitchen failed to reach. He darted through the dead zone to the blackout curtains. Once the great room was cleared, he veered into the formal dining room. Empty and again, he closed the blackout curtains.

Yes, it let whoever followed in his footsteps know he'd been there, which was better than risking some dog walker stumbling upon the kind of activity their gated community promised to protect them from. Their little war had to remain private.

The doorbell rang and echoed throughout the house. *Who the fuck?* So much for protecting the public. Whomever the unlucky bastard was, he'd leave a thank you on their headstone. The soft swoosh of a door opening alerted him to someone exiting the study on the other side of the house. Footsteps crossed the foyer, heavy, male, but he was out of position, on the other side of the room, away from the door, for any kind of shot.

Quiet as he could, he dashed across the room, guns in both hands. All he needed was a shot and— "Hank! Hank!" *Bang. Bang. Bang.* "Open the damn door. I know you're in there. You are a sorry excuse for a father, and I'm finally gonna say it to your face."

"God damn it, Bailey," Emmet muttered in disbelief. Instead of reading the memo and staying put, she'd handed herself over to the man who wanted her dead.

Locks flipped, and the door opened.

"Who the fuck are you and where is my shitty father? Hank! Get out of my way." Cold air preceded her clipped footsteps marching across the marble, drowned out briefly by the slamming of the front door.

Bailey came into view. She was windblown and breathless, her coat fanning out around her as if she'd run all the way from the shed. She stomped deep into the foyer, screaming, "Hank!"

Ivan followed her in and stopped behind Bailey, blocking Emmet's shot. "Rogers," Ivan bellowed, "Look who came calling."

"I thought you were Rogers," Bailey said, angling her head for a better view of the second floor.

"Stupid bitch. You should've stayed away. You were going to be dessert. Now, you're the appetizer." Ivan grabbed her by the back of the head and slammed her onto the table in the center of the foyer and pinned her to the surface.

Rage almost propelled him forward to rip Ivan's arm from his body and beat him with the appendage. Instinct placed a leash on his rage. Ivan wasn't a threat to Bailey, at least not until Rogers had a turn at her.

Bailey was a lot of things. Stupid wasn't one of them. She had a plan. He'd give her an opportunity to let her plan play out and pray her sacrificial lamb routine didn't get her killed.

Something thudded upstairs, a struggle of some sort, then the doors to the library opened. "Bring her up, I want to enjoy this reunion before I gut her," Rogers shouted from inside the room, not giving Emmet a shot from his location.

Library, second floor to the right. Hank had converted two bedrooms a few months ago to make the space. Entrance in the hallway and entrance through the sitting room in the master bedroom. All this information flashed at lightning speed through Emmet's brain, though he wasn't entirely sure of the interior layout of the room.

Ivan released Bailey and stepped back with his gun lowered because she wasn't a threat. Emmet knew better.

Bailey groaned and slid off the table, except the table tilted with her, which shouldn't have happened, not with how sturdy it was built. Her one hundred and twenty pounds shouldn't have budged the thing, unless…

"Dumb ass, don't get yourself killed before I have a chance to fuck you," Ivan grumbled and watched the table and Bailey hit the floor. She rolled, seemed to get tangled in her coat, and came up with the gun Emmet had tucked into the small of her back.

Firing at a target on a range never prepared you for firing at a human being close up, in your face. Bailey paused, the gun steady in her hand, though her eyes were wide, frozen, along with the rest of her. Ivan didn't freeze. He was already diving to the ground and bringing up his own gun.

Emmet stormed into the foyer. Two bullets: one to the temple, the other to the neck, and Ivan dropped. Emmet stood over the body, in case Ivan played possum. He risked a glance at Bailey.

Gunfire erupted from the second floor—from two different directions. Rogers had more than Ivan as backup. From her position still on the damn floor, Bailey aimed at someone over Emmet's head on the second floor. "Move, Emmet!" She fired, the cold-blooded intensity on her face was a definite turn on.

He ducked and kept moving forward, reaching for her.

"I want her alive!" Rogers shouted from the library. "Alive gets you an extra million. Bring me Emmet's corpse." Which bought Bailey more breathing time and Emmet, not so much.

Gunfire came from the living room behind Bailey. A bullet grazed Emmet's ear. He let himself fall to the side, his weapon on the body rushing from the living room. Two to the head and the body dropped in a messy sprawl.

Behind him, something tumbled down the staircase as Bailey lunged to her feet.

"You're hit," she said above the buzzing in his ear.

"Grazed. Not hit." He glued her to his side and headed for the living room. Once clear of the archway, he shoved her against the nearest wall and took a quick scan, grateful for the moonlight infusing the room. "Where is your vest?" he demanded.

She threw up her hands. "Well, I couldn't stroll in here like a sacrificial lamb with a bulletproof vest on."

All those flying bullets could've killed her. That's what lodged in his brain. He grabbed her by the collar, shook her hard — "I should've hogtied you," he said harshly and smashed their lips together for a fierce kiss. "Guard my back."

Emmet peered out of the archway at the two bodies leaking blood on the marble floor. "Two dead. Did you get the one you aimed at?"

"Yes."

"Good job." On your first kill, he didn't add.

Behind him, she exhaled on the back of his neck. "He would've killed you if I hadn't."

He wanted to hug her, let her know he was grateful. Now wasn't the time.

Gun went off upstairs, followed by a harsh groan. "That was a flesh wound to his thigh. He already has a knife stuck in his wrist on the hand with two fingers missing. How much more do you think he can take? I plan on finding out. Let me take off his gag so they can hear you scream."

"Go. To. Hell," Hank choked out ten seconds later.

"Only after you pave the way." Rogers laughed, followed by Hank's groan.

"Five men in total, Emmet!" Hank got out.

"You're gonna pay for that."

A garbled cry came from Hank, then cut off. Bailey fisted Emmet's shirt and buried her head in his shoulder.

"Two million to the one who brings me his daughter's head."

She gasped, and her entire body trembled against his. "Not going to happen, babe. He's not even gonna get close to you."

"He's gonna kill him," she whispered furiously. "What are we gonna do?"

He had no fucking idea. They had to get upstairs, which left them as sitting ducks, a risk he could take, but a risk he wouldn't place Bailey in.

A shadow moved to the right and melted into the theatre room. He pointed his guns in that direction only to have Bailey knock his arm out of her way. A grenade in her hand with the damn pin out, she lobbed it into the theatre room.

"Jesus!" He snatched her back and together, they headed in the opposite direction. The explosion rocked the entire house and pitched them back into the hallway. Together they skidded back into the foyer and slammed into the side of the staircase. The first explosion was followed by a second one that collapsed the ceiling and caused the Jacuzzi bathtub and shower in the master bathroom to fall through.

"What's going on? I didn't think it would be that powerful," she screamed as they struggled to their feet.

"It's not. The house is rigged."

"Rigged with what?"

"Rigged to explode."

"Why?" Single word.

"Contingency plan. Plan of last resort."

"You should've told me that before I threw the grenade!"

"I didn't know you had a grenade!"

"Grenades. Plural. I have one more."

Great! She was as crazy as Hank.

Another explosion destroyed the front of the house, blocking the exit and flinging them to their knees. A fourth explosion took out the lanai porch, destroying any chance of escaping through the rear of the house.

"The tunnel." Hands clasped, they rushed to their feet. Emmet dragged her behind him, only to stop in front of the demolished great room. There wasn't another way to the kitchen, the tunnel leading to the shed, not even to the garage.

But something wasn't right. With all the damage, the house should've collapsed already. They should've been buried. There was nothing random about the destruction. Each explosion was timed to trap the invaders. Hank may have planned to kill Rogers and himself, but initially, when he had the house rigged for a possible invasion, he planned on surviving.

"The panic room! Upstairs inside of Hank's closet." They may be able to survive inside the reinforced steel room.

He pushed her in front of him toward the staircase. Two at a time with Emmet on Bailey's heels, they climbed. A gunman appeared below. Emmet fired and missed when the staircase shifted beneath his feet.

Bailey screamed and plastered herself against the wall.

"Keep going!" he ordered as he kept firing, aware any second another explosion could kill them both.

A bullet pierced his thigh. The pain brought him down to one knee, even as his bullet took a chunk out of the gunman's neck.

Bailey rushed back to him. "Lean on me." She hooked him under his arm. The stairs rocked, about to give way.

He pushed toward the second floor and gritted between clench teeth, "Go. The stairs about to collapse."

"I'm not leaving you." She wedged herself beneath his arm.

"Go, I'm right behind you." A grating, tearing sound, and the entire staircase dipped. With the last of his strength, Emmet shoved Bailey away.

CHAPTER 32

The staircase crumbled beneath Bailey's feet. She didn't have time to think, never mind scream. Instinct and a hard shove from Emmet had her flying over the expanding gap created between the last stair and the second floor. She tossed her gun and grabbed onto the jagged piece of wood jutting out from the landing.

Bailey held on while the world crashed around her and a dust cloud rose. "Emmet!" She choked.

Dangling in the air, she twisted around enough to see the destruction below. It wasn't easy through blurry, gritty, eyes. Where was he? She couldn't see him amongst the debris, and then she found him. "Emmet," she croaked. He lay on his side, tucked into a fetal position. Not moving. She couldn't even tell if he was breathing.

He's not dead. He's not.

"Emmet!" If she let go, she'd fall and be in the same predicament if not worse. But what choice did she have? Through the debris that used to be the front of the house, the sweet sound of sirens reached her. "Hold on! Please! I'm coming for you."

He didn't utter a single sound.

She pulled herself up, shoulders burning from the strain, and — Fingers sunk into her hair, caressed her head. For a split second, she thought it was Hank, more like hoped it was Hank having a paternal moment before he saved her.

She was so wrong. A hand fisted her coat and pulled her up. Slowly, she rose, and the person holding her came into view.

"Ah," he sighed. "We finally meet. I'm Kevin Rogers. Rogers to those who know me. And you are Hank's daughter, correct?"

He was a big man. Taller than Emmet and judging by the breadth of his chest, more muscular. He held all one hundred and twenty pounds of her in mid-air as if she weighed nothing. "Emmet's dead, huh? Goodman to have at your six, too bad he picked the wrong side."

Blond mustache, close-cropped dirty blond hair. Dark, pitiless eyes. She took all this in before he flung her into the wall. Her back merged with the plaster and drywall. Shit, she hit with enough force she thought he'd flung her through the wall.

Every bone in her body rattled, and she let loose a groan, but she didn't crumble. Bailey pulled herself out of the mini crater and landed on her feet with another grenade in her hand. She'd only brought two, and she didn't hesitate to pull the pin.

Rogers aimed his gun at her chest. "I shoot. You drop where you stand. I live."

She backed up a bit to give herself some room, her grip held tight around the safety lever and grenade. "Maybe. Maybe that happens. First, you should take a look at your surroundings. One more explosion and this house will collapse."

His eyes narrowed, and he cocked his head to the side, sizing her up. "You sure about that? It seems to be holding together pretty well. Either way, I don't really care. Your father took my reason for living. He killed the woman I loved and ruined any chance I had with the agency. Now, I'm getting payback."

Step by step, she kept backing up as Rogers closed in. "Sorry to burst your revenge bubble, but if you think that'll hurt Hank, you're wrong. He never wanted me. He doesn't love me."

"You're wrong, Bailey. I've always loved you."

She couldn't pinpoint where Hank's voice came from and neither could Rogers who raced toward her. Why when a single shot would end her? Then she understood. Shooting her wasn't enough. Rogers wanted Hank to suffer, and her quick death wouldn't suffice.

To hell with that shit.

If he expected her to freeze, she disappointed him. She shoved the pin back in the grenade and ducked the fist aimed at her head. She came back with a chop to his windpipe and a knee to his groin. No blow was too low when survival was at stake. He doubled over, his free hand cupped his bruised bits, while she grabbed the wrist of the hand with the gun. Unable to breathe, pain radiating from his crotch, both injuries halted any plans he had for her. Now, if she could get the gun away from him.

Rogers was strong and easily broke her hold. He also recovered quickly and pinned her to the wall by her shoulders. Enraged, he wheezed in her face, "I'm gonna enjoy carving you up."

Bailey went limp. She slid to her knees, registered the sharp bite of something pointy digging into her flesh and delivered two hard blows to his diaphragm. Stunned, he exhaled sharply out and smashed his knee into her chest.

Fuck, I think my heart skipped a few beats. Now she was the one who couldn't breathe as pain exploded in her chest. She slumped, gravity pulling her sideways to the floor. Rogers grabbed another fistful of hair. He yanked her upright, wrapped his hand around her throat, and squeezed.

A blur in the corner of her eye caught her attention. Out of nowhere, Hank barreled into Rogers, and both went tumbling out of her field of view.

Thimbles of air she managed to sip kept her from passing out, which turned into hard gulps. Hand pressed to her chest, Bailey climbed to her feet. Jesus! Everything hurt, but that was beside the point. Hank and Rogers weren't in the half-destroyed hallway anymore. From the sounds of destruction, they'd traveled to the master suite. Her aching chest wanted her to stay put. Staggering, she made her way across a floor that was no longer level with the tilted doorjamb.

She would've thought Rogers would've lost the gun, but the bastard had a vice grip on the weapon. And Hank, he was a seven-fingered, bloody mess. Shirtless, cuts dissected his torso but didn't stop the fury of his attack. One hand held onto the gun in Roger's hand, while both men slugged it out with their free hand. Hank couldn't win. After a few hits, his strength waned. He struggled to hold onto Rogers' hand and block the body blows. The blood loss, Bailey surmised.

She stepped into the room and their gazes collided. Hank's eyes widened in surprise, or horror, she couldn't tell which. But then, his expression changed, and all the love she'd missed filled his eyes and reached across the distance separating them to fill her heart. Tears she hadn't shed in seven years ran down her cheeks because she understood. This was his goodbye. "Run!"

Bailey wasn't ready to say goodbye, and she was done running.

She launched herself onto Rogers' back and wrapped her arm around his throat. He bucked and head-butted Hank, who released Rogers' hand and went down to his knees. Rogers brought the gun around and pointed it at her father's head.

Bailey slapped her hand to Rogers' forehead and yanked as a shot echoed. She screamed along with Hank. How bad! Was he dying? She couldn't see him. She had to see him, but she couldn't release Rogers. Not if she didn't want both of them dead.

Rogers reached around and pressed the gun to the side of her ear, the hot muzzle dug into the outer shell until she let go of her hold on his neck and slid off his back. As he turned to face her, she rotated around his body to stand between him and Hank sprawled on the ground. In her hand, the grenade with the pin out again.

"That's not going to stop me."

If a grenade wasn't going to stop him, what would because she had nothing else left? The sound of an ambulance and fire department sirens filtered in from the outside. Relief poured into her bloodstream. "It's over. You're going to jail."

Rogers snorted, shook his head, and supplied darkly, "Jail? People like me, Emmet, and Hank don't go to jail. We're too valuable. Our skill set is a commodity governments line up to pay for. Plus, I came here with the expectation of dying. Going quickly in a ball of flames with both of you...there is no downside to that."

I'm going to die.

On the ground next to her, Hank coughed, a wet, garbled sound that gave her a smidgen of hope for him and herself.

This ain't over.

She needed time, time for the police to get in here and help her. Maybe talk him down and give her a chance to—what? She couldn't leave without Hank *and* Emmet. Even if that meant leaving with their bodies. A whimper threatened to crawl up her throat, but she swallowed it back down. Unraveling now would help none of them. It was up to her to get them out of this mess.

"I don't believe you. Once you've finished killing us, you'd want to live, as any man would. You want to take Hank's place. Be top dog in the agency. Have men you've trained follow your every word. The money, the wealth, the infamy. Have everything that Hank has and more, along with Hank's head mounted on your wall. You can have all of that." She held up the grenade. "If you're not dead."

Something gave way downstairs and the entire second floor

tipped, parts unseen sounded like it was being ripped away. Bailey stumbled and tripped over Hank. She fell. The dresser, a bulky contraption that probably took four muscle-bound men to bring it into the house, slid toward her. The pin went flying when she stretched out her hand as if she could ward off the inevitable. Even as she braced, she tucked the grenade close, her hand depressing the safety lever. At the last second, the dresser got hung up on a rug and spun. Instead of head-on, she absorbed a glancing blow to her shoulder.

The mantra in her head, *Hold on! Hold on! Hold on!* Directed at Hank, Emmet, and the grenade.

What the hell possessed her into thinking a standoff with a grenade was a good idea? She didn't have to worry about Rogers killing her when she was going to do the job for him.

The room dipped, tilting twenty-five degrees or more. She kept rolling through the ongoing destruction of the room and into the walk-in closet filled with suits. She tried to stop the skid, hard to do with one hand. At least all his suits cushioned the landing as she crashed into Hank's designer duds. And continued through the clothes and into a hidden room beyond. A room stocked with food, clothing, and weapons, nestled in custom foam inserts, safely locked away behind glass cabinets embedded in the walls, similar to the weapons cache below the shed next door, though lacking the volume of weaponry.

Metal cot bolted to the metal floor. Metal toilet in the corner. Five-gallon water jugs tipped over and rolled toward her, along with everything else he had stored beneath the last shelf. With one hand, she latched onto a leg of the shelf bolted to the floor, which stopped her slide into the toilet and prevented the jugs from smashing into her. She wasn't so lucky with the two Rubbermaid storage containers. They slammed into her and continued until they wedged under the sink. A metal foot locker inched toward her, and she prayed it stayed in place. On more hit and she wouldn't be able to hold on. She'd join the avalanche.

A shout snapped her head up for her to catch the sight of Rogers sliding on his ass through the doorway. His arms flailing, searching for purchase. The hand he held his gun in —empty.

He slammed into the toilet, his head connecting with a solid clang against the base. This was her chance, probably her only chance to get away. Carefully, she maneuvered over everything blocking her path to the exit, climbing with one hand and her elbow, making her way one inch at a time.

Rogers groaned and clamped onto her knee with a weak grasp. She kicked his hand away, balanced on a jug and jumped. Gripping the leg of a shelf with one hand, Bailey pulled herself up.

Just a few more feet. Thank God the room was twice the size of a prison cell with more accouterments.

Rogers clamped a hand around her ankle. This time she couldn't kick him away. All she could do was hold on as he climbed up her body. The hand holding the grenade cramping, sweating. The hand gripping the metal leg, slipping. Letting go of either meant certain death. Muscles straining, now screaming, she had to make a choice.

"You're not going anywhere. You're staying with me." Rogers reached for her.

"Okay." Breathless she managed to answer and blinked the sweat from her eyes. "On one condition…" She looked down her body and met his crazed gaze. "You hold this."

Bailey shoved the grenade into his outstretched hand. The fury on his face was a beautiful thing to see, from afar. Up close, it was chilling. Her calculated risk, balanced on the decision that at the end of the day, they all wanted to survive.

His fury morphed into terror as he depressed the safety lever and held on. Her gamble paid off.

Bailey had no time to enjoy the fear darkening his eyes. A well-placed kick to his chin sent him flying backward into the toilet again. Stupidly, she watched his impact, cringing when his hand hit the tank.

"Bailey!"

Her head shot up at the sound of her name and her gaze latched onto Emmet. Blood ran from his temple down his gray skin to his jaw and dripped onto his chest. Panting heavily, face drawn up in pain, he leaned against the jamb, in one hand, his raised Glock. His other hand clutched his bleeding thigh. Though dark, by the blood dripping from the bottom of his pants, it was soaked.

She wanted to shout with joy. He was alive... But not for much longer. He couldn't shoot Rogers, not with him holding the grenade.

"Move your ass!" he wheezed.

With focus she'd never realized she had, Bailey climbed.

"You bitch! You think you've won? I release this grenade, and we all die together."

Bailey kept her trap shut and kept climbing, using the legs of the shelf as handholds. Never had she regretted more giving up her workout regiment when she learned Taekwondo. *I'm hitting the gym tomorrow. And the mat. And the treadmill. Get me out of this, God, and I'll never skip the gym again.*

"You think I won't release it and kill us all? I will," Rogers screamed.

Another tearing sound registered, and the tilt of the room increased another couple of degrees. *Oh shit!* She held onto the leg for dear life.

The guns, secure behind the glass cabinet in the foamed insert, came free. The glass door swung open, and like manna from heaven, a Sig Sauer tumbled out. It landed with a loud clank and skidded toward Rogers.

It's empty, right? Who leaves a loaded gun lying around? A hitman, that's who.

"Bailey!" Emmet stretched out a bloody hand for her to

clasp. She wasn't even close to making the connection. The metal foot locker was wedged on a leg she needed to climb over to reach Emmet. If she could get it out of her way, she'd have a chance.

She pushed with her hand, then her shoulder, which did not a damn thing. Whatever it held kept the locker in place, even in the tilted room. She prayed a bit more weight wouldn't change that and squeezed between the top of the locker and the bottom of the shelf.

The footlocker shifted. Bailey froze.

Below her, Rogers fumbled with the gun. She couldn't see it but heard enough to know his only option was to get the weapon and tip the balance back in his favor, even as the room collapsed around them.

Bailey cleared the small space and landed on the other side, so much closer to Emmet. Now, all she had to do was stretch and grab the last leg, then pull herself up to reach Emmet. Carefully, using the locker as a stool, she balanced on the side and jumped for the final leg above her head. Which was all the footlocker needed for it to break free and ski down the sloped floor aimed at Rogers.

Dangling again, she paused to look, couldn't help herself.

"Damnit, Bailey!"

Emmet was above her, the last hope of getting out of harm's way. With her final bit of strength, she pulled herself up and slapped her hand into Emmet's bloody hand. Heat rushed up her arm the moment they touched, followed by a wealth of strength as if he gave her what little he had left.

He pulled her up, and out of the safe room, then shoved her into the adjacent wall layered with designer suits and pressed his hand to a console on the wall next to him. The door slid closed as the footlocker met flesh and bone, and an explosion rocked the room.

Emmet flung himself on top of her. The world crashed all

around them and narrowed down to the two of them, holding onto to each other, slipping and sliding into darkness.

"I love you," she cried and prayed if those were her final words, he heard them.

CHAPTER 33

Bailey went from a world absent of light and sound to her eyes peeling open on a kaleidoscope of color and a heavy metal band shredding her eardrums. Fighting to be free of it all, she punched her way to an upright position, screaming for Emmet.

Hands grabbed her shoulders and pinned her down. She didn't have the energy to fight for her freedom because everything hurt. A face hovered over her, EMT by the uniform. His lips moved, but she couldn't hear a word he said.

"Emmet. Where's Emmet?" Her throat hurt like a sonofabitch, but didn't stop her from repeating, "Where is Emmet?" Didn't he understand? She had to lay eyes on him. She had to know... The screeching in her ears cleared enough for the EMT's voice and lip movements to sync.

"He's alive, and they're working on him."

She gasped and cranked her head around to find ambulances and firetrucks, firemen running back and forth, policemen holding back a crowd, a black limousine parked at the curb, and Emmet being wheeled into an ambulance by two EMTs. Her relief was swift and short-lived.

"Hank, my father. Where is my father?" she croaked. Her vocal cords died on the last word.

"They brought him out of the house five minutes ago and resuscitated him. He's already on the way to the hospital."

He's not dead. That's all she could think of. Exhausted, Bailey flopped onto the stretcher as every bone, and every single muscle in her body suddenly screamed in vehement protest.

"She's going into shock," someone said.

And that was the last thing she heard.

~

"She's coming around, but I don't know how long that will last." The voice came from a distance, as if at the end of a tunnel. The world was a blurry, fuzzy, washed out picture, lacking definition until she blinked. A heavyset man in a jacket that had seen better days hovered over her. A gold shield and police ID hung from his neck.

"What happened? Who are you? Who was in the safe room? Who owned the house and the weapons?" Rapid fire, the questions came at her faster than she could answer.

From the corner of her eye, the flair of a white coat exiting the limousine caught her eyes. It was a woman, an African American female, no more than five feet in height, with hair the same color as her coat. Backed by men in black suits, she marched up to the officer with stripes on his shoulder bars, flashed an ID, and pointed at Bailey. The officer glared at the woman, glared at the ID, and shouted, "Detective Homer."

"Yeah?" Annoyed, the detective turned away from Bailey and shuffled over to his superior and the lady holding everyone's attention.

Bailey couldn't hear the conversation, but she could see the results. Detective Homer flung up his hand and marched away. He didn't return, and the questioning didn't resume. She suspected she'd just had a brush with a member of the agency. An important member. One with more clout than Hank.

Should I thank her? Or pray to fly under her radar? Under the radar, she decided and slid back into unconsciousness.

Ten hours later, she lay in an uncomfortable hospital bed in a private room with a guard in an expensive suit positioned at the door. A guard she didn't hire.

She had a concussion. Not news to her. Scrapes, bruises, everything hurt, even with painkillers, but she was better than Hank and Emmet. Carved up, missing three fingers on his dominant right hand, and shot in the abdomen, Hank had lost so much blood his heart had stopped, and the doctor wasn't sure he would make it. Shot in his thigh and impaled by a piece of wood through his side, Emmet was still in surgery.

Strung out from exhaustion and worry, she waited for news about her men, which Whiskey delivered four hours later when he breezed into the room. He'd come straight from the airport after flying directly from London. Calm and confident, he sat on the edge of her bed. "Emmet will be fine. He's got five broken ribs and a ruptured spleen, probably from the fall, and damage to his liver from the wood. He survived."

Her head bobbed like one of those toys stuck to a dashboard, trying to process how close she came to losing him. Too damn close. "And my father?" she whispered. Even with all the medication they pumped into her, her vocal cords were still bruised and swollen, yet better.

"He's still in surgery, Bailey." The gravity of his voice wasn't lost on her.

"He can't die, Whiskey. Neither one of them. I can't lose either of them."

He covered her hand with his rough palm. "You're not going to. Those two bastards aren't going anywhere."

Throat clogged with emotions she didn't know how to express, she croaked, "You are so right." And changed the subject because she had no more tears to cry. "Who's the suit at the door? And don't lie to me."

"The agency taking care of their own."

"Now they care?" She snorted.

He shrugged and somehow managed to look suave as he did it. "To the victor goes the spoils. We won. Now we're back on the payroll."

"We won? My father and Emmet are in the O.R. How is that winning?"

"You've lost when they're six feet under. Not before. Don't ever forget that. As long as they're breathing, and the enemy ain't, it's a win."

Daisy arrived, and Whiskey bailed. Bailey caught her up to date, well, as much as she could, and fell asleep for what seemed like three days but was only twenty-four hours.

Emmet and Hank were the only things she cared about when she woke.

"How are they?" she asked a nurse who came in to check her vitals and bring her breakfast.

The nurse lowered the guardrail and turned to retrieve Bailey's meal. "They're in ICU."

"I want to see them." She whipped the covers off and slid to the edge of the bed. The nurse was there to catch her when her legs gave out.

"All right, you're stable enough for a trip to ICU. I'll take you after you eat and get cleaned up. You're a bit ripe."

After breakfast and a shower, a volunteer wheeled Bailey down to ICU. Turns out, they were side by side in glass cubicles with matching suited men guarding their doors. The staff tiptoed by them, clearly intimidated. Fuck that.

In a hospital gown, Bailey ignored her protesting muscles and climbed to her feet. She shuffled up to the guy blocking Hank's doorway. He knew who she was, of that she had no doubt. "Move."

He paused to curl his lips into something that resembled a smirk, then stepped aside and opened the door for her to enter. Bailey burst into tears at the sight of her father hooked up to multiple machines. Bandages covered his entire chest and arms. This wasn't the indomitable man she'd loved and hated for most of her life.

"He's not as bad as he looks."

Bailey jumped at the unexpected voice behind her. A nursed rushed past her, tapping on a tablet as she studied the machines around him.

"Most of the cuts were shallow, and the burns are second degree."

Burns? Bailey hadn't considered burns. Why wouldn't he be burned with her tossing grenades and the house exploding around them. How she escaped without being charred was a miracle.

"Injured as badly as he was, he's recovering remarkably fast." The nurse was young, pretty with wavy, dark hair and an olive complexion.

"Really?" Bailed asked afraid to believe.

The nurse nodded. "He was awake earlier, making demands. I had to tell him to slow his roll. He yelled at me. Nobody yells at me. A sedative took the bite out of him."

Bailey laughed. "I like you."

The nurse moved a chair closer to the bed and patted the seat. "He should be awake in a bit."

Bailey sat but stopped the nurse before she left. "My…" Lover, boyfriend, what were they? Everything was so fresh they hadn't put a name to it. "Emmet Streeter. How is he? Do you know his condition?"

"I'm also his nurse, Lydia, and aren't you his *wife*?" She winked at me. "Because I can only give his family members any information about his condition." She winked again.

The woman was a saint. "Yes. I'm his wife."

"He woke in recovery screaming for someone named Bailey. Any idea who that could be?"

Bailey couldn't contain her smile, a smile Lydia returned.

"He wouldn't calm down, so they sedated him. He's been in and out, a bit combative, which isn't good for his stitches. When he wakes up, I'll come and get you."

"Thanks." Bailey touched the nurse's arm.

"De nada." She exited the room, and Bailey heard her say, "You get in my way one more time, and it's gonna be nighty nighty for you, big boy. I have access to a lot of drugs and sharp needles."

Bailey glanced through a part in the drawn curtain and through the glass wall into Emmet's room next door. All she could see was his feet and the nurse moving around the bottom of the bed.

Hank groaned, and she shuffled to her father's bedside. Thick bandages covered his entire chest. A mesh bandage covered a burned area stretching from his left shoulder down to his elbow. Another large bandage covered the bullet wound on his right thigh. Blood and other fluids hung from IV poles while machines tracked his vitals with steady beeps.

Tears coasted down her cheeks. "Damn it, Hank. Don't you die on me."

She gasped when his eyelids fluttered, and waited patiently for them to open. He blinked a few times, and his eyes rolled around in their sockets until his gaze settled on a spot on the ceiling. She was about to clear her throat to gain his attention when his eyes shifted, and his gaze landed on her. His lips moved, but she couldn't hear what he said through his oxygen mask. With his good hand, he pulled the mask to the side. Tears welling in his eyes, he whispered, "You alive?"

Too emotional to reply, she nodded.

"Not ghost?"

She shook her head.

He sobbed, and tears streamed from his eyes to his temples. "You real? Not dreaming?"

She nodded and took his hand in hers. "I'm here, and I'm fine."

"I thought they lied to me. I couldn't survive if you weren't here."

"Oh, Dad." The words sounded awkward on her tongue as if it had five syllables and not one. She did it for him, not for her.

"I fucked up. I know I did and I'm sorry. I'm sorry I did this to you." With each word, his voice lost strength.

She leaned forward and pressed a kiss to his cheek. "It's okay. Everything is okay. You can make it up to me when you get out of the hospital."

The tension left his body, and he sank back into the bed, his eyes still glued to her. "Sweetheart, forgive—"

"Bailey!" Emmet's bellow echoed through the glass walls.

Startled, she jumped and sought the gap in the curtains. Hank squeezed her hand. God, she'd forgotten all about him. "I have to—"

"Go to him." He finished in a raspy whisper. She could see the concern and love in his eyes for Emmet, and that was okay because she loved Emmet too. She loved both of them.

Bailey kissed her father on the forehead. "I'll be back later. I promise." His eyes were already closed by the time she pulled away and placed his oxygen mask back on over his nose and mouth.

She shuffled into Emmet's room as quickly as her aching body allowed. Lydia and both guards were trying to restrain him, but Emmet wasn't having it. He thrashed around, yanking out his IV, spraying fluid and blood everywhere. Alerts blared from the machines. Lydia saw her and said, "I have to knock him out before he ruptures his stitches."

"Wait!" Bailey shuffled past the guard and captured Emmet's face between her hands. "I'm here, Emmet. I'm right here."

Instantly, he calmed and in the nick of time. A nurse rushed in with a syringe in her hand.

"Do not give him that," Bailey ordered. "He's fine, aren't you, babe? Tell everyone you're fine and you're gonna behave."

She basked in the intensity of his icy blue eyes, eyes lit with a cold fire burning hotter than an inferno. "Hey there. Took you long enough to wake up. Are you in pain?" Her strained voice cracked with each word, but she didn't care.

His Adam's apple bobbed, then his lips parted, and he croaked, "Not anymore. Thought I lost you."

"Not possible." She kissed him gently and felt his lips trembling against hers.

"Were you hurt?"

"Cuts and scrapes. I'll live because you saved me."

He shook his head and groaned at the motion. "Not me. You. You took care of Rogers and saved us, Bailey." His eyes widened, and he gripped the rails of the bed. "Hank. Where's Hank?"

She stroked the hair off his face, attempting to soothe him. "He's next door, and he's not going anywhere. He's alive and staying that way." *Please, God, don't make me a liar.*

Tension bled out of his body, and he sank back onto the bed. "I saw him lying in remains of the bedroom and thought he was dead. I couldn't go to him. I had to find you. But damn, you did not need my help."

"I wouldn't have gotten out of that room without you." She pressed her cheek to his and basked in the gentle abrasion of his stubble.

His snort ended on a deep groan with him clutching his side where he'd been impaled. "Maybe." He managed to say after a few seconds. "But doubtful. You would've found a way because it's who you are, a tenacious badass." His cupped the back of her head and pressed her closer. "I swear I will never underestimate you again."

She eased away to meet his gaze again. "Aw. You say the sweetest things, and I'm never gonna let you forget you said that." She had one more question to ask and then she'd let him rest. "Did you hear the last thing I said to you before the house collapsed? Before everything went dark?"

His hand dropped to the bed, and his eyelids drooped. Yet a weak grin curled his lips. "Can't remember. Say it again."

Bailey kissed him, because she couldn't resist, then whispered in his ear because this was their moment and she didn't want to share. "I love you."

"Yeah, I heard it, and I love you, too." His voice trailed off at the end and then he was gone. The steady blip of the machines, the only sound in the room.

She held his hand, took comfort in the warmth of his skin and his underlying strength. He lay there, wounded, but not broken, as was Hank in the next room. She could've lost them, an unbearable possibility when she just found them.

A throat cleared. Bailey turned to find the woman she'd seen outside Hank's house in the room. The white coat was gone, replaced with continuous black, including the hat perched on her head like a small crow sitting on a cloud of salt and pepper hair. A pair of leather gloves clutched in her hand completed the ensemble. Was she in mourning?

"I came to congratulate Emmet and Hank on a successful mission, even though the clean-up continues to be messy. Hank was always good with ordnance and demolition. He did an excellent job of bringing the house down without killing himself. Though you contributed heavily to his survival, especially with Rogers little more than a gooey mess inside the remains of the safe room. I thank you for that feat, Miss Monroe. Or will it be Murray? Or perhaps Streeter in the near future?"

Bailey couldn't answer those questions. Especially the last one. Not that she needed to answer any to the stranger in her presence. The cool, though not quite neutral gaze assessed her, and Bailey didn't shrink. If this woman were here to hurt Hank or Emmet, she'd leave in pieces.

"You don't seem like much, but you've proven to be quite resourceful." She waved her gloves at Bailey dismissively.

"FYI. You don't link an insult with a compliment. And who are you?"

The woman's gaze turned condescending. "Don't ask questions you already know the answer to." She glanced around Bailey and studied Emmet, and then glanced through the now parted curtains into Hank's room.

"I'm a firm believer in DNA. However, time will tell."

What the hell did that mean?

The woman turned on the heels of her sensible black shoes and grabbed the handle of the door and paused. "The future unfolds in precarious ways. I suspect our paths will cross again, Miss Monroe, and I wait in anticipation for that day to come. The agency could use another female to balance the testosterone. That being said, offering you a job would place me in Hank's crosshairs. And Emmet's. Can't have my best operatives vying to kill me." She sighed, and her gaze turned flinty. "We've had enough of that already. Too many funerals. Take care of them." She sailed out of the room. Two men lined up behind her while a third man took the lead.

With her exit, she planted a seed in suddenly fertile soil, which was probably her intention.

Me? A hitwoman? Nah. I couldn't possibly do that…
Could I?

EPILOGUE

Two Months Later.
Gingerly, Emmet exited his Porsche 911. He tried not to favor his left side and failed. The wound on his side and the gunshot to his thigh had healed but would take time for him to return to peak form. Impossible to do with Bailey playing nursemaid.

Bailey. The mere thought of her name made warmth spread through his chest.

The only reason she wasn't glued to his side right now was because of Daisy dragging her out for an early dinner. At his suggestion. He loved Bailey; however, this was the one place he couldn't bring her—yet.

Sidewalk traffic was light for a late-afternoon weekday. No one stood out as he made a quick scan of the area. The two guns holstered under his arms were in easy reach. Rogers may be dead, and all of the men who followed him, but a man in this line of work was never at ease. Things at the agency had settled, and while he remained on the sideline healing from his injuries, one never knew who'd see this as an opportunity. After Rogers, his circle of trust included two people.

And he planned on keeping it that way.

Emmet entered the building. He flashed a gray business card that held no information other than a black rock to the security guard on duty and was led to a private elevator. On the twelfth floor of the fifty-story building, a woman greeted him when the door slid open. "Good afternoon, sir. May I take your coat?" Her fake English accent didn't quite pass muster.

"No."

She didn't expect that and barely managed to hide her surprise. "Very well, sir. If you'd follow me, I will take you directly to Mr. Pimmer." Her heels were silent on the thick carpet as they made their way through the showroom, empty not counting the three armed security guards. He noted she didn't ask for his name or volunteer hers. Strange way to conduct business, even if they were forewarned of his presence.

"No business today?" he asked.

She glanced over her shoulder at him. "As a personal friend of Mr. Morgan, we could do no less than give you our undivided attention." They passed display cases filled with the usual wares, nothing he was interested in. At a locked door, she paused and pressed her hand against a biometric scanner. The scanner beeped, she opened the door and swept aside for him to enter.

Emmett noticed the standard issue guard near the door and took in the spacious office, done in muted tones, with blackout curtains keeping the room private from outside interests. The desk was glass and draped with a black velvet cloth. On the surface, a computer, and several display cases, half filled with loose gems, the rest filled with an assortment of jewelry. He took all this in as he crossed the room to meet the man seated behind the desk, a man who was as wide as he was tall, with jowls instead of a neck.

"Mr. Streeter, a pleasure to serve you today. I'm Darwin Pimmer."

Emmet leaned across the desk for a handshake.

"Please make yourself comfortable."

Emmet lowered himself onto the leather chair next to him. He arranged himself for easy access to his weapons, sat back, and crossed his legs.

"May we offer you some refreshments? Wine, or perhaps something stronger?" Primmer flicked a finger at the woman who greeted him at the entrance. She waited by a cart laden with liquor and a variety of snacks ranging from brie and crackers to chips and dip.

"No, thank you." This wasn't a social call.

Primmer tipped his head and folded his hands on the table, between his wares. "What brings you to my doorstep this evening?"

"An engagement ring."

Primmer's broad face broke into a wide smile. "Congratulations. I hope it is not presumptuous to wish you a happy and fruitful marriage."

"Thank you."

"Nancy, if you'd please." His assistant removed two display cases filled with jewelry but left the loose diamonds and other gems. "Are you seeking something specific? A certain cut or carat?" Like a true salesman, his hand brushed the largest of the diamonds displayed while Nancy left through a side door and returned seconds later with more cases filled with rings. Emmet suspected Julius may have forewarned Pimmer about his possible intentions.

Nancy placed the cases in front of Emmet. Good lord, there were so many. Too many choices for a man whose sole piece of jewelry was a Breitling, a birthday gift from Hank. "No, and I'm open to suggestions."

Mr. Pimmer tipped his head in understanding. "Tell me about the person who will become your spouse."

Emmet gave an inward chuckle at Mr. Pimmer's adroit navigation of a social landmine. In the business of selling high-end jewelry, why offend anyone when profit had no gender or bias?

How to describe Bailey? "She's...independent, stubborn, smart." The generic description summed up half the women in the world. There was more to her than three adjectives. "She doesn't know how beautiful she is."

"Ah, but you do," Pimmer said knowingly.

Not use denying it. Yes, he did know how beautiful she was, and he would tell her so every day.

"Nancy, tray number five, please."

She pressed a panel on the wall which retracted and revealed rows of cases filled with jewelry. Pimmer was very lucky Emmet wasn't a thief because he would've cleaned their clock.

Nancy brought a tray of diamond rings to the desk. Similar sizes, different, they were all spectacular; however, one ring whispered her name. Before Pimmer began his spiel, Emmet lifted the ring from its nest.

"That beauty is a radiant cut three-carat diamond set in a platinum basket setting. The band is lined with twenty-two pavé diamonds. A radiant cut diamond is one of the rarest cuts you will ever find. See how it catches the light?"

No, all he could see was it on her finger the moment she said yes. "This one." No need to discuss price. Whatever the cost, he would have it.

"An excellent choice. We will box and wrap it." Pimmer held out his hand for the ring and passed it to Nancy. She left the room while Emmet handed over his platinum card.

"Sorry to interrupt, Emmet, but have you made your purchase?"

The voice came from the entrance. Emmet let Pimmer handle the greeting since he'd leaped to his feet and practically wobbled around the table. "Mr. Morgan. I didn't expect you this evening. What brings you here today?"

Morgan waved the man away. "No purchases tonight,

Darwin. I'm here to catch up with an old friend. Can we have the room for a few moments?" He took Pimmer's seat.

Primmer's sharp gaze darted between Morgan and Emmet, even as he bowed and waved to his guards to leave. "Of course. My home is your home." Quickly, he closed up shop, securing all the jewels back in the safe. Next, he signaled everyone to leave and with a soft click, closed the door behind him.

Emmet eyed his friend. He had an idea what this was about and didn't like it one bit. "You coulda called. The dramatic entrance was unnecessary."

Julius shrugged. "Yeah, well, I was in town, and I knew where you would be. Did you find what you wanted?"

"Yeah. I think she'll like it."

"How much it set you back?"

Emmet laughed. "I don't even know. Doesn't matter. She's worth it."

"Spoken like a man in love." He sighed heavily. "Sorry to rain on your day."

"But..." Emmet supplied.

"You owe me, and I'm calling in my marker."

Last night, he promised Bailey he was done. Told her he was out of the agency. Even showed her his resignation letter, not that he needed one. Today, he was back in. If a man didn't live by his word, then he shouldn't live. A motto Hank lived by and taught him to live by.

The engagement would have to wait. Emmet locked eyes with his friend. "My gun is yours. Who do you need killed?"

∼

Wait! Don't leave yet!

Thank you for reading *Plain Jane and the Hitman*. I hope you enjoyed the novel. Emmet and Bailey's story isn't over.

They still have to get married. Plain Jane and the Hitman's Wedding, coming summer 2019.

Before their wedding, you can expect *Plain Jane and the Marine and Plain Jane and the Bad Boy*, the next books in the Plain Jane series will be available on Amazon this spring.

*I*f you enjoyed *Plain Jane and the Hitman*, please take a moment to show your support by leaving a short review on the product page where your purchase was made. Your reviews are essential and help readers discover new books!

UNTITLED

Links
Check out my website: http://tmoniquestephens.com
Sign up for my contemporary newsletter: http://bit.ly/2Sp5dRA
Amazon Page: https://amzn.to/2zQYGZc
You can also find me on:
Facebook: https://www.facebook.com/AuthorTmoniqueStephens
Twitter: https://twitter.com/Tmoniquebooks

ABOUT THE AUTHOR

Passion changes everything, especially for the characters Tmonique writes about in her Descendants of Ra, UnHallowed, and Plain Jane series. Flawed characters who reflect the emotional baggage we all carry interests her the most. She writes complicated stories for complicated people.

She loves SyFy and the History channel, and also Asian cuisine, but her heart and stomach long for anything from the Caribbean. She'll read anything about fairies, demons, or angels. Her favorite authors are JR Ward, Gena Showalter, and Kresley Cole. She also enjoys Stephen King, Dean Koontz, and Preston & Child. At any given time, you can find her on Facebook and live tweeting her favorite shows, *The Walking Dead* and *Game of Thrones*.

Made in the USA
Middletown, DE
02 March 2025